FIRST STEPS

A Julie Armstrong Novel

Lorenda Lee Lux

FIRST STEPS
By Lorenda Lee Lux

TCL Consulting Group
Motivation Concepts Publishing
Surprise, Arizona 85374
Orland Park, Illinois 60462

ISBN-978-0615783703

Dedication

I want to thank everyone who helped with the writing process at Bard College, Hudson-on-Avon, Hudson, N.Y., University of Iowa, Iowa City, Iowa, and seminars at Ohio State University, Columbus, Ohio.

Thanks also to Lyn Valiska, Gini Hoxworth, and Sharon Welch for their helpful reviews and editing.

And most of all, I'd like to thank my husband, Tom for his total support and encouragement.

ONE

I lay worrying about what I would say to Gram in the morning, when a heavy weight on the metal doorstep outside rocked the camper. "Jack, is that you?" I sat up and reached for my cell phone only to recall it was on charge in my grandparents' house. We'd parked in the yard alongside their house. The camper rocked again as the weight dropped off. A dry palmetto frond crunched outside. I held my breath, listening. On the road our camper's a box on wheels, but once the top is cranked up and the platform beds are drawn out like drawers at either end, the sides are nothing more than flimsy canvas.

It was long past dark. Gracie, my two month old baby, slept peacefully beside me. We shared one side of a vintage pop-up camper. An old Coleman gas lantern glowed softly on the camper's tiny countertop casting shadows on my husband Jack's empty bed at the opposite end of the camper.

Gracie drew a raspy breath and let it out with a little sigh. I lay still, allowing only shallow breaths as I listened for movement outside. Gentle waves from the Gulf across the road lapped rhythmic backup to the trill of insects. It soothed me into feeling calm and I took a deep breath thinking I'd probably scared off whoever rocked the camper.

A sharp scuff on the gravel road brought me back to full alert. My heart raced and for a brief moment, I couldn't breathe. Then Gracie snuffled in her sleep and in an instant I knew I had to get my baby and myself into the safety of my grandparents' house.

I rolled off the bed and stood next to the camper's two-burner stovetop. In the dim light I spotted my heavy cast iron skillet and wrapped my fingers around its solid handle. Then I took a deep breath as I moved toward the end of the counter. A black and yellow flashlight slipped easily from its clip on the side of the counter top. Armed with the skillet and the flashlight tucked under my arm, I gently turned the tiny metal doorknob, held my breath and pushed the door open a few inches. Nothing happened so I eased the door open enough to see outside.

A large silver dish light blazed from the eaves at the corner of the back porch illuminating the canal behind the house and the back yard about half way to the road. The front porch lay in deep shadows. A field of weeds and palmettos behind the camper stretched several lot lengths to the Williams place as you head up to the point where the canal meets the Gulf of Mexico. I told myself that whoever was out there had probably gone up the road toward the point or headed back the other way toward town. Then again, he could also be lurking behind the camper. I had to know.

The camper's little metal doorstep felt cold, and the grass wet on my bare feet when I stepped outside. I tiptoed toward the end of the camper near the road so that I could peek around the corner. Hopefully whoever had been there was gone. It was too dark to see behind the end of the camper so I switched on the flashlight.

It beamed into the face of a short, heavy man with a dark vest flapping over his hairy bare belly. Baggy dark pants were cinched with a rope belt. I flew at him so suddenly that we were both surprised. I dropped the light and gripped the pan with both hands, giving my all to a heaving chop to the side of his head. With a dull clang from the pan, he crumpled like an empty laundry bag.

I stood over him, panting, trembling, with sweat trickling down my scalp, and I couldn't decide if he was going to stay down. Scenes from horror movies where the monster comes back to life played in my mind, so I whacked him in the head again with all the force in my one hundred and ten pound body. The flat part of the skillet hit the top of his head with such force that it vibrated all the way up my arm and sent the pan flying under the end of the camper.

When my breathing slowed enough, I picked up the flashlight and aimed it at his head. Blood ran in dark rivulets across his unshaven cheek onto the grass. I tried to hold the light steady but it darted around like a single disco bulb. I gently poked the hulk in his middle with my big toe. There was no response so I sprinted around to the camper door, charged in, and scooped Gracie into my arms, clutching her still fragile head against my chest while I pounded through the yard to the front porch door. The knob was slippery from Florida's ever present humidity. I managed to turn the doorknob enough to push open the door, stumble in, and slam it closed behind me, pressing in the thumb lock as soon as it was closed. I leaned against the door, chest heaving, kneecaps dancing, with Gracie clutched to my chest.

After a time my knees quit twitching and my breathing returned to normal. Fish shaped nightlights guided me through the living room and then through a wide archway into the dining room. It's a straight shot back to the kitchen where I'd left my cell on charge but I veered to my left to a short hallway where two bedrooms are separated by a bathroom. Gram, no doubt, had removed her hearing aids, so I wasn't worried about disturbing her. She slept in the bedroom on the left ever since she suffered a mild heart attach two years ago. Turning right, I entered Gramps' bedroom and put Gracie in the center of the bed. She stretched her arms and legs, turned her head back and forth a couple times .before she settled down. I sat on the edge of the bed to let my heart stop racing and my nerves to calm down.

As my mind cleared, I realized with a pang that I'd just hit someone hard enough to knock him out, at the very least. That he might die scared me all over again. I hurried to the kitchen where I grabbed my phone and stabbed 911 with shaky fingers. A woman answered. "What is the nature of your emergency?" she asked.

"I need an ambulance quick." My throat was dry and my voice croaked. I cleared it to repeat the message with more urgency.

"What type of injury did you sustain?"

"None. It's for a guy I hit in the head with my skillet and now he's bleeding and may bleed to death if you don't hurry."

"Slow down, Darlin'," she said. "I can't make heads or tails out of what you're saying."

I had to make her understand. "My name is Julie Armstrong. I'm visiting my grandparents in Holiday Park subdivision. It's the second house on Old Gulf Road. I just knocked out a man who is bleeding from his head and I'm afraid he's going to bleed to death unless an ambulance gets here fast." There was silence on the line. "Please," I begged, "we can't let him die!"

"I'll send help right away," she said. "Do you want me to stay on the line until help arrives?"

Nodding with relief, I rolled my eyes as I realized that she couldn't see my nod so I said, "Yes, please."

The phone line crackled and I heard the woman talking to someone else, hopefully to an ambulance. The woman came back to me and asked, "How did you come to strike the man with a skillet?"

"He was outside my camper, right next to where my baby slept and I thought he was after us." That sounded lame. "He didn't say anything, or make any noise. He was sneaky."

"I see," she said.

"It's late and I was afraid," I said. "But I sure don't want him to die. I can't believe I could break the Commandment, Thou Shalt Not Kill,"

"Of course not," she murmured in a voice that was, no doubt, meant to soothe.

"I mean I don't want to spend the rest of my life knowing I killed someone." I knew this as much as I knew I wasn't going to let anyone get at Gracie. Maybe he shouldn't have been sneaking around in the middle of the night but that didn't make it fair for me to kill him either. "I'm going to take a cold compress out to press on his wound until the ambulance gets here," I said. I thumbed the end button on my phone and dropped it on the dining room table as I passed it on the way to the bathroom.

The cool Gulf breeze bathed my face when I stepped out the front door with a cold wet wash cloth. After flipping on the light above the front door, I peered along the edge of the field behind the camper and saw no skulking monsters. My stomach clenched when I saw the guy still lying either dead, or hopefully just unconscious. Guilt swept over me suddenly. Maybe the guy was just some curious fisherman. After all, Jack and Gramps were out night fishing. Maybe this poor slob just thought he'd take a peek at my camper and I went ballistic. I was tired, I was ticked off at Jack, and I was scared. He had me so rattled that I wasn't thinking clearly. In fact, my feet were still bare, and I had on nothing but a sweat soaked tee top and short pajama bottoms. I should have grabbed Gramps' robe at least, I chided myself. My flashlight still lay in the grass where I'd dropped it. I played the light on the lump at the end of the camper. Fresh blood oozed from behind the man's left ear and covered his lower jaw. Kneeling next to him, I placed the flashlight in the grass between us and pressed the cold cloth against the wound. I felt his wrist for a pulse but there didn't seem to be any. I held my hand near his nose to feel for breath. I couldn't feel breath nor did it look as though he were breathing. My hand accidentally touched his face smearing blood on my hand. I gasped and my stomach heaved. I was about to throw up. I swallowed a sudden rush of saliva until the waves of nausea passed. Then I closed my eyes to get a grip on myself with a wordless prayer. My head cleared enough to realize that I should take some deep breaths. It helped somewhat. Trembling in the cold, damp grass, I tried to take stock of the situation. As far as I could tell, the man was probably dead. Then again, he might wake up suddenly. Neither thought eased the knot in the pit of my stomach.

Unwilling to give up on the man, I held the cloth against his wound. The ground was uneven, cold and damp beneath my bare legs. There's always a cool breeze off the Gulf and I felt chilly. The moon was a distant slit in the black starless sky.

Somewhere in the darkness tires crunched on the gravel road. I could almost hear each pop as the vehicle crawled over the stones. My heart beat faster as I realized it couldn't be the ambulance. It was coming from the wrong direction.

TWO

D im yellow fog lights appeared in the dark as the vehicle came closer. Soon it would be next to me as I sat in the grass a couple of feet off the road. I hated to take the cloth off of the man's wound, but as the lights crept closer, I let go of the cloth and ran into the house. After pushing in the lock, I squatted behind the daybed on the porch and peeked out the window. A shaft of light from my flashlight shot across the road as it lay in the grass where I'd left it.

A stake body truck crawled across the light and stopped beside the injured man. Its cab was faded red with wooden slat sides that looked to be loaded with boxes of various sizes. The silhouette of a large man emerged from behind the truck. He loomed over the flashlight from behind it for a split second before the light snapped off.

Faded yellow fog lights gave half a picture of what was going on. I could see the passenger door being pulled open. A bulky person heaved the bleeding man into the cab of the truck and quietly pressed the door closed. Seconds later the truck crept past the house toward town. As soon as the truck passed the Dodds' house next door, I slipped outside. No tail lights shone. Across the road I could hear the Gulf in the distance across the empty strip of land leading up to the point. The Dodds are the last house on the road before the bend that leads to Route 19 and Port Richfield.

Shivering, I crossed my arms and stared into the darkness. Would the bleeding man be taken to the hospital? The careless way the injured man was slung into the cab of the truck gave me chills. From a distance a motorboat chugged from the canal behind the house signaling the return of Jack and Gramps.

I was about to slip inside when tires spit gravel coming from town, heading toward our place. A wide arc of headlights swung around the bend followed by another vehicle. Seconds later a dark colored squad car came to a rocking stop in front of the house. An ambulance pulled up next to the squad car and stopped in the middle of the road.

Two policemen jumped out of the car, leaving the drivers' side door open and the interior lights on. "Somebody here call the police?" one of the men called as Jack and Gramps came from the back yard. A second man played a hand held spotlight around the front of the house. By then Jack and Gramps had made it to the front of the house and spotted me at the door.

"What's going on?" Jack demanded. He came to stand, hands on hips, to tower over me.

"I called an ambulance," I said looking down. For some reason I didn't want to meet his eyes. But somebody in a truck came and took him away."

"There's no one injured here than?" the officer with the light asked. I shook my head no. He ambled over to the ambulance, leaned into its open window, and said, "Looks like you guys can go back to bed."

Jack glared down at me as the ambulance turned around in the yard. The officer with the light came over to stand beside his partner who stood next to Jack forming a semi-circle around me.

Gramps cut through the line of men to wrap an arm around my shoulders. "What happened, Sweetie?" he asked. I leaned against his soft flannel shirt and the next minute I was sobbing onto it. My legs trembled, and I felt like they might give out. Gramps gently led me into the house.

Inside, Gramps wrapped his thick navy blue fleece robe around me and held me while I sobbed against his chest, my head tucked under his chin. He rubbed my shoulders and patted my back until my crying was reduced to an occasional ragged hic. He gently eased me onto a living room chair, knelt beside me and handed me one of his big white hankies. I wiped my face, and blew my nose.

Gramps stands very erect; his white hair is cut military style, and his suntanned face is always clean shaven and smells like Old Spice shaving lotion. Before they retired to Florida, Gramps and Gram lived next door to us in Owensville, Illinois. I loved it. I could always run next door for comfort, vindication, or something to eat.

"Do you think you can go back out and tell the police what happened now?" Gramps asked finally. I nodded. He rose, put his arm under mine and guided me out to where Jack and the two policemen hunched around a weather-worn picnic table at the edge of the canal.

The two officers rose awkwardly balancing between the bencheat and picnic table. A tall, thin officer wore jeans and a tee shirt. His shorter beefy partner wore jeans and a short sleeved plaid shirt. The only thing that resembled a uniform was the badges pinned to their shirts.

"This is Officer Braxton," the taller, thin policeman said indicating his partner who nodded before slumping back onto the bench. "I'm Officer Daly," he said reseating himself carefully so as not to bang his knees on the picnic table.

Deep creases in Officer Daly's narrow face stretched with a smile. His light brown hair blew in wisps in the breeze. He and Jack sat on the side of the picnic table facing the camper, their backs to the canal.

Officer Braxton, stocky and sporting a dark brush cut, sat opposite Jack and Officer Daly. He moved down so I could sit next to him. I wrapped Gramps' robe around my legs and wedged between the bench and table. Gramps folded his long legs under the end next to Jack. In the glare of the dish light, the canal looked black and thick like the blood in the grass. I felt nauseated and lightheaded.

"So tell us again why you dragged these guys out here," Jack said. His sarcasm exploded into our midst so much so that even he had to hang his head and mumble something about being tired from driving all day and it being so late.

I batted my eyes to keep them clear of tears and said, "Somebody started to come into the camper. At first I thought it was you but when nobody came in, I got scared. I mean, you hear about crazies and I was all alone with Gracie." I looked to Gramps for understanding and he nodded. "I took my iron skillet outside to see who was there and when I saw somebody lurking near the road, I hit him over the head with the skillet."

Everyone looked at me a few beats before Jack said, "You sure you weren't dreaming?"

I yanked the ends of Gramps' robe from around my legs and swung my legs around the end of the bench. "He fell over there," I said getting up and trailing the robe in the grass as I headed for the side of the camper near the road. The others followed. "He was unconscious and bleeding right here." I pointed to the end of the camper.

Officer Daly switched on his spotlight. A circle of congealed blood glistened like a fresh patch of tar. Officer Daly bent over and lightly ran his forefinger over the pool. "Looks like blood, all right," he said sniffing his fingers before he rubbed his thumb and forefinger together. He finished by wiping them on his jeans. I gagged. "You say you hit him with a skillet?" His eyes were soft brown and he looked sympathetic but confused.

I spotted the skillet under the camper and pointed. Officer Daly reached under the camper. His long arms easily reached it. "You say you hit a guy with this?" He gauged its weight by hefting it from one hand to the other. Then he ran his finger along the rim and rubbed his thumb and forefinger together when he felt blood, repeating his investigation with another swipe on his jeans.

Insects droned around the porch light, and chirred in the field next to us. Waves softly swooshed from across the road. I suddenly felt so drained all I wanted to do was go to bed.

"What did the guy look like?" Officer Braxton said. He held a small note pad open ready to take notes.

"Big and hairy," I said softly. "Another man came in a truck and took him away. I didn't see either man clearly, but I did see the truck well enough to see it had a red cab and wooden sides." I thought a minute and added "The back was full of boxes, I think."

The policemen looked at one another, shrugged, and Officer Braxton stuffed his note pad into his shirt pocket. "If you think of anything more, let us know," he said. They headed for their car. "We'll fill out a report in the morning," Officer Daly called over his shoulder. "Call if they come back." The squad car made a U turn before it roared away.

"If the guy I hit comes back for another bonk on the head, I'd be pretty surprised," I said. I felt giddy with exhaustion.

Gramps insisted that he sleep on the daybed on the front porch, Jack should sleep out in the camper, and Gracie and I should sleep in his bed. Although Jack was less agreeable to the idea, I didn't need any encouragement. At this point I didn't care about anything but getting into bed. On the way into the house, I thought I'd call the local hospital in the morning to see if anyone with a head wound was brought in for treatment. I hoped so. At this point, I assumed this event was over and I could focus on the important issues in my life. Instead, it was only the beginning of a summer from hell.

THREE

The house was quiet when I woke up and Gracie was not in her carrier. Rested for the first time in months, I stretched and spread out on the bed. After a few minutes, I got up heading for the bathroom. From the hallway, I glimpsed Gram rocking Gracie snuggled on Gram's ample bosom, one tiny hand resting beside her neck. Gram's face radiated such bliss that I could see why artists often depict a halo around mother and child pictures. Not wanting to disturb them, I ducked into the bathroom to take a shower,

Hot water streamed through my shoulder length hair and down my back relaxing my body, but my mind wouldn't let go. I desperately needed Gram's advice. Maybe if she understood how awful our marriage had become, she'd say it wasn't worth fighting for. Ha! I didn't know what Gram would say, but I knew it would not be to give up on it.

By the time I stepped out of the shower, the tips of my fingers were wrinkled. I wound my hair in a towel and put on Gramps' robe. Gram looked up smiling when I came into the dining room. The rocker angled so that it sat in the alcove created by the wide archway between the living room and dining room. Gracie rested on Gram's shoulder and I kissed them both before I went into the kitchen for a cup of tea and something to eat.

I brought my tea and a couple of pieces of toast to the dining room table. From my place at the table, I could eat breakfast and still visit with Gram. Homemade strawberry jam dripped from my thumb and I slurped it off. The night before Jack and I had driven straight through from Owensville to Florida to visit my grandparents

The day before we left, Jack had come out of the bedroom that was supposed to be Gracie's nursery, tucking his shirt into his jeans. He was dressing for his usual trip uptown to Chuck's Bar and Grill.

"Can we come with you tonight?" I'd asked even though I was dead tired and knew he'd stay until they closed. I had Gracie dressed in a cute little dress and I wore my hair down the way he likes it.

"Are you crazy?" he said. "Getting away from you two is the whole point of going!" Then he slammed out of our apartment and tromped downstairs in a huff. It had hurt so much that it felt like a physical blow in the middle of my chest. I thought about poets writing that they could die of a broken heart, and I knew what they meant.

At first I cried, but after a few minutes, I got mad and loaded Gracie into my mini-van to go anyway. But when I got to Chuck's, Jack wasn't there. Later he claimed that he saw me follow him and he had gone somewhere else. I knew in my heart that couldn't be true considering how long it took me to get there. I knew then that there was no way I could live with Jack the way things were. Not for the rest of my life. It hurt too much. My one last hope was to get help from Gram. When I suggested a visit, Jack agreed. He practically never refused to visit them and, in fact, often suggested we go see them.

"Thinking about it hurt all over again. I have to tell you," I said to Gram, "I don't want to go to town with Jack to make a police report. I thought I wanted to talk with him, but now I'd just rather skip it." Gram nodded that she understood, but she didn't offer any comment. I knew she and Gramps could see how things were between us.

Gram rocked to the ticking of the grandfather clock in the corner of the living room. We sat a while, not saying anything. I finished my tea and took the cup and saucer to the kitchen. While I rinsed the cup under hot water, I thought how safe and peaceful it felt at Gram and Gramps' house. It was always a safe haven. If only I could stay with them instead of going back home with Jack.

I set the clean saucer alongside the cup in the dish drainer and went back to the living room where I curled up on the couch at the end next to Gram. I closed my eyes and let my head rest against the back of the couch. It had been a long time since I'd been completely relaxed and rested. We sat for some time without speaking. Finally I said, "I know you love having us come here as much as I love being here." Gram smiled at me and kissed the top of Gracie's blonde furry head. I bit my lip hating to spoil the moment, but I had to figure out what to do. "I need your advice," I said.

She waited, rocking, her face held close to the top of Gracie's head. "Jack and I don't get along anymore." I began. Now there's a news flash, I thought annoyed with myself. "I know divorce isn't usually right." I forced myself to continue. It was a lot harder to talk about our marriage than I thought it would be, even to Gram. "Anyway, we don't really have a marriage, Gram." When my eyes filled with tears, I wiped them on the corner of the towel wrapped around my damp hair.

Gram turned her face to the window opposite me without comment and rocked steadily. I waited. She looked down at Gracie and inhaled Gracie's sweet baby scent. She sighed and finally faced me. "It's pained your grandfather and me quite a bit to see the way you two treat each other," she said. Her pale blue eyes were stern behind her bifocals. "But your duty is to Gracie. If it was just you, it would be one thing, but it's not anymore. You have to think about your baby first."

"I know," I whispered. I had to get up and do something before I burst into tears so I got up, shook out my heavy damp hair and took the towel into the bathroom before I went out to the kitchen to fix myself a second cup of tea. When my emotions were under control a little better, I returned with the steaming cup of tea and sat on the couch again. I sipped tea lost as to what I needed to do when it occurred to me that some day Gracie would see Jack and me the way my grandparents did.

"Do you think it's a good idea to raise Gracie with role models like us? I mean, without love?"

Gram blinked and quit rocking for a moment. Sunlight poured in through the windows at her side and glinted off the wire frames of her glasses. "Maybe not," she said slowly. She looked down at Gracie and resumed her steady rhythm, a rhythm that let one sleep in total safety. More than anything, I wanted Gracie to have the security that I had growing up.

"Thank you for being there for me when I was growing up," I said softly. "I don't know what I would have done without you and Gramps." Gram nodded, absently stroking Gracie's back. "Mom and Dad were so old when they had me that I knew they resented having a kid so late in life. I'm grateful that you and Gramps were always there for me." It wasn't an indictment of my parents really, but what I considered to be family knowledge.

"Your parents love you very much, Julie." Gram sounded stern, as though that would make me believe her. "And both of your parents want you to be happy." I knew there hadn't been a lot of love lost between my mother and Gram, but they got along for the sake of the family.

"Jack doesn't want us to be a family, Gram." I faced it as I said it. "In fact, he'd probably be just as happy visiting Gracie once in a while. It's not like he spends any time with us now. He's rarely home anyway."

"Where does he go?" Gram stopped rocking and sat up straight, shifting Gracie to her shoulder.

"He goes out to be with his buddies." Gram's lips tightened and I knew she didn't like that. Going out to be with the guys isn't grounds for divorce but it would let her see what my life was like without making her think too badly of Jack. "I can't seem to make him stay home with us. And believe me, I've tried." Gram kept her eyes down, but rocked gently once more. "Speaking of Jack, where is he, anyway?"

"He went to pick up the mail and a few things from town." Gram answered. A pang of guilt shot through me at sight of her furrowed brows. I knew I shouldn't be upsetting her. Besides, I felt like I was tattling on Jack. I should be working things out for myself. I really didn't want Gracie to grow up without a father, and I wasn't sure I could handle being a single mom, either.

My cousin Andrew came to mind. He'd left his wife, Brenda, and their two-year-old son for a bimbo who knew at the time that Andrew was married. I remember Brenda had to work all the time and scrape to make ends meet. Every time Andrew came over, Andy Junior acted like it was a visit from Santa Claus. Andrew would bring toys that Brenda couldn't afford. Afterwards Brenda would cry a lot. The solution to the problem had seemed simple to me then. I told her to give the kid to Andrew so she could get a good job and be the one with enough money to buy stuff. Her reaction made more sense to me now. She'd screamed at me, "Are you nuts?" At that point I thought maybe Andrew was right in leaving Brenda because she was probably the crazy one. I marveled now at how naïve' I'd been at eleven.

"On the other hand, a father can be just as loving from a distance." I said thinking out loud. I've often been reminded not to "think out loud," as my family puts it. "I mean," I continued ignoring what was no doubt sage advice. "We don't actually have to get a divorce, just a separation." I looked to Gram to see what she thought of the idea. But before she could tell me how dumb she thought that was, Gracie opened her eyes, stuffed her fist into her mouth and began to suck furiously. That was her cue that if a bottle didn't turn up in a few minutes, she'd give everyone a red-faced howling until the bottle was produced. She rarely had to resort to that and I wanted to keep it that way.

Gram got up and handed Gracie to me. "Let's think on all this," she said. "Meanwhile, I'll get Gracie's bottle."

Jack and Gramps came in while I was putting Gracie to bed in Gramps' room. She'd been fed, burped, and changed. I had gotten dressed and made a quick call to the Port Richfield Hospital.

I set the table while Gram ladled out her wonderful soup. She puts leftover vegetables and meat into a blue enamel pot she keeps in the fridge. Somehow she knows what to add to make it taste just right. We ate bread and soup with thick slices of Gram's peach pie for dessert.

We were finishing our pie when Jack said, "Mrs. Krueger at the post office said there's been a rash of robberies in our area." Jack doesn't usually contribute to the conversation, so we all looked up from our plates. When he went back to wolfing pie, it was like we'd had our nickel's worth from the talking machine and now it was over.

"There wasn't anyone brought in last night with a head injury," I said buttering a slice of bread. "I called just before lunch."

"You probably just knocked the guy out," Gramps said. "And when he woke up, he was fine." He winked at me and I smiled. He was probably right. I wanted him to be right.

"Do you think he was in cahoots with the thief?"

"Gramps nodded yes. "I doubt if they'll try anything again in this neck of the woods, though, now that you showed them what happens to those who bother this family." Everyone laughed but I couldn't. They didn't see the way the injured man was crammed into the truck. Even if the driver was trying to stay hidden, when he picked up the flashlight, he could have at least checked to see if the guy was alive.

"Our little town hasn't seen much in the way of crime," Gramps said. "I expect it's going to be the topic for quite a while."

"Did Mrs. Krueger say anything about somebody being injured?" I asked.

"Nope." I watched Jack shovel pie into his face and felt the urge to kick him. It must have shown on my face because Gram frowned over her glasses at me like I'd been a naughty girl.

"I think you and Julie should go make that police report in town this afternoon, Jack," she said briskly. "I'll take care of Gracie, of course." She got up abruptly and picked up some empty dishes from the table. "It's nap time for both of us." I stared at her back when she left for the kitchen. Then Gramps surprised us by grabbing some dishes from the table, something he hardly ever does, and he followed Gram into the kitchen with them.

Jack was clearly irritated but he said, "Gct yourself ready than. The bus leaves in two minutes." With that he pushed away from the table and went into the bathroom. I was glad everybody left the room because tears flooded my eyes and it took two napkins and a lot of effort to blink them away. The knot in my throat remained there, but at least nobody could see it. I got up to "get ready," which amounted to grabbing my wallet from the diaper bag. As much as I wanted to talk with Jack, I didn't think it would be a good time to say anything when he was already in a bad mood. Still, we would have the time together on the way to town. He might tell me what was wrong and try to make peace for the sake of Gracie.

FOUR

It took me less than two minutes to grab my wallet from the diaper bag and check on Gracie who was awake, red faced, and grunting. It looked like she was creating a fresh load of "big girl" for Gram to change. Gram would croon over the smelly mess and tell Gracie what a nice job she'd done, while I, on the other hand, would not enjoy it nearly that much.

After I kissed Gram and Gracie, I left through the back porch to where Jack sat in the idling van. We drove up Old Gulf Road past the Dodds' house and the weed and palmetto stretch of land before we turned right at the bend and headed into town. One thing I didn't want to do, I reminded myself mentally, was to think out loud. I wanted to choose my words carefully so I waited until we turned onto Route 19. It would be a while before we got into town. That seemed like the best time to talk, if ever there was going to be one. Once Jack had negotiated onto the four lane highway leading to town, I asked, "Can we pull over and talk before we get to the cop shop?"

"What's there to talk about?" He speeded up.

"Is it possible for us to get back to that place where we were before we got married? You used to be sweet and loving, and I miss that, Jack." A familiar lump formed in my throat so I looked out the window at fields of palmettos and the occasional stand of pine that whizzed by.

We rode in silence until it was obvious that Jack wasn't going to bother to either answer or pull over. I felt red hot anger swell inside and my heart thumped. I said, "If you want a divorce, you can have it. In fact, that's what I think is going to happen anyway. We might as well get it over with."

"You can forget that idea," he said without turning his eyes from the road.

"Why?" I felt dumbfounded. "I know it can't be because you don't believe in divorce. You never go with me to church." He stared ahead as though I wasn't in the car with him. Suddenly I felt hollow and sad. "You don't love me anymore," I said quietly. All the anger had turned to something painful in the center of my chest. "Why don't you want a divorce?"

"For somebody who's good with numbers, you ought to be able to figure it out." I stared at his profile totally confused.

"What does that mean, Jack?" He didn't say anything. We just kept barreling toward town. I tried to make sense of his response. Numbers? What numbers? I looked at Jack's soft dark brown hair and handsome profile, hoping he'd soften, say something, anything more, but he didn't.

Instead we pulled into a slot in front of the police station. The narrow weathered shingle building huddled between a newer yellow brick post office and a sprawling whitewashed cedar bait shop. Jack jumped out of the car and slammed his door. He sauntered toward the run-down little building while I sat there so stunned that my mind was a complete blank.

After a couple minutes, I got out of the car and followed Jack into the building. Thick dust motes swirled in the sunshine from the plate glass window that took up most of the front wall. I squinted, batting at the dust while I tried not to breathe too deeply. A single cell furnished with a cot and a stainless steel commode occupied the back of the room. Between the window and the cell, an old gray metal desk, a rusty tan four drawer file cabinet, and two mismatched wooden straight back chairs completed the décor.

"Can I help you?" a cheerful voice came from behind us. "Oh, it's you." Officer Braxton smiled recognizing us. He nodded to me and shook hands with Jack. "Let's hope you can pick a winner from our little photo album?" He had a low amusement level, evidently, because he roared with laughter. Jack chuckled. I squeezed out a smile.

"Let's go on over to the bait shop with this," Officer Braxton said after he tugged a thick brown book from the top drawer of the file cabinet. "That way we can have a cold drink too."

We followed him outside into the blinding sun, across the tiny yard to the front of the building next door. A wide porch wrapped around the front and one side of the bait shop. Three white bait bins lined one side of the porch. Having been to the bait shop many times with Gramps, I knew they imprisoned live bait fish, and one was a freezer stocked with frozen brine shrimp and other delicacies for the finicky fish palette.

We climbed the two wide wooden steps to the front door, but instead of going inside, I was offered a springy metal chair toward one end of the porch. I shrugged and sat. Immediately the heavy book was handed to me. The front screen door squeaked open and Officer Daly came out carrying dripping wet, cold sodas for each of us

Jack sat on the opposite end of the porch and talked with the two officers while I flipped through the book. Faded photographs were almost too faint to be clear by the end of the dusty tome. I didn't see anyone who looked like the man I'd hit in the head. "Did you check the hospitals in nearby towns?" I asked dropping the book on the seat of the chair as I stood.

"Yep." Officer Braxton spit off the porch into the scrub grass growing in patches around the building. It irked me that he was about as communicative as Jack.

"Is there any reason why I can't leave town and go back home?" I dropped my empty Pepsi bottle into a blue plastic rack leaning against a bait bin and wiped my hands on my jean shorts.

"None that I can think of." Officer Daly stretched his crinkly face into a smile. He was probably only middle aged, but his skin was slow roasted by the sun into creased leather. "We'll contact you if anything turns up, but I doubt it will. I think whoever it was will steer clear of this neck of the woods since you bopped him with your killer skillet." All three men laughed. I winced at the word killer.

Officer Braxton chuckled his way to the rack for empty soda bottles. Too thick in the waist to bend over, one leg shot out behind him as he tipped over from the hip to drop his empty soda bottle into a slot in the rack.

The two men turned to go inside the bait shop. Jack stepped off the porch, slid behind the wheel of the van and honked the horn. I got in beside him. "That was a waste of time," I said. Jack pulled into traffic. It was late afternoon so traffic was light. "I really hoped we could talk about maybe getting along better."

Jack exhaled loudly through his mouth, but ignored me otherwise. After several miles of silence, I decided that if he didn't want to talk to me, we might as well split up. The first thing was to get home and then get my two older brothers to help me give Jack the boot. He could find somewhere else to live, somewhere where I didn't have to pretend we were married anymore.

"I'm taking Gracie and we're going home tomorrow," I said. It didn't stop the pain in my gut when I said it, but it felt a little like some kind of relief.

"You're not going anywhere until I'm damn good and ready." Jack answered, again not taking his eyes off the road. I looked at him with new eyes. He still had the same hair and face, the same wide shoulders, but now I knew how somebody who is ugly inside can look ugly on the outside too. A lot of things popped into my mind to say to Jack, but I felt so angry that I preferred to let my actions speak for me. I wasn't sure what actions I'd take yet, but given some time, I knew I'd come up with something.

Jack stalked straight into the house when we got back. Gramps was sitting on a faded redwood lawn chair pulling old fishing line from a reel. He did this periodically. I asked him one time what he was doing and he'd said he had to take off old line to replace it with fresh line. I knew it was so if he caught Moby Dick, the line wouldn't break because it was old and worn out.

I hugged Gramps' shoulders and dropped onto a nearby lawn chair. Gramps smiled and went on pulling string, using both hands in an overhand motion. I watched a few minutes. His movements were swift and sure, but then he'd had years of practice.

"Gramps, when you and Jack fish together, does he ever say anything about us? Or me?

"Sorry, Sweetie," Gramps shook his head no. He quit pulling line and met my gaze. "Jack's real quiet when we fish, but then you don't want to scare away the fish. About all we discuss is fishing and the weather. Why?"

I dropped my eyes. "I just wondered." He went back to ripping off line. Part of me wanted to tell him that I couldn't live with Jack anymore but a bigger part didn't want Gramps to think less of me. "I almost forgot that you can't talk when you fish," I said. "No wonder I don't like fishing." He chuckled and I tried to laugh with him but it didn't come out like a laugh. It sounded more like a sob to me. I hugged him and headed inside.

The house was cool and fragrant with something Gram was cooking when I stepped into the kitchen from the back porch. Gram was busy getting a cello bag of carrots from the refrigerator so I knew Gracie must be asleep. Thank God she was a good baby.

"I need to lie down," I said to Gram. She held out her cheek for a kiss without taking her eyes from the carrot she'd begun to peel. I was grateful that she would wait until I wanted to talk to hear about what happened at the cop shop.

Gracie was on Gramps' bed so I snuggled around her. My mind reeled. I had no earthly idea what to do. I knew I could always call my two older brothers, Shawn and Kevin. They'd come and get me. But I wasn't sure what would happen then. I didn't want a bitter divorce. I didn't want Gracie to suffer strained holidays and fights over who got to have her on weekends and during the summer. Plenty of my friends in school went through all that and more. The idea of Jack taking Gracie anywhere alone didn't seem likely. He never had. Still, just for spite he might.

I must have drifted off to sleep because the room was dark when I woke up. Gram rapped on the open bedroom door. I sat up and rubbed my eyes. Gracie was no longer asleep beside me. Gram came in and sat on the edge of the bed. "I guess you really are worn out," she said. She took off her glasses, wiping them on a hanky she had tucked in the pocket of her cotton dress.

When she finished, I put my arms across her shoulders and gave her a hug. She wrapped her arms around me, pulling my head to her shoulder where we rocked on the edge of the bed. It was as close to being rocked in her arms as I'd come in years. It was heaven. Gram let go suddenly. Jack loomed in the doorway. "Gramps told me supper's ready." He took up most of the space in the doorway before he turned away. Gram followed Jack out to the dining room. It took me a few minutes to fight off the urge to rush out and belt Jack with something.

Together, Gram and I served a pot roast with carrots, potatoes and gravy, corn on the cob, and homemade stewed tomatoes. I knew I'd get some private time with Gram later, when the men went out to take on six to eight inch long grouper.

After supper the men went out to fish while Gram and I did the dishes. Afterwards we fed Gracie and gave her a bath. Sharing bath time with Gracie and Gram lifted my spirits for a while. No matter how I felt about Jack, I'd do it again to have her. I put Gracie to bed for the night. Gram made green tea with a disk of peppermint candy in the bottom of our cups. That's how we both like to relax while we watch television. We carried our cups to the living room to get comfortable. The living room is small but warm and cozy. Across from

Gram's rocker, along the wall on the opposite side of the wide archway, a soft leather chair angles to face the TV. I tuned on the set, pressed the record button on the digital record box, and then muted it so I could get right to the point.

Gram settled in her rocker. I set my cup on the coffee table, took a deep breath and blurted out, "I asked Jack for a divorce and he said no." I couldn't look at her so I leaned my head back on one of the throw pillows that Gram had cross-stitched. I closed my eyes and hoped that I wouldn't cry while I waited for a response. The rocker creaked but she didn't say anything. "Jack's way different than when we got married," I finally added.

"Nobody stays the same." Gram sipped her tea.

"We live like strangers, Gram. He sleeps in what was supposed to be Gracie's room and I sleep in what's supposed to be our bedroom. And he's never home. He only comes home when he wants supper or clean clothes." It sounded like I was whining. I blew out a breath and took a sip of hot tea. For some reason I couldn't get a handle on what to say or how to convey what I wanted her to understand.

"How did it come about that he sleeps in Gracie's bedroom?" she asked.

"You know I was sick all the time when I was pregnant, so eventually it was a relief not to have him moving around in bed with me." It sounded like Jack was trying to be a gentleman when actually he'd set up a bed in Gracie's room so he didn't have to listen to me puke into the plastic waste basket I had to put next to the bed.

I was about to explain that when Gram said, "If you're not sleeping together anymore, maybe that's why he's behaving the way he is. You aren't doing your duty as a wife, dear."

My hand shook holding my tea cup and I think my hair stood on end but I directed my gaze into my cup. All the red stripes on my mint had dissolved and only a fragile white disk remained

When I was able to look up, I said, "Jack's made it clear that he doesn't want to sleep with me."

She sipped her tea and looked out the windows. On TV Images of a young couple holding hands on a garden path walked across the muted screen. "I think you need to give it more time." She looked at her hands. "Sometimes the mere passage of time changes things. He's obviously angry with you. I suspect he's frustrated and that's why he's so upset with you. One thing I do know is that your place is by his side and in his bed." When our eyes finally met, she added, "For Gracie's sake."

I couldn't stop a rush of tears. They slid down my cheeks and my nose clogged up. I always love the part where snot covers the part of your face that your tears miss. I reached for the hanky Gram held out, wiped my eyes, and sniffed until I could breathe better. "You know I believe in God, Gram. But I don't think Gracie should grow up with us as role models. In my Life Skills class at school, they talked about how important parents are as role models. I want Gracie to learn how to be a loving, caring person and I'm afraid that can't happen with parents with no love between them. Besides, I don't want to be a prisoner the rest of my life." I finished in a voice husky with newly forming tears.

"Do you love him?"

It took a while to answer. My first instinct was to say no, but I did love the old Jack, the one I married. "I did love him. But he's so changed," I managed to answer.

"You've let this go on far too long. I can see how you two might have drawn apart when you were too sick to do much above taking care of yourself and the house, but now it's different. You should go home, get back into his bed, and see if you can't make your marriage work for the sake of your family." It sounded simple. I go home, Jack jumps on and bingo, one happy marriage. "I guess I could try it," I said. I sure didn't have a better plan. It sounded like a stupid plan to me, but at least it was something.

FIVE

Gram and I didn't talk anymore about my problems with Jack. We watched a couple of television shows, but I wasn't really paying attention to them. My mind was numb. Nothing made sense. We turned in early but I lay awake next to Gracie trying to will myself to sleep. Suddenly a pinpoint beam of light from the window at the foot of the bed crawled across my legs. I froze, squinting. The strip of light moved up my body. I shut my eyes completely when the light reached my face. I didn't move. When I sensed the light pass my eyes, I opened them a slit. The thin shaft of light cut into the room. When it moved away from the bed enough, I gently rolled over on my side, facing the nightstand. The light flicked back to the bed, held, and then cut across Gramps' dresser and chest. My cell phone lay within inches of my hand on the night table. By moving my hand very slowly toward the phone, I was able to pull it under my cover. The light flicked off abruptly. I held my breath, waiting for something to happen. When nothing happened, I pressed 9-1-1 with my thumb, slipped the phone to my ear and softly said. "I need the police."

This time it was only a matter of minutes before I heard tires on the road. When headlights flashed past my window, I eased off the bed, and I scooted over to the window where spotlights flared between our house and the Dodds' house next door. Gramps poked his head in at the door and asked, "You all right?" I nodded and he withdrew in response to a knock at the front door. I flipped on a lamp. Gracie drooled from the corner of her mouth as she lay in her carrier, her tiny fingers uncurled at each side of her head. My fingers trembled as I scrambled into the shorts and top I'd left on a nearby chair.

In the dining room, Officer Daly was speaking with Gramps. Officer Braxton leaned on the dining room table, his left hand curled around his note pad as he wrote. His short, dark hair looked uncombed, and his face was dark with stubble. The screen door slammed on the back porch and Jack came in then through the kitchen. Officer Daly's thin sandy hair lay in limp wisps, the lines in his face deep and pronounced.

Officer Braxton straightened up, readjusted his pants beneath his overhanging belly, and flipped his note pad closed after I explained about the light from the window. "Did you leave your bedroom window open at all?" he asked. I shook my head no, surprised at the question.

"We have the air conditioning on," Gramps said.

"I thought as much," Officer Braxton said. "We noticed that the window is open part way and there's a hole above the lock. Looks like someone put his hand through the hole and unlocked the window. He must have been in the process of opening it when something scared him off." I gulped audibly. Gramps looked surprised but Jack scowled like he'd been up to something. I'd seen the look before and wondered what he wasn't saying. "We'll stay in the area," Officer Braxton said.

The two nodded to me and shook hands with Gramps and Jack before they left out the front door. We followed them outside. The squad car worked its way up the road, its spotlights flaring over the strip of vacant land on their left and the Dodds' house on the right, followed by several empty lots until the road turned toward town and they were out of sight.

Inside, the three of us settled around the dining room table like startled birds returning to a row of high tension wires. Jack looked strangely agitated but said nothing, rubbing his jaw as he does when he's upset or angry.

"As I recollect," Gramps said, "Port Richfield only has the two policemen and I think they're considered part time.

Seems to me they work for the bait shop unless called on, but I could be wrong."

Jack stared into his clasped hands. My gut told me he knew something.

"What do you suppose the prowler was after?" I directed my question to Jack.

He leaned an elbow on the table, cleared his throat and mumbled while he looked down at the table, "Maybe I'd better get Julie and Gracie out of here. We'd better go home in the morning." My mouth fell open but he didn't look up.

Gramps shook his head and pushed up from the table. "I guess I better go nail up a board over the window before turning in." Gramps was a carpenter by trade, like my dad and two older brothers. "I think Julie will feel safer, Jack, if you sleep inside with her tonight," Gramps said from the kitchen doorway. Then he left for the back porch to look for a board to use on the window without waiting for a response from either of us.

Jack pushed away from the table and slammed the bath-room door behind him. He and I hadn't slept in the same bed since I got pregnant with Gracie. I went into the bedroom to put Gracie into her carrier to make room for him on the bed. When Jack came in, I brushed past him on my way to the bathroom and when I crawled into bed, Jack faced the wall

I was too upset to sleep. I thought about how much fun our engagement had been. Tears burned my eyes and my nose clogged so I reached for a tissue from the night stand determined not to let Jack hear me cry. Before our wedding, Jack had been attentive and sweet. He took me to all kinds of fun places like downtown Chicago to several theatres, a concert, dancing at the Willowbrook Ballroom, the museums and he even went shopping with me.

Jack and my brothers, Shawn and Kevin were buddies. My brothers tried to discourage me from hanging around with Jack. They said it was because Jack was ten years older than me. I didn't see that as a problem. In fact, it was like a dream come true when Jack gave me an engagement ring last spring, during my senior year in high school. It had all been very exciting. For a wedding present, Dad and my brothers built us an apartment over my parents' garage. It was more an assembly of leftovers from their carpentry jobs, but it's a great apartment and I love it.

After the wedding my parents took off to follow their dream of touring the country in a Winnebago motor home. They left me the old camper and Dodge Caravan. My brothers live in the house and take care of it for them.

Our marriage didn't go bad until I got pregnant. What happened was that it was only a couple of days after my period last year. Jack wanted to have sex while I was on the pill and also on an antibiotic for a sore throat. Turns out antibiotics cancel out the effect of the pill. Anyway, I was so nauseated that I couldn't be fun or sexy anymore. When Jack moved into the room that was going to be the nursery, I felt relieved because he couldn't even turn over without making me feel queasy. I assumed it was only temporary.

But two weeks ago I came home from my six weeks checkup and told Jack that he could sleep with me again. Instead, he said that there was "no hurry," and he chose to go out to Chuck's Bar and Grill like he'd been doing all winter. Since then it seemed like he was angry at me for something all the time.

I lay beside a man that I didn't even know anymore. After a while I slipped out of bed and went into the bathroom to cry so Jack wouldn't hear me. It was late, and I knew nothing would be solved thinking about it as tired as I was so I closed my eyes and whispered a quick prayer for guidance and went back to bed. We slept back to back until morning.

Next morning, we ate breakfast, kissed Gram and Gramps and loaded Gracie into the van. Gram had packed us what she calls a "care package." She sent us off with ham sandwiches, chocolate chip cookies, six jars of her homemade jam, some bottles of her stewed tomatoes, and a bag of oranges and grapefruit from their trees.

To show Gram that her advice was at least worth a try, I wore a low cut tee top, shorts, and had my hair down instead of clipped up off my shoulders. Who knew? Sometimes simple things work. All I needed as we hit the road was a singer twanging out a song about winning back my man.

An hour into the trip, however, I ran out of topics to tempt Jack into a conversation. I gave up and we drove home listening to Jack's crappy heavy metal CDs. For the most part, Gracie slept, Jack drove, the music blared, and I fumed.

SIX

It was after two in the morning when we finally reached Owensville and pulled into our driveway. We climbed the outside enclosed stairway leading to our apartment above the garage too weary to even unpack the van. I put Gracie in her crib against the wall next to my bed and then I tumbled into bed way too tired to even consider inviting Jack to join me.

After Gracie's six o'clock bottle the next morning, I went back to sleep until she woke me up for her ten o'clock bottle. It was Saturday and Jack was not in his room when I got up. Jack's an electrician and, like many tradesmen, he often takes a side job on weekends so I assumed that's where he'd gone.

I had a lot of things to keep my mind off of my problems. After I fed Gracie, I made myself some cereal, took a shower, unloaded the van and went to pick up the mail and get a few groceries. The rest of the day I spent getting laundry done and going through the mail.

When Jack came home for supper, I forced myself to be cheerful. I served his favorite supper, chicken and biscuits. He ate without comment; unless you count the grunt he gave me in response to whether he enjoyed his meal.

Things started to look up after supper though. Instead of leaving, Jack turned on the TV in the living room and sat on the couch with a beer while I cleaned up the kitchen. I'd put on makeup and I wore a hot pink tee shirt that showed ample cleavage. Gracie cooed from her carrier in the living room. When I finished with the dishes, I went into the living room to join my family.

Jack's beer bottle dangled between his knees as he leaned over Gracie. She made a cute little sound and Jack chuckled. He leaned back, took a swig of beer and smiled at me. My heart melted. I leaned over him, bringing my low cut top close to his face and said, "We make good babies, huh?" He nodded and ran his finger along the rim of my tee shirt. I smiled and he cupped my chin for a kiss.

The theme song from ROCKY played in my mind when he reached for me, and afterwards, I lay in bed next to him and decided Gram was right. I was relaxed and reached over to kiss him when he rolled out of bed and headed for the bathroom. I followed, needing to use it myself. When I came out of the bathroom, Jack was in his bedroom instead of ours so I went to the doorway and said, "I thought you'd want to sleep in our room now. We need to be together," I added, "for Gracie's sake at the very least."

He sauntered over to the door, leaned over me and said, "We are as together as we're gonna get, kid." Then he pushed the door closed, forcing me to step back.

It ticked me off so much that I beat my fists on the door. "What's going on with you, damn it!" There was no answer. "Get out here and talk to me!" When I got tired of beating on his door without getting any response, I crawled into my bed totally confused. What else did he want?

Sunday morning Jack left before I got up. I went to church and spent the afternoon catching up on my part-time bookkeeping. During my senior year at Owensville High I'd gotten Kline's Department store, Al's Auto Body Shop, and Tom's True Value Hardware to let me do their bookkeeping part time. Together they pay enough for me to get along and put away a few bucks each month.

When Jack didn't come home for supper that night, I made myself a cup of tea and reached for the phone to call my friend Margie. I needed to tell her we were back and to catch up on all the local gossip.

There wasn't much going on in town. I griped about Jack leaving his stuff all over and the fact that we were not really able to talk together much, but I couldn't share what happened last night. Margie told me she was also mad at her husband, Brad. "I made Brad so mad at me last night that he gave me a little shiner." She laughed and sounded downright jovial about it. It made my skin crawl. I thought Brad always seemed a little rough, but now I saw him in another light. The idea that he hit Margie, and that she was so matter of fact about it, gave me a sick feeling. I thought back to the occasional bruises I'd noticed and the time she had a really bad swollen lip, and I wondered if Margie was trapped in a miserable marriage too.

After we hung up, I watched some TV and went to bed after the evening news. I lay in bed not only mad at Jack now but Brad too. My mind darted around like a ball in a pinball machine. I knew that if I went for a divorce, Gram and Gramps wouldn't like it and everyone in town would hold it against me for walking out on my husband, especially since we had Gracie. But, I told myself, this marriage wasn't the kind of family life I wanted for my baby or for me.

I turned over to try to go to sleep. Something scratched at the window in the living room. I thought fleetingly that it might be the person who cut a hole in Gramps' window in Florida, but that didn't seem likely. What made more sense was that a branch from the green mountain ash tree growing next to the apartment was probably rubbing against the window in the living room. The scraping stopped. That would happen if the wind died down. But as I listened, my muscles tense, waiting, it happened again, I was too aggravated to waste any more time wondering about it. I knew I wasn't going to get any sleep until I checked it out. I yanked my covers back and turned on the small reading light on my headboard.

This just made shadows around the bedroom. I thrust my feet into my scuffs by the bed, got up and turned on the overhead light. That felt better. I reached for the light switch on the living room wall outside my bedroom to turn on the lamps. No boogeyman from Florida in the living room. Jack's room is adjacent to mine, so I stepped into his room and turned on the overhead lights. Nobody there either.

I walked quickly through the lighted living room to the kitchen and flipped on the wall switch. It too was empty. The only room that remained was the bathroom off the kitchen. I hit the bathroom wall switch. The shower curtain was pulled closed to dry after my shower, but I marched over, whisked it open, and rolled my eyes. I was creeping myself out.

On my way back through my apartment, turning off lights as I went, I added myself to the People Who Deserve a Swift Kick in the Butt list. I swatted off the headboard light and I got back into bed. When the tree branch scraped again, I asked myself what a glass cutter might sound like. Damn! I didn't check the window either. The red digital numbers on my clock glowed 2:30 A.M. I could always call my brothers to come and check things out but if I called at this hour, there'd better be somebody there or I'd be called a wuss forever.

Once again I jammed my feet into my scuffs, stalked into the living room and hit the light switch. My drapes were drawn closed across the double windows, so I yanked the corner pull cord so hard the drapes flapped open. The window panes reflected the light from the room, except for a circle above the lock the size of a softball, black against the night. I huffed back into the bedroom to call my brothers at the house.

I heard Shawn's muffled hello and yelled, "Somebody's trying to break into the apartment by the tree!" Since I'd just been through the place, I knew no one lurked in the apartment. But I thought if a guy came into the window now, I'd rather not be close at hand. I grabbed Gracie and my cell phone and hot footed it down the enclosed stairway to huddle against the door until my brothers came outside. I punched in 9-1-1 while I waited.

Kevin pulled the door open. "Is somebody up there?" I shrugged and he pushed past me to take the stairs two at a time. I held the door open prepared to run. It didn't take long for Kevin to tromp downstairs, past me and Gracie, and call to Shawn. "See anything?"

Shawn answered from the back of the garage that it was all clear so far. Kevin went into the garage for a flashlight. The siren from Owensville's one and only police car wailed in the distance and finally screamed into our driveway. The siren and their searchlights insured that all of my neighbors would be up and out.

Gracie slept on my shoulder probably thinking she heard her father's heavy metal noise. I stepped out as our neighbors, in various stages of dress and undress, congregated on our oversized asphalt driveway. They were a conglomeration of senior citizens, in sleep bonnets, smashed perms, missing false teeth, and liver spotted bald heads. Most of them had bought their homes at the same time as my grandparents.

Behind the throng, the movement of an old red truck with wooden sides pulled out of the Dairy Queen parking lot across the street and caught my eye. "Hey!" I pointed. "There goes the truck I saw in Florida!" But it was out of sight by the time anybody turned around to look.

Shawn, Kevin, and Hugh, one of Owensville's three cops, came from the side of the garage. "I think I just saw the truck that the thief in Florida drove!"

"There's a ladder leaning against the garage, right below the hole you saw." Kevin announced to everyone.

"The guy from Florida's here?" I repeated the question a couple of times as if somebody had an answer.

"Take it easy Brat." Shawn cuffed my shoulder lightly. "We'll take care of him for you. Don't we always?" I blew out a deep breath and nodded. My tummy unclenched.

"So we're down one window pane and up a ladder." Kevin, on stage for the neighbors, flashed a two finger victory sign. The remark amused the neighbors, but his cavalier attitude worried me. But then, neither of my brothers had ever been unable to bully his way through whatever problem came along.

Naturally everybody wanted to hear all about what happened in Florida, so I brought the town's policemen and the neighbors up to speed on the bizarre prowler and the truck with the man who picked him up. I ended with the hole cut in the window.

"Oh my!" Mrs. Costanza next door spit-gasped. Her false teeth were out and her head bristled with tufts of gray hair. Mrs. Costanza is probably the oldest person in town. Nobody knows how old she is, but nobody in town can remember her not being older than them either. Mr. and Mrs. Costanza bought Gram and Gramps' house. Right after Mr. Costanza made his first mortgage insurance payment, he died of a heart attack. Now everyone in the neighborhood looks after Mrs. Costanza.

"We'll watch your back," Mr. Spinoza said. Short, bald on top, and proud of his Italian heritage, he has plenty of spunk. He lived next door to us on the other side all my life. Everyone made similar offers of comfort and encouragement.

"Thanks," I said to everyone, "I appreciate any help I can get." Eventually, when nothing else happened, everyone but the police and my brothers drifted away. Shawn had gone to school with our three-man police force. My brothers refer to our policemen as Huey, Louis, and Donald Duck. Their names, in fact, are Hugh Hanover, Lewis Grayson, and Donald McNulty. They talked with Shawn while Kevin went into the garage chuckling about needing a piece of plywood for my window to keep out the bugs, the birds, and the bad guys. I had to admit that my brothers probably could take care of this problem for me now that it was on our turf.

"Where is our old buddy, Jack?" Shawn asked. The squad car backed out of the driveway, lights and siren on for the thrill of it.

"I assume he's at Chuck's."

Shawn didn't look happy to hear that but then he and Kevin spend a lot of time at Chuck's Bar and Grill too. Kevin came out of the garage with a piece of plywood and went to hammer it over the window. "Go to bed, Brat," Shawn rubbed the top of my head. "We'll take care of everything." I slept as soundly as Gracie the rest of the night.

SEVEN

I must not have heard Jack come home because when I got up to feed Gracie in the morning, Jack came out of his bedroom scratching his broad, bare chest. His pajama bottoms hung loose on his slim hips. I used to think that looked sexy. Now I wondered if part of his attraction had been the fact that he was new in town and every girl under menopause was hot for him. I won the competition. Now I didn't even want to have a conversation with him.

I wasn't sure how I wanted to handle the situation with Jack, so I'd have to be careful not to think out loud or lose my temper. Gracie's future depended on it. Jack had to go to work so I made him eggs and toast for breakfast, packed his lunch, and left the kitchen as soon as I finished, leaving him to read the paper and eat alone. I went in and made my bed and sorted laundry until I heard Jack leave. Whenever I'm upset, I like to keep busy doing housework. The activity helps me think somehow. While I wrestled with what to do about Jack, the guy who cut holes in my window lurked in the back of my mind too.

I finished getting my clothes ready to take over to the house to wash and decided I'd get Jack's too. It wouldn't help much to pick a fight over stuff I didn't care about until I'd decided what exactly I wanted to do. I found most of Jack's dirty clothes on the floor at the foot of his bed. A pair of dress slacks hung on the doorknob of his closet. His slacks were badly wrinkled and needed to go to the cleaners. I rolled them up and set them on his bed after I'd made it up. I picked up the rest of his dirty clothes, scooping up his wet towel from off the floor and the dress slacks. In the kitchen I dumped his clothes in the pile of Gracie and my stuff, and I put his slacks on the corner of the counter to take with me to the cleaners when I did my errands. After I hung up his towel in the bathroom, I did the dishes and cleaned the kitchen. Finally I settled at the kitchen table with a cup of tea to drink while I talked on the phone with Margie. The local grapevine would have spread the news about somebody cutting a hole in my window last night, but Margie would get a first-hand account from me.

"Why on earth would somebody follow you all the way from Florida just to break into your apartment?" Margie asked when I finished my tale.

"Beats me. But unless it's the newest craze in home burglary, it has to be the same guy. The hole was exactly like the one in Gramps' window, same size, and same place above the lock. The truck looked like the kind that stopped to pick up the injured prowler I hit over the head. I can't imagine why he picked up the man, nor what he'd want from me."

"Got any idea what you own that anybody would want real bad?"

"Not a clue."

"Where was Jack?"

"Chuck's, I guess." As I said that, Jack's dress slacks on the corner of the kitchen counter, spoke to me. Dress slacks? For Chuck's? I couldn't explain the intruder, but all of a sudden the penny dropped, and I could explain what was going on with Jack. The wife may be the last to know, but I decided she's probably the first to suspect.

"You up for an early lunch at Chuck's today?" I was as casual as possible considering my thumping heart. "My treat." Margie never turned down an offer like that. After we hung up, I called myself all kinds of stupid while I fixed a bottle for Gracie, took my shower, and got dressed Growing up with brothers like Shawn and Kevin, you'd think I'd have immediately put two and two together. I came to the conclusion that I must have been sleepwalking all year, but I knew that I was awake now.

By the time I'd dressed and had Gracie ready to go, Margie's rusty blue Cutlass pulled into our driveway. We're the only ones in the neighborhood with a garage as big as a barn and a driveway that reduces the back yard to a strip of flowers along the fence. But then none of us likes to cut grass anyway, so it works for us.

Margie's chestnut curls frame a great big grin complete with dimples. I slid open the side door of my old Caravan and Margie expertly snapped Bradley Junior's car seat behind the driver's side so she could reach back to him. I put Gracie behind Margie who had already climbed in front. "Do we have time to stop at the DQ?" We usually began our ventures together by getting an ice cream cone for her baby at the Dairy Queen first.

I cranked the ignition, and stifled a gasp at the heavy make-up beneath her swollen left eye. "Of course," I said casually, but she knew I'd noticed her eye. She didn't say anything as we pulled out of the driveway. It was hard to keep my mouth shut but I knew when she wanted to say something about it, she would.

The business section of Main Street is encroaching into our neighborhood and since our house is only half a block from Main Street, the Dairy Queen is now located directly across the street from my parents' house. With a practiced sweep, I backed out of our driveway and wheeled into the drive-through for a small cone for Bradley. He'd reduce it to goo all down his front, but part of his everyday outfit includes a big plastic bib with a pocket on the bottom to collect the big stuff.

We waited for Bradley's ice cream cone while I told Margie what I suspected. "Jack would be nuts to fool around with anybody with your brothers around." Margie said. The ice cream cone and my change were handed out the drive through window. Margie twisted in her seat and handed a miniature vanilla ice cream cone to her five-month-old son.

"I don't know where Jack was last night, but he came home after the police and everybody left so it had to be after two o'clock. I bet Chuck knows what bimbo he was with."

Margie's eyes widened and her dimples faded. When I didn't add anything further, she said, "You don't look all broken up."

"To tell the truth, all I feel right now is stupid and embarrassed. If he has actually been screwing around, everybody must know."

"I haven't heard anything but everybody knows I'm your friend."

"If anybody knows, Chuck will. I'm going to have a talk with old Chucky boy, but first I think we should have lunch, don't you?" I forced a grin. She smiled back relieved.

We passed the WalMart and crossed the tracks into the town's main business district. I angled into a parking space next to Chuck's Bar and Grill. The owner's son, Chuck, runs the place for his father, who retired to Arizona. My brother Kevin went to school with Chuck. Kevin is ten years older than me, and Shawn is twelve years older. The family joke is Mom thought she was in menopause and refused to go to the doctor until I kicked her in the ribs.

By the time I was out of the van and came around to the sliding door, Margie had Bradley's car seat unhooked. I unlatched Gracie's carrier and followed Margie into the dimly lit restaurant.

Six black Formica topped tables with chrome and maroon chairs are sandwiched between a wooden bar the length of the restaurant and a row of booths patched with duct tape... There are no cloths on the tables, some aren't even level, but the kitchen behind the bar produces the best pizza and Italian beef sandwiches around.

Margie put Bradley's car seat on the floor at the end of a booth after she slid onto the seat. I sat across from her with Gracie in her carrier on the floor next to me. I was glad that the place was empty since it was so early. At noon, the stools in front of the bar and every chair and booth would be filled. Besides having great food, Chuck's is the only restaurant in town.

Margie leaned over and deftly wiped ice cream and bits of soggy cone from Bradley's face. Then she snapped open a clean bib from her diaper bag on the seat next to her, and with a few expert moves, she had Bradley ready for his next mess.

"Bradley's really getting big" I commented. "Let's hope he learns to walk before you can't lift him anymore."

She rummaged around in her diaper bag on the seat until she fished out a pacifier. "We're lucky we have such good babies," she said as she clipped one end of the pacifier to Bradley's bib. She popped the other end into Bradley's mouth and he promptly closed his eyes.

"Man," I grinned, "that plug is like a sleep switch." Margie's loose brown curls bounced when she shook her head and laughed. I envy her natural curly hair. My hair is long, and as Gramps once said, "It's straight as a yard of pump water." The only good thing about my hair is that it's thick. Well, and people have said It's a nice honey color.

"How about a nice fat Italian beef and a Pepsi for both of us," I called to Chuck. Chuck doesn't "wait" on customers. Instead he stands behind the bar and people call out what they want. The place isn't really that big, and he really is that lazy.

Margie's husband, Brad, is such a tightwad that she doesn't usually have anything left over after buying groceries and necessities. My three bookkeeping jobs work well enough so that I can occasionally splurge. There are other advantages too. I can pick up the company bills and receipts when I'm out running errands. As long as I pay the bills and make out the payroll checks on time, I'm golden. Of course I also have to keep the bookkeeping ledgers up to date for the quarterly audits. I can do the work at home too, which is another perk. The downside is that since they're all considered part time, I don't get any fringe benefits like insurance. I do get in-store discounts, though, so that helps.

Chuck went through the swinging doors behind the bar into the kitchen to make our sandwiches. I smiled at Margie without saying anything. It isn't that I wasn't hurting; I just didn't want to be like a member of my brother's silly "bimbo squad."

In public my brothers are very gallant to all women, even old Mrs. Costanza next door. They open doors, pull out chairs, and fawn over them. At home they laugh and joke about them unmercifully.

One time Shawn was in bed, while some dumb girl sat on the couch in our living room reading a magazine like she was in the waiting room of a doctor's office or something. I went down to Shawn's bedroom in the basement, told the lump under the covers he had company, and all he did was roll over and say, "She'll wait." And she did.

My brothers are both over six feet tall and very muscular from carrying heavy stacks of wood. They have competitions with one another to see who can carry the heaviest load. Our family has always been competitive. All three of us have blonde hair and blue eyes. Shawn is a little heavier than Kevin, and his hair is darker blonde than mine or Kevin's. We grew up listening to people tell my parents what beautiful children she had. In school girls used to tell me how great it would be to live with Kevin or Shawn. If they only knew.

After Margie and I finished eating, Margie carried Bradley out to the van while I went over to the cash register at the end of the bar carrying Gracie's carrier, my diaper bag slung over my shoulder. I didn't know exactly what I was going to say, but I knew I'd think of something.

I handed Chuck a twenty. Chuck has a big, mushy bran muffin face. He always wears droopy pants under an apron tied somewhere beneath his beer belly. I'm five six and figure he's maybe three or four inches taller.

Chuck," I said looking directly into his dark little raisin eyes, "I know Jack is screwing around on me." He looked like I'd stepped on his toe. "Before you deny it, let me point out that either you are with me, or against me. Now if you are siding with Jack, then you'll have to take whatever consequences my brothers dish out to Jack when I tell them about it."

"I don't know nuthin', honest!" He spoke an octave higher than normal, and his raisin eyes plumped up big and round. "He don't tell me his business. He just comes in here for a few beers!"

"Yeah, well keep what I said in mind." I turned to walk out. At times like this I'm glad I can count on my brothers. As a kid, I was spoiled by them. They bought me toys and were enthralled with having a little baby sister. As I got older and demanded more bathroom time, they got a little less enthralled. But if anyone ever gave me a hard time, all I had to do was tell them and it was taken care of so well that I never had to worry again.

One time I was on a date with Karl Oberman who pushed me down on the front seat of his father's Chevy. "Stop it, Karl," I said squirming back up. "I'm saving myself for marriage."

Karl paused long enough to ask, "Why?"

"Because," I told him, "before I give my body to a guy, he has to give me something too. He has to prove he loves me enough to stand up in front of God and his mother and say he loves me and he'll take care of me and any kids we have." Karl laughed and shoved me down again.

So I belted him in the face. While he tried to stop his nosebleed, I walked to a nearby house and called home. I was a freshman then. The next day Karl was all beaten up. He said he'd fallen down but nobody ever gave me any trouble after that. I joined clubs, played softball and worked on the newspaper. I had lots of dates and hung with Margie, her husband, Brad, and a group of kids I'd known all my life.

I was pretty sure if Jack was getting interested in someone else, Chuck would find a way to get a message to him to knock it off before my brothers found out. Instead, after I turned to go, he said in a barely audible voice, "Charlotte Hooper." I knew Charlotte from high school. Two years ahead of me, she was known as the school "mattress."

"That's good thinking, Chuck," I said without turning around. My legs felt wobbly as I pushed through the door of the restaurant but I don't think Chuck noticed. I stepped out into the bright July afternoon, temporarily blinded by the sun shining in my blurry eyes. I wiped the traitor tears away with the back of my hand.

EIGHT

Margie had already buckled Bradley into the back seat of the van when I came out of Chuck's. I put Gracie into the van and slammed the side door. I enjoyed slamming it so much that I slammed the door a couple more times before I got in behind the wheel. Bradley set up a squawk and Gracie stirred a little. Margie replaced Bradley's pacifier and he settled back to sleep. Then she turned to me and waited until I could speak.

"The bastard! Chuck just told me that Jack's been with Charlotte Hooper."

Margie gasped, her eyes wide, her hand at her mouth. I peeled into traffic, my tires squealing a moment but immediately I slowed to a safer pace for the sake of my passengers. We drove in silence a moment before Margie asked, "Do we kill him, or leave it to your brothers?"

"My brothers sniff every tail that comes down the road too." I was mad at them too for some inexplicable reason. I hit the steering wheel with the side of my fist. All I could think about was how everybody must know. "I can hardly believe it."

"Me neither. He's got to know your brothers will kill him." She looked at me and I knew what she was thinking.

"They must have known." I made myself concentrate on driving in hopes that the ache in my middle would subside. When it didn't, I wondered if it ever would. I didn't feel any pain when Chuck told me about Charlotte. So why did it hurt now? Was it a delayed reaction? Or was it because my brothers knew and didn't tell me?

Margie interrupted my thoughts. "I have a confession to make, Julie." I listened half heartedly until she said, "Brad cheated while I was pregnant with Bradley."

"What!" I slowed the van to a crawl, oblivious to cars whizzing past on my left. "Why didn't you tell me?"

"I wanted to, but I couldn't I guess I was too embarrassed. You're the only one I've ever told." I pulled off the road into the WalMart parking lot and shut off the engine.

"You went through this pain and I didn't even notice?"

"But the thing is, it's okay now." I felt a breeze in my mouth and shut it. "We worked it all out. Brad said it was because our sex wasn't good when I was so big, and well, men have needs."

"So do women! Don't they? Don't you? She looked down at her hands and picked at the cuticle on her thumb. When she only shrugged, I decided that maybe she didn't get the hots for every good looking guy she met the way I do. I always harbored a suspicion that I wasn't normal where sex was concerned.

"Besides, aren't you afraid of what Jack might do if you try to leave him?" Margie said.

"That never entered my mind. Is that why you stayed with Brad? Because you were afraid of him?"

"Of course not!" I was about to apologize but she said, "I don't believe in divorce. It's just an excuse to run away rather than work things out."

"You love Brad, right?" I said. Margie pursed her lips and agreed with a nod. "I don't believe in divorce either," I continued. "But remember when we read ROMEO AND JULIET in English class?"

"Yeah?"

"You know how silly it seemed to everybody in class when Miss Olsen told us in ancient times parents picked out who you married whether you loved the person or not. We thought it would be awful to spend the rest of your life with a person you didn't love just because your parents picked him out?" She nodded. "Well, I feel like that's my marriage. I'm trapped and I don't want to be a prisoner the rest of my life." I couldn't look at Margie but I could imagine her wide eyed stare boring into me. I don't want a prisoner for a husband, either," I added. I'd just put into words what I'd been feeling -- finally!

"I know my grandparents want me to try and make things work out," I continued thinking out loud, but I'm not sure I can do that." Margie bit her lower lip. There didn't seem to be anything else to say, so I put the van in gear and headed for home.

"I don't know what I'll do yet," I said when we pulled into my driveway. I turned to Margie. "Don't go home yet, okay?" Margie nodded. We unhooked Gracie and Bradley and hauled them upstairs in their carriers. Margie put the tea kettle on while I put Gracie in her crib. Bradley, Jr. slept peacefully in his car seat by the kitchen door.

"I think you should tell your brothers to take care of Jack and your problems will be solved," Margie said.

"Can they force him to love me?" We looked at one another across the table. She sighed and dipped her tea bag into a steaming mug of water. A cup of tea steamed in front of me but I couldn't sit still so I got out a plate and took a long time arranging some homemade brownies that I'd made earlier. I like to cook and bake a lot. My mother never did, but Gram does. Gram taught me before she was whisked out of my life to live in Florida. I felt homesick for Gram and Gramps like I did when they first moved.

"My life is filled with people who leave," I said feeling tears well up in my eyes. I plunked the brownies on the table so hard that it jarred them all crooked after all of my careful arranging. That was it. Tears splashed out so fast I could hardly soak them up with the tissues Margie fed me from a box I keep on my counter.

"First Gram and Gramps left," I said collapsing onto my chair, "then my parents," I took another tissue, "and now Jack!"

"Sounds like you think your relationship with Jack is over for good."

I sagged inside. I put my head down on the table and sobbed. I knew I was on the pity pot, but I didn't care. It was ugly. I let myself bawl. Margie came around to my side of the table and smoothed gentle circles on my back with the tips of her fingers. When I heard her sniff too, I felt sudden anger at Jack for causing her to suffer too. I held my head back and beat my fists on the table top. My nose was so plugged up I had to breathe through my mouth.

I honked, "Why should I let some pea brain make both of us miserable?"

"Now that's the Julie I know and love," Margie gave my shoulders a little squeeze before she blew out a breath and returned to her place at the table across from me. "I have to tell you, Julie, that everybody's noticed you and Jack don't seem to have much going on anyway."

"I know," I blew hard into a tissue, getting a little air through one nostril. "I'm thinking I shouldn't let that jerk ruin one more second of my life. Not one second!" A dimple flickered on Margie's cheeks.

"I'll make him sorry!" I felt myself inflate inside. "He may be screwing Charlotte, but he's about to be screwed by me!" Margie flashed full dimples.

"In fact, I don't need him for anything. I can take care of myself and he can take a flying leap!"

"Good for you!" my cheerleader clapped.

"I'm ready to be a free woman and kick the creep out!" My spirits were taking off. I felt like I was talking my way through a tunnel of pain and out into a world of freedom. It helped a lot.

"Are you going to tell your brothers, or what?"

Plop went my insides. "I don't know yet. I think I'll just wait until Jack gets home and play it by ear." I took the plate of brownies from the table and wrapped plastic wrap over it. "Why don't you take the brownies home for you and Brad."

Margie glanced at her watch, bit her lip, and took the plate. I knew she was prepared to stay as long as I needed her there. I also knew it was getting late and she had a family to feed. The shiner she'd so carefully covered had tiny purple lines in the cracks of the caked-on make-up. I felt a pang of remorse that we hadn't gotten around to talking about it.

"You need to get home to fix supper, and I need time to think," I said. "Go ahead; I'll be okay."

"You sure?" I nodded yes. We hugged and I walked her and Bradley Jr. downstairs to her car. Gram's hollyhocks bloomed next door making a rainbow of colors along the chain link fence between the houses. "Life has so many good things to offer," I told Margie through her open car window, "and Jack's just not one of them." She left smiling at me. I didn't know what I could do about the prowler, but I knew what I had to do about Jack.

It was almost four o'clock in the afternoon. Jack and my brothers wouldn't be home until around five unless they stopped after work for a beer at Chuck's. I wondered if Chuck would warn Jack. For some reason I felt totally drained, but I wanted to be alert when Jack came home so I took a nice long shower. Then I turned on the TV and fell asleep on the couch.

The door at the bottom of the stairs slammed and Jack's footsteps stomped up the stairs. I was instantly awake. I flew to the door in the kitchen before he could get to the top of the stairs and I twisted the deadbolt. "That's not cute, Julie!" Jack yelled through the closed door while he twisted the knob. I heard him search for his keys. "What'd you do that for, anyway?" He inserted a key into the lock.

"If you open that door you'll run into my meat cleaver!" I yelled, thinking on my feet. No sound came from the other side. "I know about you and Charlotte." He pulled the key out of the lock. "Take your butt back to your whore, 'cause you don't live here anymore."

He didn't answer but I didn't care. Every now and then I find myself in a position where I have to lie and then prove it. That way it isn't a lie. I slipped over to a cabinet drawer to pull out my meat cleaver and snuck back to the door. I stood in front of the door with my heavy meat cleaver held overhead and flashed back to when I hit the prowler with my skillet. I gulped. Suddenly Jack charged back down the stairs and his car squealed out of the driveway. I was so relieved that I dropped the meat cleaver, missing my foot by an inch. I didn't know what to do next, so I wandered back to the bedroom, kicked off my shoes and climbed into bed. I prayed for the strength to do whatever I needed to do and fell asleep.

Gracie woke me up for her six o'clock bottle. I got up energized. After I fed Gracie, and put her back in her crib, I grabbed the roll of trash bags and took them into Jack's room. I started dumping Jack's stuff into a garbage bag, taking special delight to toss his heavy metal CDs in first, followed by his retro stereo equipment. I used four bags, but I stuffed all of his magazines, clothes from the chest of drawers, clothes from the closet still on the hangers, shoes, sweaters from the closet shelf, a bowling ball in its case, and everything from the closet floor into the bags without worrying about possible damage.

When I finished, I stood outside Jack's room, panting and sweating, with all four bags of Jack's garbage tied up and stacked along the living room wall. I was pumped! It took me four trips down the stairs with each one of his bags bumping along behind me. I pulled them along the asphalt to line up in front of the garage door.

I stood a moment in front of the bags with my head back so the cool air could circulate through my sweaty hair. No lights were on in the house, so my brothers weren't home yet. Then my heart skipped a beat. What if the window cutter was out here! Yikes!

I made a quick dash for the stairway, bounded upstairs, slammed the door, and threw the deadbolt. I didn't know who was scaring me, but he was doing a pretty good job of it.

A car pulled into the driveway. I ducked down, goose-stepping over to the window over the kitchen sink and peeked out at the driveway below. Shawn got out of the old pick up my brothers use as a work truck. Kevin pulled up in his four-by-four behind Shawn.

It was after seven, so I figured they'd stopped off at Chuck's. I wondered if Jack went there. I felt a flood of embarrassment and then a sense of satisfaction that now everybody would know I'd kicked Jack out, and why. My kaleidoscope of emotions ended with a sudden sense of joy. I now had a perfect excuse to put an end to our sham of a marriage. Jack was cheating! Even in the Bible you can divorce someone for cheating.

"Hey," Kevin called when he spotted me at the open window, "What's with all the garbage?"

"It's Jack's stuff. In case you haven't heard, I kicked him out."

"We heard." Shawn shook his head and went into the house. Kevin stared up at me a minute before he followed Shawn. Their response was less than I'd expected. But then, Jack was their friend too. I wondered if he still was.

It didn't matter. I dropped a slice of bread into the toaster and fired up the tea kettle although I wasn't really hungry. Instead I felt drained of energy. I thought a bite to eat would help. I stared at the glowing lines inside the toaster and thought maybe my brothers were mad at me too. It wasn't like them not to poke their noses into my life, especially when something was going on like me kicking out Jack.

The phone rang and jarred me out of my reverie. "This is Officer Braxton from the Port Richfield Police Department. I thought you'd like to know, a man with injuries like the ones you described last week turned up in the hospital in Clearwater."

I was surprised to learn that the two good old boys from Florida had actually done something to check on my story. Before I got a chance to ask how the guy was doing, Officer Braxton said, "The father of the victim is wanted for questioning with regard to some robberies in our area. We think it was probably a father-son robbery team. We're on the lookout for him but he hasn't picked up his mail or come to the hospital to visit his son either. But he'll turn up eventually."

"I think he's here," I said.

"Ma'am?"

"Somebody tried to break into my apartment last night by cutting a hole in the window like the one in Florida. And afterwards I saw a red truck that looked just like the one I saw in Florida pull away from my house here in Illinois."

"Well I'll be switched," he said. "In that case, Ma'am, I'll be in contact with the other pertinent agencies, including your local police." Neither police department inspired much confidence on my part, but I thanked the deputy for calling and promised to let him know if anything new came up.

My toast popped up and startled me. Then heavy footsteps clomped up the stairs. I ran over to the door to double check that the door was still locked. "Julie, it's me," Kevin called through the door. I don't know if I was ticked off at Kevin or at myself for being so jumpy.

"I thought you two weren't interested when you went into the house."

"Yeah, well, let us in." I twisted the deadbolt back and Shawn came in behind Kevin. He pushed past me and headed straight for the fridge where he pulled out two beers. Kevin straddled a chair and accepted one of the bottles of beer, twisting off the cap and tossing it onto the table. He watched it spin while Shawn pulled out a chair, plunked his bottle on the table and sighed audibly. "We decided maybe we'd better come over here and have a talk with you," Shawn said.

Now what, I wondered.

NINE

The tea kettle started its shrill whistle. I caught it while Shawn and Kevin settled around the kitchen table. They sprawled out to look casual, but Kevin held his chin against his chest and Shawn twirled his beer bottle on the table. Neither of them could look me in the eye. My hackles went up. I knew them well enough to know something was up and I'd probably not like it.

I got tired of waiting for them to say something, so I said, "The hospital in Clearwater has the man I hit in the head." Kevin had straddled his chair, and hunched over the back. His thick blonde hair hung in his face. Shawn angled his chair so that his legs extended into the room so that I had to walk around them to make my tea.

Once I had a cup of tea and a piece of toast on a plate, I sat down at the table. Whatever they had to say was apparently stuck in their respective craws. Neither of them looked at me. "I hate that somebody's trying to break into my house," I said to give them an opening. I thought I'd go for a subject other than Jack. No response.

"I also hate that Jack's been cheating on me." They nodded and studied their hands. "I hate that everybody in town is probably laughing at me too." I felt like slapping them both but I was determined to be civil. I waited a few beats and they still slumped there without offering anything. "So what's with you two?" I yelled smacking the table. So much for civility.

That, at least, made them look at me. Shawn sighed like he does when he's about to jump off the high dive at Memorial Park. "We talked with Jack while we were at Chuck's," he said. He stood up and came around the table to stand next to me. He took one of my hands. That's always trouble. "We think you should give Jack another chance, Julie. Let him come home."

"What?" I flung his hand away, jumped up and clipped Shawn in the chin with my head. I hardly felt it. "How could you take Jack's side against mine?" I felt tears start. "Give me one good reason why I'd want to?"

"Because he's your husband," Kevin said quietly. "And you've got a kid."

Shawn paced around the kitchen. He stretched his mouth open, moving his jaw from side to side so I knew it hurt but he wouldn't admit it.

"Oh, well of course, if you're married to an unfaithful asshole and you've got a kid, by all means, bring him back." At this point I was screaming and my head pounded with rage. "What difference does it make where he dips his dick if he's got a kid and a wife at home?" Are you two out of your flip flaming minds?"

Shawn took his seat and a swig of his beer. Kevin said, "Look Julie, people make mistakes. Everybody's not as perfect as you. You could at least try to forgive him. It's not like dropping a boyfriend, you know. He's Gracie's father."

"But he's impossible to live with!" I said in a more normal voice, "and he doesn't love me."

Shawn reached across the table for one of my hands but I pulled it away. "You don't know what it's like being married to him." I batted my eyelids like mad to keep tears away by sheer will power. I lost.

"Jeez," Kevin got up and tried to put his arm across my shoulder but I elbowed him somewhere I couldn't see through my tears. After a quick intake of breath, he swore softly, bent over and hobbled back to his chair.

Listen, Julie." Shawn gave me his older-brother-I'm-going-to-tell-you-how-it-is voice, "if you guys have problems then you need to work 'em out. See a counselor or something. You could go to Reverend Hanover."

"Jack quit going to church after our wedding. I don't think he'll pay any attention to The Reverend anyway." I reached for a tissue and blew my nose.

"Aren't you worried about what Gracie will think when she grows up?" Kevin asked. "What's she going to think if you don't even try to make a go of your marriage?"

I held a wad of tissues over my eyes although there was no longer any reason to. I'd stopped crying or feeling anything. He made sense. I said, "Fine. Tell him to come home. But make good and sure he knows he needs to talk to Reverend Hanover with me."

"I think you and Gracie will be safer with Jack here, anyway," Kevin said. He chugged his beer in noisy gulps.

"I wish I knew what the guy from Florida is after," I muttered. "What have I got that's worth chasing me all the way from Florida for?" I had one elbow propped on the table, my chin against the back of my fist. I felt like I'd been in a fight and lost. "Shoot, I'd gladly put a 'please steal' sign on my old TV, and my second hand computer." I noticed my brothers were fidgeting in their chairs. "Got any ideas?" I said pointedly.

Shawn cleared his throat and exchanged a look with Kevin. Uh-oh. I'd seen that look before and it usually meant bad news for me. Kevin clinched it by saying, "Let's go in the living room where we can be more comfortable." My brothers both got up and flanked me, helping me up by slipping a hand under each elbow. I let Kevin put his arm around my back and steer me to the living room, knowing full well that they were also steering me into something else, and I probably wouldn't like it. I felt like I needed to know what, so I went along quietly with them.

My brothers plopped on either side of me on the couch. They each took one of my hands in theirs. My guard was way up at this point, but I listened. "What do you know about the weed farm?" Shawn asked.

"What farm?"

Shawn swiped his hand over his face. I noticed he perspired although I didn't feel too warm. "Jack didn't tell you, huh?" he said. I stared at him. He cleared his throat and said, "Jack's been getting a little weed from a farmer in Florida. The guy grows it for a few of us and Jack sells it for a few extra bucks. It's no big deal." He took a swig from his beer, burped into the air above his head, and added. Something must have happened between Jack and the farmer."

It felt like someone threw ice water in my face. I yanked my hands free and shot off the couch. "You mean to tell me you knew all this and never thought to mention any of it?" I stood against the opposite wall facing the couch, eyes glaring, maybe smoke coming out of my ears.

"Don't get all hyper." Kevin said. He got up and put his arm around my shoulder but I shrugged it off. "Look, smoking a little pot's like having a beer, or a cigarette." He reached for my hands but I slapped them away. He heaved a martyred sigh and plopped on the couch, draping an arm over the back. "It's no big deal," he said to the ceiling.

"Let me get this straight," I said through clenched teeth, "while Gracie's father was out catching cooties from Charlotte, and everybody in town was laughing at me, you thought it was no big deal?

With a sudden brain jolt, I knew what Jack's willingness to visit my grandparents in Florida was all about. His willingness to run errands for Gram and Gramps was really an excuse to meet some marijuana farmer so he could get the town's pot supply.

My brothers scowled up at me from the couch. I was trembling and felt all hollow inside. "Does everybody lie to me?" I said softly. Tears gathered in my eyes and I blinked fast.

"Look, Brat," Shawn said, "you're making this into something that it's not. You know we're responsible. We go to work every day and we don't get so high we get girls pregnant or drive when we've been partying. Nobody in our crowd is irresponsible. It's not like we're drug addicts."

Kevin nodded and pulled back his outstretched arm from along the back of the couch to mirror Shawn who leaned forward, arms resting on their thighs.

"Yeah, I know," I said. "It's harmless as all get out." I took a few steps closer to stand over them. "You think some drug dealer is after Jack and you want him here with Gracie and me." I felt like aliens had stolen my brothers.

"You don't have to worry about him, Julie," Kevin said, "When we talked with Jack last night at Chuck's, he said the weed farmer is some fat, old dude who's perfectly harmless. He's just trying to scare you."

"He's doing a good job of that." I said. I began to pace a little, trying to absorb all this.

Shawn said, "Jack is really sorry that he ever got tangled up with Charlotte. He says it wasn't much of a thing, anyway. If you two get back together, I'm sure he won't be seeing her anymore. Plus, if he's here, he can deal with the weed farmer."

"So where is Jack now?" I asked. They looked at each other for answers and shrugged.

"Maybe he crashed with Chuck," Kevin suggested.

"Or maybe he crashed with Charlotte." I pointed out.

"Oh, he won't be seeing her anymore," Shawn said with conviction. "Like we said, we had a little talk with him last night at Chuck's." He turned to Kevin and said, "I think you'd better go get Jack. I'll stay here with Julie until you get back."

After Kevin left, Shawn watched a White Sox baseball game on TV, while I fed and changed Gracie. I didn't doubt that my brothers could make Jack come home, and even stay away from Charlotte, but I had my doubts about their ability to make him into a real husband or father. Still, I wasn't about to have anyone say that I didn't at least try to save my marriage.

I made two turkey and cheese sandwiches for Shawn. It was supper time but I was too upset to be hungry. I put the sandwiches on a plate with some chips, along with a tall glass of iced tea, and dropped it all on the end table next to Shawn in the living room. He reached for a sandwich without taking his eyes from the TV.

I needed to do something to keep busy so I cleaned the kitchen. I scrubbed the floor and washed the window. Cleaning usually helps me to think, but tonight, while my body was on auto pilot, my mind reeled.

Kevin and Jack drove up while I was outside putting the garbage in the trash cans behind the garage. They were halfway upstairs when I rounded the corner from behind the garage so I followed them upstairs. They each carried a bulging plastic bag of Jack's belongings in one hand. Kevin dumped his two bags on the floor beside the kitchen door. Jack went on into his room where he left his two bags before he returned to the kitchen. He went directly to the fridge for a beer without so much as a nod in my direction.

"Welcome home," I said. "Shawn and Kevin tell me you've been the local dealer for the neighborhood."

"Julie, for Pete's sake!" Kevin said. For a second I thought Jack was going to bolt back out the door. He clenched his fists and his jaws but he gulped half a bottle of beer and blew out a long belly belch.

"We told her," Kevin said.

"No shit, Sherlock," Jack snatched up the two bags by the kitchen door and stalked back to his bedroom with them.

"Look, Julie," Kevin said. He held my shoulders and bent his face down toward mine. "We know the dangers of weed. We don't do it with women during sex. We don't do it when we know somebody's got to drive. We never miss a day of work." He straightened up and let go of me. "It's not like Jack sells hard drugs or something."

Just then Jack loomed in the doorway glaring at Shawn. "And," Jack said, "it's not like you'd ever have known if it hadn't been for your brother's big mouth." He sauntered over to the fridge and helped himself to another beer. He twisted off the bottle cap and flipped it into the sink.

"Oh yeah, it's much better for me not to know what my husband does."

"Just for the record," Jack said, "It's like Kevin says, I don't buy hard stuff, just a little bit of grass from a farmer who I've known for years"

"Can either of you explain why somebody from Florida cut holes in my windows?"

Kevin said, "I bet it's got something to do with that prowler you conked over the head in Florida." He walked over to Jack and stood toe-to-toe in front of him. "You're sure you told us everything." They stared at each other for a minute exchanging some male voodoo message by way of an answer.

"Okay," Kevin said stepping back. "You're both going to see Reverend Hanover and get straightened out, right?" He looked at me for confirmation. My heart wasn't in it, but I nodded agreement.

"If you say so," Jack muttered. He took a pull on his beer ending with a swipe across his mouth with his sleeve. Kevin nodded and joined Shawn who stood out on the landing of the stairway. They stomped down the stairs, slamming the door at the bottom. Jack turned on his heel and stalked into his bedroom, slamming his door too. I slumped onto a chair and put my face in my hands, my elbows on the kitchen table. I felt like someone stuck a pin in me and let all the air out. I thought about Gramps frequently telling me to forget how I'd like things to be, or how I think things should be, and ask myself what's best for everybody given the way they are now. So what's best right now, I asked myself. Gracie needs a bottle soon, and she needs me to take care of her. My bookkeeping is getting behind and I need to do some work or I'll lose my jobs. I can't do much about Jack, my brothers, the weed farmer who wants to scare me for some reason. I took a glass of ice water with me and went into my bedroom where I keep my desk and sat down to work on my bookkeeping ledgers. It was something I knew I could do until Gracie woke up for her bottle. I hoped it would keep my mind off of all my unanswered questions.

TEN

I worked at my bookkeeping, poring over ledgers on the built-in desk in my bedroom. My nerves settled down and I felt grateful for the diversion. I was in the middle of a column of figures when the fridge door rattled. "Do I get any dinner around this dump?" Jack yelled from the kitchen. I ignored him. It didn't work. He stuck his head in the bedroom door and in a more conversational tone asked, "The guy you belted with the frying pan, what exactly did he look like?" I tossed my pen on the ledger and gave up. He backed up when I pushed past him and headed for the kitchen. Jack trailed me into the kitchen where he straddled a chair.

"You were there," I said. "Like I said, the guy was big and hairy." I took leftover stew from the fridge.

"I wonder if you got Old Man Grady's son with your killer skillet." Jack got up and paced into the living room before returning to stand in the kitchen doorway.

"Who's Old Man Grady?" I asked dumping the stew into a microwave dish. .

Jack turned away to circle the living room some more and to give his jaw a good massage. "Now I know why Grady's trying to break in here, he said. "You got him all pissed off when you hurt his kid and now it's payback. You got nobody to blame but yourself."

"What was his kid doing sneaking around the camper in the middle of the night?" I opened the microwave oven after it dinged and gave the stew a stir.

Jack yanked his chair away from the table, flipped it around and plopped down in front of the steaming bowl of stew I'd plunked in front of his spot at the table. "Damn it to hell, anyway, Julie." He jabbed his fork into the food and started to shovel it into his face. I put another bowl of stew on the table for myself. We ate without comment; he wolfed down two bowls while I picked my way through part of a bowl. My appetite was completely gone. When Jack was pretty much finished, I asked, "Where were you last night?"

His eyes narrowed. "Do I have to report my every move to you now?"

"Look Jack, do you want to live together like this forever? If you want to marry Charlotte, I'll give you a divorce right now."

"I told you I don't want a divorce!" He shoved up and took a few steps toward the kitchen door leading to the doorway.

"Is Charlotte still in the picture?"

He turned back to face me. "No!"

"I don't understand you at all," I said from my chair. "I did want us to get back to where we were when we first got married." I looked at him and all I felt was disgust. "Now I don't care anymore." I picked up our bowls and spoons and took them to the sink. "If I call Reverend Hanover, are you going to go with me to talk to him," I asked after a few minutes. I turned to face him as he reached for the doorknob. "Are we seriously going to try to make our marriage a real one?"

"Just go ahead and call your minister and quit needling me about it." He yanked open the kitchen door.

"So where are you going now?"

He faced me, one hand on the door. "To talk to Chuck, if that's all right with you. I know you didn't find out about Charlotte from your brothers." He slammed the door and clumped downstairs.

I filled the sink with hot sudsy water. It didn't seem like anything changed between us, I thought. What had changed was I had a name for the man in the truck in Florida. I'd hit the son of "Old Man Grady," Jack's weed farmer.

When the clean dishes were in the drainer, I went online and got the phone number of Clearwater General Hospital.

"I'd like to know the condition of one of your patients, please," I said. "His last name is Grady."

"Are you a relative?" the woman who answered the phone asked. When I didn't answer right away, she said, "We can only divulge patient information to a relative."

"He's my brother," I lied. It wasn't an out and out lie, I told myself. I mean, all men are our brothers, right?"

"I'll connect you to the floor nurse."

"I'm calling from Chicago to inquire about my brother," I told the nurse who answered. Nobody's ever heard of Owensville, and since we live in the Chicago Metropolitan area so it's easier just to say I live in Chicago. "My brother suffered a head injury. He has a gash behind his left ear and a bump on top of his head. Can you tell me how he's doing?"

"Perhaps you should speak with his doctor."

"Oh, good," I said relieved.

"May I have your name, please?"

"Armstrong, Julie Armstrong." I gave her my address and phone number just to keep the lies down to a minimum. "Look," I said after a long silence. "How many people named Grady do you have with a gash behind his left ear and a lump on the top of his head?"

"I'm going to have to transfer your call. Hold on please." Her voice definitely had a get-me-out-of-this tone to it.

Several minutes of classical music while I was on hold gave my heart time to slow down before a man's voice said, "Dr. Sutherland here," his voice seemed crisp and professional. "You say you're the sister of my patient?"

"Yes sir."

"The nurse tells me you've described my patient's wounds and you're calling from Chicago. Is that correct?"

"Yes sir."

"Well, I'm sorry to have to tell you that your brother is in a coma. There's a chance that he may never fully recover. It would be best if you could come here as soon as you can."

"Yes sir," I said softly. "And thank you." I hung up. Not only did I have to have Jack back, but I might be a killer.

I spent the evening watching mindless TV. The news ended and Jack still wasn't home. The phone rang as I was getting ready for bed. A woman's slurred voice rasped, "You think you can screw up my life with the snap of your little finger, don't you, honey? Well, watch your back." Then she hung up. I recognized that it was Charlotte, drunk as usual.

Great, I thought. I seem to be making friends all over the place. First somebody named Grady, and now dumb Charlotte. She must be upset because Jack broke it off with her. I wondered why the thought didn't make me feel any better.

In bed, instead of falling asleep, my mind drifted to stories in the newspapers about crazy women who kill the wives of their lovers. That was a comforting thought. It also didn't help to think about the man whose son I'd put into a life threatening coma either. He, at least, had a reason to hate me.

Every squeak and creak became the sound of a window being cut. I got up every few minutes to check the windows and finally wound up watching some more TV. When I couldn't hold my eyes open anymore, I left all the lights on and climbed into bed but I tossed and turned until Jack came in. I hated to have to admit to myself that I felt a sense of relief that he came home.

In the morning Jack got up and got ready for work without a word about where he'd been. I made breakfast, packed his lunch, and filled his thermos with coffee for which I got not even a nod or grunt of acknowledgement. I had tried to get Jack to talk to me some more about Grady during breakfast, but he ignored me so I gave up and began to plan what I wanted to say to Reverend Hanover. Maybe the Reverend would have some advice to help me reach Jack. Or maybe after some times passed, he'd get over his anger and we'd get along better. I felt like I had a heavy load stuffed inside my chest that I couldn't seem to shake.

After breakfast, Jack gathered up his lunch pail, his thermos and the toolbox he always dumped beside the fridge. Then he left.

I did the usual chores, beds, dishes, picked up the laundry, and took out the trash. When I finished, I knew I should get back to my bookkeeping. Instead I picked up the phone and called Margie.

"What are you up to?" I asked.

She sounded breathless. "I've got to get some errands done this morning and one of them is to get to the cleaners before eleven or Brad's slacks won't be back in time for his bowling banquet tonight."

"I've got to get out of here," I said. Think you could meet me at Chucks for lunch?"

"Really? Chuck's?"

"I'm not about to forego a good Italian beef sandwich just because Chuck is Jack's bartender." Margie laughed and agreed to meet me for lunch.

Ten minutes before noon, Margie bustled into the restaurant, her face glistening with perspiration. "Oh – my – gosh," Margie said as she plopped onto the booth across from me. "It feels so good to sit down."

Chuck had looked surprised to see me when I came in but he didn't say anything. I didn't bother to say anything to him either but just went to our favorite booth. After we ordered, Margie told me how Brad had given her a list of things she had to get done this morning. "By some miracle, I've done them all." She smiled.

"I'm guessing it's more like you worked your butt off to get it all done," I said.

"It's hard to keep the peace sometimes," Margie said to her lap.Chuck brought our sandwiches over to us and placed them in front of us without comment. He went back behind the counter and proceeded to wipe it off with a big white cloth. Margie squeezed the end of her sandwich with her fingers enough to get the end into her mouth. "I try to do everything the way Brad wants me to," she said between bites. "But it seems it's getting harder and harder." I hoped Margie would talk about her eye injury. It was shades of red, blue, green, and purple muted behind her make-up.

"I guess you can't miss my shiner," she said finally. I nodded. We ate a few minutes before she said, "The official story, you know, for my folks and everybody, is that I ran into the corner of the cabinet." I couldn't look at her, concentrating instead on keeping my soggy beef sandwich intact enough to get it to my mouth.

"But the truth is," I looked up and she had tears in her eyes, "Brad slammed my face into the corner of the cabinet."

"Oh my God!" I choked the food in my mouth and had to cough into a napkin and clear my throat several times. Margie waited until I sipped my Pepsi and nodded that I was all right.

"I'm lucky it hit below my eye." She looked down, sighed, and picked up her sandwich, nibbling off some overhanging meat. She didn't look at me but I couldn't help staring at her. I'm pretty sure my mouth hung open too.

Finally I said, "Maybe you should tell your folks, Margie." I was stunned that she could say that and continue to eat. When she didn't look up, I said, "Or I could tell my brothers and have them take care of it for you." She looked up wide-eyed, a look of horror on her face.

"I mean it, Margie. I've never asked my brothers to go to bat for somebody else, but I think it's the perfect solution for your problem. Brad won't do anything to hurt you again if they get a hold of him."

"I think we ought to leave well enough alone," she said shaking her head no. "It's over now, and I don't think it'll happen again. Brad feels really bad about it. So tell me, how are you doing?"

I told her about Charlotte's call. Then I told her about Jack dealing with a weed farmer who he said was trying to scare me by cutting holes in my windows. I didn't tell her that my brothers were also Jack's customers. I filled her in on the call to the hospital, and how the doctor said Grady's son might not make it. I ended with, "I can't believe that I might have actually killed someone. Pray for him not to die, will you?" Margie shook her head and placed a hand on mine on the table. "And," I said after taking a ragged breath, "I don't want to spend every night worrying about whether or not I'm going to be attacked in my sleep by someone sneaking in my windows."

Margie looked at me with misty eyes and just shook her bouncy curls. She drew some of her Pepsi through a straw before she picked up her sandwich to negotiate another bite of the thick Italian beef. "I can't tell you what to do, of course," she said after eating a while in silence. I nodded encouragement. She chewed, swallowed, and wiped the corner of her mouth with her napkin. "If it were me, I think I'd be more worried about whether or not Jack is still seeing Charlotte."

"The truth is, when I thought he and Charlotte were together, I felt relieved." Margie's left eyebrow raised but she didn't comment. "On the other hand, I have to admit I was also relieved when Jack came home last night."

Margie and I ate in companionable silence for a while before I said, "If we do get a divorce, I think I'll have to move back to the house with my brothers. At least I'll be able to sleep at night."

"Oh pa-lease!" Margie threw her soggy napkin on the table. "You hated living with your brothers, remember? You told me getting your own place was one of the things you liked best about getting married. You want to go back to, and I quote, cooking and cleaning up after pigs? And what else? Oh yeah, you had to put up with their bimbos running around the house at all hours and their crappy music." She picked up the remains of her sandwich and finished it. She sighed audibly and rolled her eyes. Then she wiped her fingers on the wadded up paper napkin, tossed it onto her empty plate and said, "Maybe you should get a big dog."

"I don't need a dog. I've got two already – Kevin and Shawn, remember?" We laughed. It felt good to laugh with Margie. Our eyes met and we howled with laughter again. It struck us so funny that several people gave us annoyed looks, especially Chuck. Good, I thought. Let everybody know that I'm not sitting home crying over anything Jack pulled.

"You know, I don't know what I'd do without you." I reached over and put my hand over the back of one of Margie's on the table.

Margie nodded and smiled. "Yeah, it's good we've got each other." Even though her marriage is far from perfect, I had to admit, Brad works steady, brings home his paycheck, and he only stops at Chucks on Friday nights when all the guys get together after work. In our crowd, that makes him a good husband. And somehow Margie still loves Brad. It was hard for me to wrap my mind around her wanting to even stay in the same house with Bradley. How could you love someone who hurt you, I wondered. If I were in her place, Brad would have to spend the rest of his life with his back to a corner and his eyes open because as soon as he closed them, I'd think of something to make sure he never hit me again. The memory of the night I used my skillet on old man Grady's son filled my eyes with sudden tears. How could I kill someone? What kind of person was I? My insides went hollow every time I remembered what I'd done that night.

ELEVEN

Gracie's diaper bag doubles as my purse so I was in the process of worming my hand inside the stuffed bag for my car keys.

"Hey, isn't that Charlotte's car?" Margie asked directing her gaze toward the plate glass window at the front of the restaurant. Charlotte's dark green SUV angled into a parking slot in front of the building. We stared at the van wondering where Charlotte was since the passenger door stood wide open. We scanned the room for Charlotte. "She must be in back using the bathroom," Margie said. I nodded and went back to locating my keys.

I squeezed my fingers past a protrusion in the bottom of my bag and snagged my keys just as Gracie's carrier was suddenly whisked into the air. Charlotte was halfway out the front door with Gracie in her carrier before I realized what had happened. Charlotte wedged the carrier on the floor of her SUV between the dash and front seat. She slammed the door and was behind the wheel by the time I made it to the curb. She took off with Gracie as I reached for her door handle. I was too late.

"Oh my God!" Margie shrieked. My keys were still in my hand, thank God. I turned and bolted for my van without missing a beat. By the time I screeched out of the parking slot on to Main Street, Charlotte was turning left all the way up on High Street.

My heart raced but my hands were steady on the wheel. I charged through traffic and turned on High Street without slowing down. I barreled down the quiet residential street, slowing just enough at each crossroad to scan up and down before gunning it to the next stop sign. Charlotte's SUV was nowhere in sight.

When I reached the cul-de-sac at the end of High Street, I felt a wave of dizziness. Where had she turned? My hands trembled on the steering wheel. I blew through eight stop signs on the way back to Main Street where the tail end of the Owensville squad car partially blocked the street in front of Chuck's. I maneuvered around it and shot away heading north. I didn't want to waste time talking with Huey, Louie, or Donald.

I thought maybe Charlotte had turned on High Street and headed away from her house to throw me off the track. She lives down the hill, across town, near my neighborhood. I wondered just how drunk Charlotte had to be to pull a stunt like that. I couldn't imagine what she had in mind but I knew she had my baby and I had to catch her.

I flew across town to her house. The only car in her driveway was on cinder blocks near the back of a long driveway so I turned around, and peeled out toward Route 43 that runs along the outskirts of town. I had an idea. I sped along Frontage Road, crossed the railroad tracks, and headed up the hill at the edge of town where the road ends on a bluff overlooking the highway.

At the summit, I hit the brakes, shoving it in park so fast that I banged my chest against the steering wheel. I was out the door, sprinting across the grassy knoll by the guard rail along the edge of the highway before I felt the pain in my chest. On the highway below, a green SUV triggered a surge of energy so strong I may not have touched the ground as I flew back to my van.

My back wheels skidded on the shoulder when I yanked the van into drive and floored it. Traffic was still light after lunch when I reached the highway. I kept the accelerator on the floor, closing the gap between us. The van started to shimmy. It shook so much that I was afraid the van would conk out. I didn't let up until I was within a few car lengths from her and I could slow down to match her speed.

We sped along for several more minutes. Suddenly the SUV turned onto a gravel road leading to farms outside of town. The SUV picked up speed. So did I.

Dust and gravel flew in the wake of the SUV. Her back wheels fishtailed on the gravel only righting itself when she slowed down. My heart was in my throat. Soybean fields flickered through clouds of dust on either side of the van.

She made a sharp U-turn at a crossroad and would have passed me going the other way except I stopped dead center in the road. She either had to stop or kill us all. Instantly, I wanted to change my mind, but it was too late. She locked her brakes. Gravel and dust splattered my windshield. When I opened my eyes, her SUV had skidded to a halt within inches of my front bumper.

Before her SUV stopped rocking, I was out my door and I yanked Charlotte's passenger door open as she shifted into park. She dropped her head onto her arms against the steering wheel. Her back heaved.

"You insane moron," I screamed. "What were you thinking?" I held Gracie's carrier by then. Gracie opened her fists but not her eyes. She stretched, and shifted into a more comfortable position in her carrier.

Charlotte turned her head to face me, her head on her arms like it was too heavy to pick up. "Jack may be married to you." Her upper lip curled, "But he loves me." I backed away with the carrier in my arms. Her voice rose. "If you'd only give Jack a divorce, we could be happy. We could have our own baby."

I turned around to squint at her in the glare of the sun. "But no," she picked up her head, her voice stronger, more shrill. "You think if you keep him there, he'll love you. Well, Missy, he'll never love you 'cause he loves me!"

"Listen you drunken idiot." I yelled at the top of my lungs. "I asked Jack for a divorce! He said he didn't want one."

"You're lying!"

I went back to the SUV and rested Gracie's carrier on the edge of her passenger seat. "Why would I lie? All he has to do is buy a few groceries, and he's free to spend the rest of his check on you!" After a mental head slap, I continued. "He doesn't want a divorce because he's got free rent, cheap vacations, no bills, and somebody cooking and cleaning for him." So that's what Jack meant about numbers. They all added up in his favor.

I removed Gracie's carrier and started to walk away feeling like a bigger moron than Charlotte. I hate being bested. Always have. Then I had an inspiration. "If you don't believe me," I called turning around, "I'll prove it. Come home with me and when Jack gets home from work tonight, I'll tell him I want a divorce and you'll see." I knew it was perfect the minute I said it. "Come on, Charlotte," I said heading for my van. "Follow me and we'll wait for Jack together."

Charlotte has always been too plump, wore too much make-up, and drank too much. But her biggest problem has always been her lack of brains. Apparently she saw the wisdom of my proposal, however, because she backed up and turned around to follow me.

When I turned onto my street, the squad car, Margie's Cutlass, my brothers' truck, and an assembly of neighbors covered our driveway so I had to park on the street. Charlotte pulled in behind me and stayed in her SUV

"Hey, there they are!" someone yelled as I stepped out of my van with Gracie in tow. The crowd surged out to the street. People waved, applauded, yelled, wiped their eyes, and slapped one another's backs with relief.

"We're fine!" I shouted above the sudden din, "It was all a mistake!" You'd think I'd managed a group slap in the face. Everyone shut up at once. There was a few seconds of stone silence before people rolled their eyes, shook their heads, and left, some grumbling about being disturbed by me entirely too often.

I took Margie's hand, did some back and forth glancing in Charlotte's direction and said, "Let me call you later." Before she left, Margie picked up on my signals and helped convince the police she'd made a mistake by calling them.

Shawn wanted to know what kind of mistake caused Margie to call the cops and Charlotte to grab Gracie. "Charlotte's so drunk she thought it would be funny to grab Gracie and then give her back," I said

"She should be locked up before she hurts somebody!" He yelled at me like I was responsible for what happened. We stood beside my van. Kevin walked over to Charlotte's SUV and bellowed into her open window, "If you ever pull a stunt like that again, I'll break you in half, you hear me!" She nodded and her head swayed. I wondered how drunk she was.

Finally Shawn and Kevin screeched off in the work truck and Charlotte climbed upstairs behind me. I put Gracie in her crib and started the tea kettle. Charlotte wanted a beer instead, so I gave her one. I made myself some tea and drank it down to help fight a sudden slump in my energy level.

We sat across from one another at the kitchen table. I sipped a second cup of tea and she chugged her beer. I couldn't help but ask, "What did you think would happen when you took Gracie?"

"I thought I could trade her for Jack." She slugged back a gulp of beer. Now there's a real well thought out plan, I thought. She looked at me with her dopey brown eyes and shrugged. It struck me as so stupid that I started to laugh. I laughed until tears streamed down my cheeks. When dumb Charlotte joined in, I could hardly keep from falling off my chair. When we finally wound down, I wiped my eyes, blew my nose, and pressed my hands against the ache in my belly from laughing so hard. I looked at the clock. It was only four in the afternoon. "Jack doesn't get home until five-thirty or six," I told her.

Charlotte patted her wet mascara with her fingertips. I had to hand it to her. Her make-up might look like she put it on with a trowel, but it was perfectly in place even after laughing so hard she cried. If anyone ever needed some industrial strength make-up, she'd be the one to ask where to get it.

"So tell me," I asked to pass the time in conversation, "how did you two meet?"

"Well, you know, I went to Chuck's one night and got him to buy me a drink. Then from there it was all pretty much love at first sight."

From there he jumped your bones and you fell in love, I thought. I could picture it. I had no feelings of anger or hurt or anything, which surprised me. I sat there looking at her swill beer. If anything, I felt a sense of relief.

"Do you think he'll marry you?" I felt quite amiable toward her in spite of what she'd just pulled.

She smiled broadly. Her teeth were too big for her face but they were sure nice and white. "Oh yes! Once he's free I know he'll marry me." She drained her bottle and shook it to signal it was empty. I got her another. She got up, took it, and went into the living room where she flopped on the couch to watch TV. Another conversationalist, I thought. Yep, she and Jack were made for each other, all right.

I couldn't imagine what Jack would say when he walked in and saw Charlotte, but I was pretty sure it wouldn't be, oh goody. However, now I could get rid of Jack without feeling guilty. It occurred to me, as I watched Charlotte tip back her beer bottle, her pale blonde perm propped up on the end of my couch, that Jack probably wouldn't be any more faithful to Charlotte than he was to me.

I worked at my bookkeeping in my bedroom while Charlotte napped until we heard Jack clump up the stairs. Charlotte sat up on the couch and ran her fingers through her hair to fluff up the curls. I came out of the bedroom and guided Charlotte into the kitchen where I stood next to her so we could greet Jack together.

"Guess what?" I said to Jack as he dropped his tool box on the floor next to the refrigerator by the door. "You get to take Charlotte out for dinner and then you can take her as your wife."

Jack's mouth hung open, his eyes froze, and he didn't move, even when Charlotte pranced over to wrap her arms around his neck and plant kisses on his face. He pulled her arms off and flung her aside without taking his eyes off of me.

"We're getting a divorce after all." I giggled. I felt downright giddy. "Feel free to go home with Charlotte right this very minute. In fact, you're no longer welcome here, so unless you want to face my brothers, you can get your stuff, and get out for good this time. Charlotte here can help you."

He started toward me, head lowered, eyes up, glaring under his brows like a charging bull. I scampered into my bedroom, slammed the door, hopefully in his face, and pressed the thumb lock. While I propped my desk chair under the doorknob, he beat on the door a couple of times with his fist and yelled, "What the hell's going on here!" Then he hammered on the door with both fists. "Get out here and tell me what the hell's going on!"

"Charlotte and I decided to make a trade," I called through the door when the pounding stopped, "She gets you and I get a divorce."

"Like hell!" he roared.

"Jack!" Charlotte's voice was pitched higher than an air raid siren, "What's the matter with you? This is our chance! Are you crazy?"

"All right! All right! Pipe down! What happened here?" I sat on the edge of my bed and grinned. Yeah, Charlotte, I thought, explain it all.

"Well," I heard her say in a little girl voice, "she and I kind of got together and she said she wants a divorce now. Maybe she didn't before but now she does. So why aren't you happy?" She conveniently left out the part about taking Gracie. Did she think everyone in town who knew us wouldn't tell Jack? What a ditz.

"You bitch!" Jack started banging on the door again.

Safe with the door and a chair between us, I couldn't help but yell, "I know you can't be talking to me."

"Come on, damn you," Jack said presumably to Charlotte after he got tired of beating against my door. I waited, listening as their footsteps receded down the stairs. I unlocked the door when tires squealed out of the driveway.

Gracie's next bottle wasn't due yet so I picked her up, and carried her and her bottle over to the house. My brothers weren't home yet but I expected them to turn up any minute. I ordered a pizza to be delivered so I'd have pizza ready for them as sort of a peace offering. I did want their help when it came time to keep Jack away from me permanently.

TWELVE

I sat at my parents' kitchen table waiting for my brothers to come home. Gracie cooed in her carrier on the floor next to me. I had several pieces of paper spread out as I worked on some numbers that would benefit me for a change. Shawn pushed through the door but stopped with his hand held on the doorknob when he spotted me. It took a couple seconds before he said, "Hey Brat. What's up?"

Kevin came in behind Shawn, eyed the plates and napkins I'd put out, and said, "Looks like dinner's on. They exchanged hands down slaps with each other. "That's good 'cause I'm starving."

"We stopped at Chuck's and heard you kicked Jack out again." Kevin said over his shoulder. He and Shawn jostled one another at the kitchen sink, vying for the water to wash their hands, both too stubborn to leave and use the sink in the bathroom. The doorbell rang. I went to answer it while my brothers squirted water on each other.

"Jack was at Chuck's," Kevin called from the kitchen.

"What, not home with Charlotte?" I took the money I had to pay for the pizza from my jeans pocket.

"He said to tell you he's coming for his stuff tomorrow."

That sounded promising. I wondered what story Jack was passing around. Old Mr. Thompkins, who delivers the neighborhood news with Chuck's pizza, greeted me at the door with a broad smile. "Hey, I hear you gave your old man the boot again." His toothless smile split his face in two like a Muppet.

"Yep," I said as I held out a twenty.

Shawn stepped up from behind me and held out his twenty. Mr. Thompkins took Shawn's cash. I shrugged and pocketed my money. Shawn said, "Keep the change," and took the pizza back to the kitchen. I was going to close the door, but Mr. Tompkins clearly wasn't ready to leave.

"It's about time," he said with a short laugh that sounded like a hen's cackle.

"What do you mean?" I asked in spite of myself.

Mr. Thompkins turned and waved on his way back to his Dodge Dart. Before he got in, though, he turned and called out to everyone within earshot, "He's been cheating on you with Charlotte Hooper." He climbed in his car and grinned from his open window. "I coulda told you he wasn't no good. You did the right thing, dearie." I slammed the front door so hard it rattled the little glass shelves that held Mom's knick-knacks on the adjacent wall.

My brothers' mouths were full, and a large section of cardboard under the pizza was already visible when I got to the kitchen. "Mr. Tompkins just handed me the latest gossip. Guess what it was?"

"Uh, let's see," Kevin said. "Jack's either coming or going?"

"He said that everybody knew about Jack and Charlotte." I stood in the doorway, hands on hips, glaring at them. They wolfed pizza but didn't look up. "You knew too, didn't you?" I said softly as I realized it was true. "How could you not tell me?"

Shawn tossed his half eaten slice of pizza on his plate and ran his hand down his face.

Kevin winced as he swallowed. He took a slug of Pepsi and cleared his throat. "We didn't know how," he finally said.

I didn't know what to say. Shawn finally looked up under hooded brows. "We told Jack he'd better make sure you got everything you needed. We thought he'd get Charlotte out of his system."

Kevin said. "I mean, she's dumb but available. Porking her a couple times while you were sick and all is one thing, but he has no intention of marrying her."

"Oh really?" I said as I came into the room and sat down. "Did you know that he's been telling her if I'd divorce him, he'd marry her?" The look they gave each other told me he hadn't. "Anyway," I said wanting to change the subject. "I've thought about it while I waited for you guys to come home. I'm still going to go see Reverend Hanover tomorrow." They didn't ask why out loud, but they did with their eyes. "I'm going to need counseling because I'm getting a divorce."

Shawn rolled his eyes and ran his greasy fingers through his hair. Kevin came over to me and pulled my head close, tenderly poking me in the ear with his belt buckle. I guess they were probably miserable and didn't know what to do about it either. "Eat your pizza," I said pushing Kevin away. I'll live."

We poked around at our food in an uncomfortable silence. I got to thinking about my life before I met Jack. "Do you remember when I graduated from eighth grade?" They looked at me nodding but they both looked like I might have lost it. I continued, "Well, I asked Dad if he'd help me go to college. I wanted to be a CPA." Looks of surprise answered my question. "Dad said I had three choices: get a scholarship, get a job, or get a husband. According to Dad, I'd just get married, have kids, and stay home anyway, so all the money for college would be wasted."

Kevin nodded at Dad's logic and waited for a point. Shawn said, "Yeah?" He looked at me under a swinging flap of hair. "So?" He shook loose a piece of pizza welded together with cheese. I could see they really were "splinters off the old plank," like Dad used to say.

I had to admit that in our crowd, girls usually did get married and guys went into a trade. I took a deep breath and blurted out what I'd been working on when they came in. "I'm going to take some college courses." I felt a surge of excitement when I said it. They both stopped eating and looked at me like a pelican just landed on my head. Gracie bleated a warning so I got up to make her bottle. I took Gracie and left my brothers with their pizza stuffed mouths hanging open.

I chose a comfortable arm chair in the living room to feed Gracie. It was good to relax and contemplate myself as a college student, and even better, as a college graduate. The prospect of being a single mom wasn't as scary as it had seemed at first. I had free rent, and low utility bills. My work paid enough to get by and leave enough to "pay myself first," as Gramps taught us all to do. He instructed everybody in the family to open a savings account and put aside some part of each paycheck, no matter how small the amount. I guess our Scottish heritage or maybe our relatives are to blame for my need to save money so religiously.

Once Gracie was finished and changed, she cooed in my lap a few minutes and then went back to sleep on my shoulder while I patted her back to see if she needed to burp any more. I carried her back to the kitchen hoping the boys had saved me some pizza. Kevin had a big grin on his face when I came into the room with Gracie in my arms. "Whether you stick it out with Jack or not," he said, "if you want to go to college, I'm going to pay for your first class."

"And I'll take you over to Owensville Community College and pay for another one," Shawn said. "Just tell me when you're ready." I gave each of them a one handed hug from behind and felt a collective return to our comfort level.

Shawn flipped a bottle cap on the table. He called "tops," to see which one would be first to get the shower. It landed bottom side up, so Kevin went first. Shawn held his arms out to hold Gracie. He chucked her under her fat chins to hear her giggle, but she didn't wake up. I cleaned up the mess on the table and took Gracie to head for home.

It was a muggy, warm evening. The sun was down but it spread pink and orange fingers across the horizon as though it was not quite through with the day. I walked back to my apartment with a plan for college within my grasp and felt like a kid looking forward to Christmas morning.

On the short walk across the back yard, I thought about why I ever got mixed up with Jack in the first place. Part of it was because he was older and looked sexy. And it was fun to wear his ring at school and to plan the wedding. I knew he wanted in my pants but I thought he wanted a home and a family too. Mom had commented once that she was afraid that I was in love with love. It didn't make sense then but now I understood.

I reached the top of my stairs a lot wiser. Then I let out a huge gasp. The kitchen was a mess. Cabinet doors hung open, their contents scattered on the floor and counter tops. Overturned drawers lay amid the rubble on the floor. My owl cookie jar was broken. Shards of glass, tea bags, jam, flour, rice, and detergent all mixed in the debris at my feet and were tracked onto the living room rug.

It took a second to catch my breath. Once I did, I beat it down the stairs to .the house. Shawn looked up from where he lay on the couch in front of the TV. "Somebody broke into the apartment!" Shawn took off out the back door. I heard Kevin in the shower.

Marylou Sanders, the receptionist at our police station, answered my phone call. "This is Julie. Tell whoever's on duty to get over here! My place was broken into!"

Kevin came into the kitchen in jeans, drying his hair with a towel. "What's going on?"

I held the phone away from my mouth and told him, "Somebody trashed my apartment!" He dumped his towel on the floor and took off after Shawn.

"Are you hurt?" Marylou asked. I'd almost forgotten that I was still on the phone. "Where are you now, Julie?"

"I'm okay. I'm at my folks' house with my brothers."

Marylou didn't bother to use their intercom "Hey, Lou! Julie's place has been broken into." Marylou was sympathetic when I described the mess and offered to come help me clean it up. I declined, telling her that I'd have plenty of help from my brothers, although I knew the only way that that would be true was if I bribed them. I thanked her anyway and hung up.

Lorenda Lee Lux

This evening Gracie chose not to stay asleep. Instead she squirmed in my arms. I put her on the couch next to me and she kicked her legs and flailed her arms a while and blew spit bubbles. This activity didn't last long before she started to cry. It wasn't like her hunger cry; it was less intense, less demanding somehow. Gram had warned me that sometimes babies have to cry to strengthen their lungs and not to worry every time she did. Still, I wasn't sure if she was in pain or something. I paced around the house rocking her and patting her back. All the while, I watched out the windows and door for my brothers or the police. It seemed like Gracie wasn't going to quit crying. But just as Gram predicted, it took about five minutes for Gracie to settle down and go to sleep on my shoulder.

Once again our town clowns took the opportunity to use their police siren and lights. Neighbors streamed from back porches and cut across yards. Dogs barked, and people asked one another what was going on.

I stepped outside to join the gathering crowd. I held Gracie, now asleep, on my shoulder. Shawn and Kevin had come out my stairway door. "Kevin told everyone milling around our yard and driveway, "Somebody broke into Julie's place and trashed it. They got in through the back window. It has a hole cut in it like last time. Looks like the hole was so he could reach in and unlock the window and come in that way. Only this time he took his ladder." Unlike last time, Kevin wasn't making jokes. Instead he had a scowl on his face and looked like he wanted to punch somebody. He turned away from us and hurried into the house for his shoes.

"Maybe if you had a husband at home, you wouldn't have so much trouble." Mrs. Arnott from a couple doors down said. Old Mrs. Seidell nodded agreement. They glared at me under bristly gray eyebrows.

"You think somebody's trying to break into my place because I kicked Jack out?" It dawned on me that maybe they didn't know the whole story. "He cheated on me with Charlotte Hooper," I informed them loudly.

"Lots of folks manage to work those things out and have good marriages in spite of it," Mrs. Costanza said. Many of the women nodded agreement. I wondered how many of them had actual experience in that area.

"We'll all help you clean everything up in the morning," Mrs. Arnott said. Most of the ladies nodded agreement, even though, like Mrs. Arnott, they all have their own health issues. Mrs. Arnott is so bent over that she has to walk with a cane.

I hugged her and got teary eyed. "I'll get it cleaned up tomorrow," I said. "It's not that big a place." They nodded with sympathy in their eyes and relief in their postures.

The group dispersed when Louie gave everybody the official signal that nobody lurked nearby. He said he'd make out a police report and the police left too.

Kevin and Shawn stood beside me on the driveway. I said, "Are you guys sure you don't know what's going on?"

"Beats me," Kevin said. "It's not like you keep the books for the mob or something."

At the mention of my bookkeeping records, I handed Gracie off to a startled Shawn, who took her against his belly like a football. I took the stairs two at a time and crunched through the broken bits on the floors to my desk in the bedroom. Its contents, along with my dresser and chest of drawers, were thrown all around like the kitchen. I searched through piles of clothes and papers for my bookkeeping ledgers. The heel of one of my black pumps hung out of my smashed computer monitor. Glass was embedded in the fabric of my lilac quilt. My bookkeeping ledgers were nowhere to be found.

The computer tower under my desk was tipped over. I set it upright and pressed the power button. It whirred to life. I sent up a quick prayer, held my breath, and popped out the disk that held all of my records. "Wheew," I whispered. Thank God!

"They stole my ledgers." I said when I heard Kevin and Shawn crunch their way into the bedroom. Gracie slept on Shawn's shoulder.

"My books are gone." I couldn't get over it. "What would anyone want with my bookkeeping ledgers?" I squatted next to my computer tower, looked up at my brothers, and hoped they could give me an answer. When they just stood there, I said, "It's like Kevin said. None of the people I work for are in the mob. They're not secret agents or government agencies. Who would want the books from a hardware store, or a clothes store, or an auto shop? Stealing my computer would make more sense."

Kevin shrugged. Shawn shook his head. I pulled my bare mattress straight on the box springs and sat down. "Do you think Mr. Kline sells knock-off dresses, or that Al runs a chop shop?" I stared at the mess and up at my brothers. They looked as bewildered as I felt. "And what could a hardware store cover up? Hot tools? Al running a chop shop makes the most sense, except I haven't heard of any stolen cars in the area. Have you?"

My brothers looked at each other, then at me and shrugged. Shawn walked over to the crib with Gracie. "The bastard even messed up the crib," he said. Gracie's blanket lay on the floor with her sheet. Kevin crunched something underfoot and swore. He headed for the kitchen while I went into the bathroom, leaving Shawn in front of the crib with Gracie, his brain apparently frozen. I found a clean sheet in the linen closet, which was untouched, and put it on the crib. I wondered absently if Shawn would have just stood there with Gracie sleeping on his shoulder all night if I hadn't come up with a clean sheet.

Bottles rattled in the kitchen. "Good news," Kevin sang out, "Your refrigerator is safe. We have beer."

"There's a relief," I called back. Shawn put Gracie in her crib. She flapped her head back and forth a couple of times before she settled down. Her pale blonde hair lay in fine wisps and her eyelashes were dark and lush. Her body reminded me of a stuffed doll in her soft pink sleeper/

"Listen, Brat," Shawn said, "don't worry about this mess tonight. You can sleep in my bed and we'll help you clean up in the morning. Then me and Kevin will find whoever did this and take him apart."

"Thanks, Shawn," I hugged him briefly and said, "It sure doesn't make sense to leave something that you could sell, like my computer, and take my bookkeeping books."

In the kitchen, Kevin was scraping stuff into a pile with the side of his work boot when Shawn and I went to see what the clinking sound in the kitchen was all about. Kevin circled a sizeable pile of broken dishes and glassware, kicking the debris from around the room with the side of his work boot.

Shawn turned abruptly, walked back to the bedroom where he scooped Gracie out of her crib. "Kevin will board up your window," he nodded toward Kevin who returned the nod in agreement. "You and Gracie will sleep in my room tonight." Then he strode out the door with Gracie without waiting to see if I agreed. I followed Shawn into the house to sleep in his grungy bed. I was too bone tired to care how it smelled. I sank into bed grateful just to forget everything.

THIRTEEN

The less than fresh odor of Shawn's bed recaptured the events of the night before. Gracie slept peacefully in a desk drawer that Shawn had pulled out and placed on the floor. He'd cleverly lined the drawer with his pillowcase. Fortunately I woke up before Gracie so she didn't have to suffer the indignity of lying on Shawn's sweaty pillowcase. My brothers have impeccable hygiene when it comes to their personal grooming, but their housekeeping is nil. I go over and clean up the place more for the sake of my parents than them. I also throw their bedding in with mine occasionally just in case the odor seeps over to my place. I have to admit they usually are appreciative, giving me some extra grocery money or bringing home pizza sometimes.

I made a mental note to strip their beds if ever I got my own place back in shape. I picked up Gracie and walked back to my apartment before she woke up for her six o'clock bottle, assuming any bottles were left unbroken. Luck was with me because I'd made up several bottles and put them in the fridge where they were still safe. The intruder hadn't bothered the refrigerator or my linen closet, nor did Jack's room suffer any damage. There were clean crib sheets and a blanket so I could put Gracie down in her crib after she finished her bottle.

Nothing in the living room was upset but then there's not much in that room. My parents' old blue couch and matching chair, a neighbor's old coffee table, and end tables, and two lamps I'd picked up from Wal-Mart were about the extent of the décor. Most of the mess centered around the bedroom and kitchen. I picked out pots and pans, silverware, plastic ware, and anything that hadn't been broken like my measuring cups and a couple of heavy bowls from the litter on the kitchen floor. After I had the sink and counter top full of salvageable items, I got the snow shovel from the garage and scooped my broken glassware, favorite pitcher, and cookie jar into a large black trash bag. My stainless tea kettle was fine as were a couple of cups that somehow managed to stay intact. I made a cup of tea and found a pad of paper that was still intact except for the first few pages. I sat down at the kitchen table to start on a list of replacement items in the kitchen that I'd need to buy. It would cost me plenty to replace the lost dishes, food, plus a new computer monitor. I couldn't face the bedroom at this point, so I didn't know what else I'd have to buy. I couldn't miss the heel of my black pumps stuck into the broken computer monitor when I fixed Gracie's crib though.

I was on the verge of tears when the phone rang. "How you doing, Brat?" It was Shawn.

"You don't want to know. Buying new everything, dishes, food, and even my monitor is going to wipe out my savings completely."

"Well cheer up. After work me and Kevin are taking you to the stores for food and dishes and stuff so you can cook again."

"What's the catch?" Past experience told me that it would cost me somehow.

"We buy whatever you want, and you cook us supper for a month."

"Deal!" I hung up and cheered. It would be easy to make meals to share with my brothers. Cheered by the thought that I could get some new stuff for the kitchen and pick out new dishes buoyed my spirits a lot. I got busy cleaning my rug in the living room, first with the vacuum and then with a scrub brush. The bedroom was mostly just a mess. Glass shards were embedded in my quilt from a broken bottle of cologne. I'd have to replace that and Gracie's quilt too since hers had been thrown onto mine and then trod on together.

While I scrubbed floors and cleaned, my mood plummeted again when I tried to figure out how much work it would take to get three new bookkeeping ledgers up-to-date. Fortunately I'd made back up records on my computer. But I'd have to buy new ledgers, and then recopy three books from January through July. Then too, my ledgers would have to be audited again, maybe at my expense. It's not like I have a lot of bookkeeping knowledge. I had a high school bookkeeping course and some help from old Mr. Kramer, Owensville's only auditor. He was not a patient man, but he did bark out information about what I needed in order to comply with tax laws. Sitting through an audit with Mr. Kramer was always an ordeal that I dreaded. .

It was just past four-thirty when I finished relining my cabinets and drawers with a roll of leftover wallpaper I had stored in the linen closet. Even though the last thing I wanted to do was talk to Mr. Kramer, I figured there was no use putting off the inevitable. I picked up the phone to call Mr. Kramer's office for an appointment. I wanted to have everything in order before I saw my bosses. Somehow I managed to seem competent to them, even though I always felt like I was one step away from falling on my can.

I smiled to myself while the phone rang with the knowledge that soon I'd be going to college. My business career would be for real. I savored the thought while I waited for Mr. Kramer's secretary, Joyce, to answer the phone.

"Hey, Joyce," I said when she answered. Did you hear what happened to me last night?" Joyce was a few years older than me. I liked her a lot. How she could stand Mr. Kramer every day was beyond me.

"I did," she said. How are you holding up?"

"About as well as expected. I guess I have to make an appointment with Mr. Kramer to have my books audited again. I also need to ask him some questions about a couple of receipts that were damaged pretty badly."

"Mr. Kramer retired," she answered. "His practice has been taken over by Mr. Dillon."

I was so shocked that I couldn't say anything. After a few seconds of silence, Joyce must have assumed that I knew all about it and so she said, "I'll put him on."

"Did he have a retirement party? Why wasn't I invited? "Wait!" I yelled to Joyce

A rich, baritone voice came on the line and said, "Excuse me?"

"I'm sorry. I was trying to get Joyce's attention before she connected you, but I was too late."

"Would you like me to transfer you back?"

"I really need to talk with you," I said, "but I guess I wanted Joyce to fill me in on what happened to Mr. Kramer first. I've known him all my life. What happened?"

"You must know how he could be," Mr. Dillon chuckled. "He didn't want any fuss or bother. He just wanted to slip away quietly to Arizona so he sold his practice to me last month."

"Oh," I said. "That sounds like Mr. Kramer." He'd been so unsociable that I thought it was likely he didn't have any friends to invite to a retirement party. I felt sad for him. "If you give me his new address, I'll send a retirement card," I said.

"Joyce can do that," he said and the phone clicked.

"Wait!"

"What?" Joyce said.

"I want Mr. Kramer's address, but I need to talk with Mr. Dillon too. But first," I said quickly before she could send me back to him. "What's the story on the new guy?"

"We-ell, you know Mr. Kramer. He wanted to get away without anybody making a fuss so he advertised in a trade journal for a replacement. It was all done quickly too. Wait until you meet our Mr. Dillon." I could hear the happy in her voice. "He's got brown wavy hair, and really deep blue eyes, and I swear, when he smiles I get goose bumps all over." Since

Joyce is a very large woman, I'd say about two people's worth, that's a major patch of gooseflesh. "I love to come to work these days," she giggled. I waited until she refocused.

"His wife died two years ago in a car crash. No kids. They lived in Evanston. He's been a CPA for five years, he's twenty-eight, and totally eligible."

"Anything else?" The last thing I cared about was his eligibility.

"Hmm. Let's see. He likes spice drops, peanut butter cups and Fanny Mae Meltaways." I began to wonder if he was really hot, or just liked the same food groups Joyce liked. We made an appointment for Monday morning at eleven and she gave me Mr. Kramer's new address.

I woke up the next morning in a much better frame of mind. For one thing, it was Thursday, the best day for shopping for groceries because all the sales start then and the shelves are all stocked for week-end shoppers. First I went to WalMart. It was fun to pick out new dishes. There was a good sale on comforters with matching dust ruffles and pillow shams. I chose a set with roses that sort of matched the pink quilt I chose for Gracie's crib. Then I shopped for groceries which took most of the morning.

After lunch I drove to the nearby town of Sherman Oaks to the Office Max supply store for new bookkeeping ledgers. Since I'd made the trip to Sherman Oaks, I decided I might as well look in the stores at the mall for something that looked professional to wear for my meeting with Mr. Dillon. The truth is I worried that maybe I wouldn't be able to ask questions of Mr. Dillon like I had with Mr. Kramer. It was possible that I'd lose my jobs. I had to make a good impression.

When I saw the price tags on the only things I really liked, I decided I'd find something at home in Kline's Department Store where my employee discount makes it hard to beat. Still, I like to look around the mall. I also got my hair trimmed. I wear it below my shoulders in back but I keep it tapered around my face.

True to his word, Shawn came home from work at 4:30 and took me to Owensville Community College. Our town isn't big, but we have a really nice community college campus that serves Sherman Oaks as well as a couple of other nearby towns.

I signed up for Introduction to Business, and also Composition 101. Classes would begin the first week in September. My classes would meet on Tuesdays and Thursdays from 4:30 to 9:30 PM. This schedule meant that Gracie would only need one bottle before I got home to feed her at ten. When Shawn reminded me that either he or Kevin would watch Gracie, I felt a flood of tenderness for my brothers. It made me aware of how much I rely on them.

At seven that evening I met with Reverend Hanover. Rev. Hanover and my dad used to be on the same bowling league. A short, stocky man with thin brown hair and a very large head, Rev. Hanover always reminds me of my Mr. Potato Head game. However, he was sympathetic and he gave me the name of an experienced divorce lawyer, named Emeryl Arnash. Reverend Hanover assured me that I could trust Mrs. Arnash and that she was a good Christian lady. It surprised me that he didn't try to talk me out of divorcing Jack, but then he knew about Charlotte too.

When I got home, I made an appointment to see Mrs. Arnash Monday at two-thirty in the afternoon. I expected my meeting on Monday morning with Mr. Dillon would be over before lunch.

Friday afternoon I met Margie for lunch at Chuck's She had been too busy to talk on the phone so we had a lot to catch up on. "You look better than you've looked in quite a while," Margie said as she slid onto the booth seat across from me.

"I'm excited," I said. "I have so much to tell you that I don't know where to begin. I knew I didn't have to tell her about the break in. The neighborhood hot line had taken care of that. "Do you want to hear about me going to college or about our new auditor first?"

Margie stopped spooning baby food down to Bradley's upturned face from his car seat on the floor beside the booth. "You're going to college!" she shrieked. That got the attention of the people around us. I smiled all around, shaking my head yes. Everyone smiled and some gave me a thumbs up before they went back to eating. Margie and I shared a high five.

Margie smiled all over herself when I told her about college registration and the classes I'd be taking. "You know you can always bring Gracie over to my house when you need some freedom. Bradley loves her company, don't you sweetie?" Bradley yawned and drooled grey-green chunks down his chin. When I couldn't think of anything more to say about my future in college, Margie said, "I didn't hear anything about a new auditor."

"Mr. Kramer retired."

Margie's jaw dropped. The baby's spoon hung midair and Bradley let out a howl at the food slowdown. We had to laugh. Margie went back to spooning food down to him. "When was the retirement party?"

"You know how standoffish Mr. Kramer was. He just wanted to sneak off to Arizona without one, so Mr. Dillon slid into his spot without any notice."

"You'd think somebody would have noticed!" Margie sounded highly offended. I had to laugh. Somebody finally put one over on the town gossips. "Where's the new guy staying?" She scraped the remains of the chunky food from a jar into Bradley's open mouth.

"I don't know," I admitted. "I forgot to ask Joyce." It wasn't like me not to get all the details. "Anyway," I continued, "Joyce is on cloud nine over Mr. Kramer's replacement. He's young, single, and Joyce says he's really hot."

"Oh-ho," Margie bobbed her eyebrows. "So he's young and single you say."

"Don't even think it," I responded dryly. "The only aisle I'm going down is in a classroom."

When Margie was finally through feeding Bradley and had given him his pacifier, she rested her crossed arms on the table and said, "You know, the one thing nobody can figure out is why somebody would want to steal your bookkeeping records."

"I can't figure that out either. Shawn and Kevin think the guy from Florida is probably the one who took them and trashed my place, to get back at me for hurting his son."

Margie leaned in closer to me from across the table. "Wait 'till you hear this. Brad has a theory." She rolled her eyes, leaning forward with a smirk. "There's only three people who might have a problem if something bad was discovered in your books, right?" I nodded. "That would be Mr. Atkinson from True Value Hardware, Mr. Kline, from Kline's Department Store, and Al, from Al's Garage. We all know Mr. Atkinson and Mr. Kline wouldn't do anything shady, but Al's not above suspicion, at least in Brad's mind."

"Tell Brad I'll take a closer look at Al's bills and receipts when I'm working on my books." We shrugged together. Anything was possible.

FOURTEEN

After lunch I drove down Frontage Road past the front of Al's Garage. One bay was empty. The other bay had two mechanics under a small brown foreign car hoisted up on a rack. Not many mechanics stick it out with Al. For one thing, he's got a rotten temper and he only pays minimum wages. The only reason he pays me a decent wage is because I do the payroll, so I know how much he can afford. Before I started keeping his books, he'd had a succession of bookkeepers who left his records in a shambles. The only thing Al has going for him is that he's good at fixing foreign cars. Since I needed to talk with all of my bosses about the break-in, I figured that I might as well get Al out of the way first.

I parked next to Al's Porsche behind the building and entered the tiny office through the back door. In order to keep from getting the bottom of Gracie's carrier covered with sludge from the office floor, I spread a plastic WalMart bag on the floor for Gracie's carrier. Years of filth are embedded in the cement floor. The desk is equally grimy under the bills and candy wrappers. A vending machine that is perpetually out of order, a faded calendar with a naked lady on the front, and a filthy desk chair complete the office decor.

The place reeks of automotive grime so I'm always in a hurry to get out of there. Many of his bills and receipts had wrinkled corners, coffee rings, and sticky spots on them but I slid the mess into a plastic bag from a stash I keep in my van.

Al entered the office from the garage, smearing grease around on his hands with a filthy rag. Dirt outlined the creases in his face like someone etched him in charcoal. "I came by to tell you in person about the break-in at my house. You do know the books for the garage were stolen, right?"

Al squinted and clenched his fists which didn't make me feel like a friendly conversation might ensue. "It's not a problem for you," I hurried on to say while I forced a smile. He still didn't look too happy nor did he respond. I waited a beat and added, "I had everything backed up on my computer."

He rolled phlegm around in his throat, spit out the back door, and turned to face me, his head tilted up from a slightly stooped position. "So that means all my business is floating around out there in somebody else's hands. I don't like it, Julie."

"I don't like it either, Al, but there's not much I can do about it. There's nothing in the books that would matter if someone knew about it, is there?" I hoped I sounded cheery and innocent.

He shifted his sullen gaze from me to the floor and said, "I just don't like folks knowing my business."

"I'm sure the police will do whatever they can to find the thief," I said, knowing as he must, that those ledgers were probably history. Huey, Louie, and Donald are not considered crack policemen by anyone I know. They mostly direct traffic and catch the occasional speeder, which is about all that our town usually needs. "I'll have new ledgers done soon," I said. I finished stuffing the plastic WalMart bag with his receipts. Al turned abruptly on his heels and stalked back into the garage so I left too.

The aroma of a pot roast I had in the oven lightened my mood when I stepped into my kitchen. Whenever I get home from Al's, I feel like I need a shower. Telling Al that our police force would get my ledgers back only reinforced my conviction that I'd never see them again. It irritated me that my bosses insisted on old fashioned ledgers instead of being satisfied with computer printouts. Their "reasoning" was the same – it was the way they'd always done it. I wanted to keep them happy so I could keep my jobs, so I double entered everything, once in the computer and then into the ledgers.

I took a quick shower and then I phoned Bill Carmichael, a friend of mine who has a thriving used computer business in his parents' basement. "Hey Bill," I said. "I need a good cheap monitor."

"So which do you want, good or cheap?" I waited patiently until he finished nasal snorting at his own sense of humor. "I thought you'd be calling me when I heard about your place being trashed. I got a monitor put aside already." Bill's around my age. He rebuilds computers and he also teaches people how to solve basic computer problems, even offering short lessons when needed. He's helped me out plenty of times, especially when it came time to set up my spreadsheets.

After supper Kevin went with me to Bill's and carried the monitor up to my bedroom for me. I hooked it up and started the long process of printing out all of the stolen records so I could copy them onto ledger sheets. I didn't want to try to read the monitor for every entry since I'd need to place a ruler along each entry to keep my place and not pick up the wrong data. My printer is slow, but it's dependable. I watched TV until after the ten o'clock news and went to bed glad that I could retrieve all of my bookkeeping information, even if it was going to take days or maybe weeks. Tomorrow, I'd begin to copy ledger sheets.

In our circle of friends, people often go to one another's homes for dinner after church and then watch the Bears, Bulls, Cubs, or Sox games. Older women attend church circle meetings while younger people tend to hang out with friends or go to the mall. Ordinarily I'd meet Margie at Sherman Oaks Mall. We'd window shop and get a frozen latte.

After church today, however, I sipped tea at my kitchen table while Jack took his stuff from my apartment. I watched him to make sure that he didn't do anything weird out of spite. It wasn't at all relaxing. He passed through the kitchen carrying his stuff without looking at me.

I considered what I would tell Gracie someday as Jack went back and forth from the bedroom to his car. He carried his clothes on hangers and most of his things in plastic grocery bags. I wanted to tell Gracie someday that she comes from good people. Plenty of kids at school had problems because their parents were bitter enemies. I didn't want that for Gracie. She shouldn't have to suffer ugly fights on holidays and family functions. I told myself that I may not be able to control my feelings when I'm around Jack, but I knew I could control my behavior, for Gracie's sake.

It seemed to me that if we could agree on how to split our stuff and we both love Gracie, then we ought to be able to be civil when we're together. As an imperfect person, Reverend Hanover had pointed out, I had made a bad choice when I married Jack but I didn't want Gracie to suffer because of it. Maybe Reverend Hanover's talk this morning in church about how hatred only eats up the one who hates got through to me. Anyway, I intended to talk pleasantly and reasonably with Jack.

When it looked like he was on the last trip to his car I said, "Would you sit down and talk with me about how we're going to handle the divorce?"

Jack paused on the landing with a few clothes slung over his arm. He turned around, heading back into the kitchen. "Yeah, I guess." He dumped the clothes on the table and straddled a chair across from me.

"I'm going to see a lawyer tomorrow that Reverend Hanover told me about. He said if we could get our act together, we won't have to pay an arm and a leg to get a divorce. If we can agree on who gets what before we see a lawyer, then all that the lawyer has to do is make it legal." Jack didn't say anything so I continued. "We don't have a lot to divide up. I say you take your car and the stuff that's yours. I get my van, my folks' camper, and the furniture, since it came from my parents and neighbors."

He shrugged. "I don't have any place for furniture anyway." He rested his forearms on the table over the back of the chair, smiling one of his formerly heart stopping smiles and said, "I'm staying with Charlotte now and she's got her own furniture." He said it like he thought I'd feel jealous. Instead I thought, I'm getting my freedom and she's getting a scumbag. And the winner is?

He left and I took some roasted chicken and noodles I'd made over to the house. My brothers weren't around, so I left it in their fridge. I assumed that I'd heard the last of Mr. Grady. On my way back upstairs, I contemplated my new status. I was now a separated, soon-to-be divorced, soon-to-be college student. It probably wasn't normal to feel so happy about a divorce, but I'd had to tiptoe around Jack so long that it felt good to be done with it. I slept like Gracie Sunday night.

With Gracie around, I never need an alarm clock. At exactly six o'clock Monday morning she fussed, so I padded into the kitchen, made her bottle, and sat on the couch with her. When she was finished with the bottle, I put her on my lap where she stretched and yawned. She kicked her chubby legs vigorously and waved her tiny fists. She was almost exactly the length of my lap now. I grinned at her, and chucked her under her chin. She batted her long lashes and giggled.

We played together a while. I made her giggle, snuggled her close, and rocked her in my arms. She smelled so good I inhaled deeply. When she closed her eyes and sighed into sleep, I decided that being married to Jack was worth it to have Gracie.

I took a long shower and put on a tailored skirt and blouse. One heel on my black pumps was pretty scuffed but a little black shoe polish fixed the problem if you didn't look too closely. The outfit looked pretty much what I thought was right for a visit to the new auditor; clean and professional. I loaded my printouts and Gracie into the van and headed for Mr. Dillon's office. I parked behind the single story, red brick duplex. The auditor shares the building with Bud Hinkley, the State Farm Insurance man. With my diaper bag stuffed with printouts as well as Gracie's necessities, and Gracie in her carrier, I opened the glass door in back of the building. Mr. Kramer's name had been replaced with Mr. Dillon's name stenciled in black script

"Hi Julie," Joyce grinned at me in a conspiratorial way from her desk. She had to swivel sideways to greet visitors because her desk was situated against the wall immediately when you entered. Two small offices on the opposite wall are set up so that one is for a conference room if you need more space to spread out. The other is, or was, Mr. Kramer's office. "Go on in," Joyce said. "Jason, that's Mr. Dillon, is expecting you."

When I stepped into the office, sunshine glared through the open windows behind Mr. Dillon's silhouette as he sat at his desk facing the door. I stood in the doorway with Gracie's carrier and shaded my eyes. Mr. Dillon reached back to roll down the Venetian blinds. "Sorry," he said. "It's such a great day outside, I just wanted to bring in as much of it as possible."

Tall, lean, muscular, and clean-cut, he had wavy brown hair, and a drop dead smile. I set Gracie's carrier by the door. "Hello," I strode across the small office with my hand outstretched. He took it in both of his and held it. I felt tingly and warm inside. His eyes were like magnets. "I'm Julie Armstrong," I said in a voice that was so calm it surprised me. Instead of ripping off my panties and climbing his frame, I was moving and talking like a sane person!

"I'm Jason Dillon," he smiled as he held my hand. I wanted him to keep holding my hand. It was warm and soft. He did for a long moment but then he gestured to a chair facing his desk.

"You can call me Jason," he said. His deep blue eyes wouldn't let me go. "Joyce told me that your place was trashed and someone stole your ledgers but that you had everything backed up on your computer. Did you bring the printouts?" he asked. I handed them across his desk and stared at his short, shining hair while he leafed through the printouts. His thick brown hair looked soft and I was wondering how it would feel to run my fingers through it when he looked up. I smiled feeling somehow guilty.

"I hope everything's in order." I said.

"I'll have to look these over more thoroughly, of course," he said, "but it looks like you've given me all of the information I'll need. After I complete the audit, I'll call you." He rose and walked me to the door. It was over.

I picked up Gracie's carrier and we shook hands again before he closed his door. As soon as the door was closed, I put Gracie's carrier down and I leaned against it in his outer office fanning myself with the back of my hand. Joyce grinned knowingly. "You weren't kidding, Joyce." I said. We chatted a few minutes before I left for home and then my appointment with Mrs. Arnash, the lawyer. On the drive home I chided myself about getting all worked up over someone just because he was good looking. Jack was good looking.

I had plenty of time before my appointment with the lawyer so I put together a meatloaf for supper. I wanted something that could bake on low while I was gone, so I put some potatoes, acorn squash, and a green bean casserole in the oven with the meatloaf. Then I fixed myself a tuna sandwich and a glass of milk. After lunch I was ready for my meeting with the lawyer.

I backed the van out of our driveway and into the parking lot across the street for a grape Mr. Misty drink from the D.Q. The air was warm and sunshine flooded through the windows of the van so that I almost needed to crack out my sun glasses for the season. It seemed a shame to waste such a lovely day filling out divorce forms, or whatever you do, I thought. Since I didn't actually know what to expect, I was a little anxious that it would go well.

I wound my way into the upscale, quiet streets of Butterfield Creek where large homes sat well back on lawns manicured by professionals. The address Rev. Hanover gave me appeared on the ornate wrought iron mail box in front of a single story home with a U shaped drive in front. For a minute it didn't look right, but then I remembered Rev. Hanover telling me that Mrs. Arnash was retired and so coming to her home made sense. I drove up to the house and got out of the van, unsnapping Gracie from the back seat afterwards. The dark brick and frame ranch nestled among large, rounded evergreen bushes reminding me of a house in a picture book I had as a child where the house nestled among mushrooms. I walked up the polished stone walkway with Gracie and pressed the doorbell beside one of the beveled glass panels set on each side of the oak double doors.

A fragile looking lady in a lavender pant suit opened the door. "Come in, come in," she smiled, "You must be Julie Armstrong, and this little cherub must be Gracie." Reverend Hanover had asked Mrs. Arnash to handle my divorce even though she's retired. She took it more as a favor, I think, for the Reverend.

I stepped into a spacious foyer the size of Gracie's bedroom. It contained a round pedestal table with a large flower centerpiece, a grandfather clock, and a side table with an elongated mirror above it. I followed Mrs. Arnash into an inviting office off to one side of the hall. Sun streamed in the windows lining the back wall. A large oak desk placed to one side of the room had a comfortable leather armchair next to it where she indicated that I should sit. She sat on a matching oak swivel chair before her desk. I put Gracie on the floor next to my chair and sat down. For an older woman, Mrs. Arnash looked pretty impressive. Her shining silver hair was cut short in a modern style and her makeup was impeccable.

"My husband is out playing golf," she said. "Can I get you something to drink? Iced tea, perhaps?" I shook my head no, so she took one of my hands in hers, and said softly, "Now tell me everything." She leaned toward me, patted the back of my hand, and waited.

It was as though she opened a zip lock bag of melted ice. By the time I finished, I'd gushed through half a box of tissues.

I talked through some things that I didn't even know I was worried about. What would happen to Gracie if anything happened to me? Would Jack get her? I slobbered and jabbered all afternoon.

At one point Mr. Arnash poked his head in. A slight man in navy pants and a white golf shirt, he acknowledged us with a two finger salute, and went on down the hall. I looked at my watch. I'd been there almost two hours. "I'm sorry to have taken up so much of your time," I said. I wiped at my tear streaked face. "You haven't even had time to get your husband any supper."

"Don't worry, dear," she patted my shoulder. "We'll pick up something later. I think everything will be all right." She smiled so warmly that I took a deep, ragged breath, feeling like she was right. The worst was over.

"You've done the right thing by getting Jack to agree to an easy settlement. All you need to do now is get everything down in writing, specifying exactly what you will get, and what he will get. Then you need to decide if you intend to receive half of his retirement, or a one time settlement.

"I'd prefer the one time settlement. I don't want any more connections with him." I said. "He can have his stuff, and I'll take mine, and we'll just call it even. I don't want to make it more complicated than necessary."

"You need to think about your child." Mrs. Arnash said firmly. "Jack must pay child support until the child reaches eighteen years of age, or is legally adopted should you remarry." I hadn't thought about Jack having to pay child support. "And you're entitled to alimony," she continued. "Later you'll be entitled to part of his pension, unless you remarry. You should not have to change your lifestyle."

"I don't want alimony. He didn't change my lifestyle anyway. We didn't have a joint checking account. I paid the bills and he bought the groceries. I don't even know what he makes to tell the truth."

"I can draw up a legally binding agreement that will spell out what you each will receive but Jack must be made aware that I can only represent your interests. If he signs the agreement, I can have the divorce petition served. Since you say he's already agreed to a settlement, I can set up a court date right away. Normally you must live in a separate residence for six months. But I think we can allow the time he's been with Charlotte as the six month period and go forward." Yep, there's nothing like a small town. I thought feeling grateful.

Mrs. Arnash walked me out the front door and waited while I put Gracie's carrier in the back seat before she waved good-bye and shut the door. On my way home I reflected on how she had worked out the agreement papers so that her fees would be paid by Jack. I thought it was only fair that he should pay since he's the one who wanted to play.

It was late afternoon and my brothers would be home soon, so I went home to serve the meal I'd planned. It was a relief to tell someone about my marriage but now I was beat. Actually, I'd told her a lot more than I'd ever divulged to Reverend Hanover or even Gram. I'd even told her about the guy I put in the hospital in Clearwater. She agreed that it was bizarre that the guy hadn't been taken to the hospital right away.

In retrospect, the last year seemed more like an ordeal than a marriage. The only good thing to come out of it was Gracie and I'd do it again in a heartbeat to have her.

FIFTEEN

Next morning I decided to go see my other two bosses and reassure them that their records were safe. I'd also pick up any bills and receipts that had accumulated

After breakfast, I took Gracie and drove down Main Street. I pulled into the slot at the curb in front of Tom's True Value Hardware Store and was about to unsnap Gracie's carrier when Ethel Vandergarden hurried out of the store waving both hands above her head. A small plastic purse flapped around one frail arm. Ethel's life centers around a high backed stool behind the old cash register at Tom's hardware store where she's been the cashier ever since the place opened, at least fifty years ago. Her biggest claim to fame is that her cash register and receipts always balanced.

She probably weighs less than a hundred pounds. Today she wore neon green stretch pants, old penny loafers without socks, and an orange and red diagonally striped polyester top that hung to one side on her bony shoulders. Her knuckles made her fingers look like she had marbles inside each finger, but she could still punch the keys on the store's antique cash register. I always felt this was why my plea for a computerized register was a waste of time. Everybody knew that although Tom Atkinson owned the place, Ethel ran it.

Tom would often ask Ethel where things were. She'd know. He wouldn't. I'd heard him myself one day when he yelled to her from an aisle in back of the store, "Hey Ethel, how much we charging for these?" When she told him, he looked surprised and said, "Wow, that much?" She said yes so he shrugged and told the customer the amount she said.

Now she was heading for my van in a panic. "Oh Julie, thank God you're here. Tom's had a heart attack! The ambulance just left and I've been waiting for someone to show up who could take me to the hospital right away."

"I immediately opened the front door of my van. Her mouth was a thin line in a face full of lines, her scalp pink in the sunlight through her thin, auburn tinted hair. For a brief second I wondered if she'd lost her mind.

Then she said firmly, "An ambulance took Tom to the hospital. You're the only customer and I need to get to the hospital right away." With that she grabbed the front seat that came to her shoulders and tried to lift a leg onto the floor without success. I lifted her onto the passenger seat and buckled her seatbelt.

We sped down Main Street toward the hospital in silence. Her gnarled fingers clenched and unclenched her tiny pink plastic purse. She strained forward in her seat as though it would help the van's forward momentum.

I parked in front of the emergency doors. Ethel had the van door open and was sliding off the seat onto the pavement before I could get around it to help her. Inside, Judy Calamine, a petite middle-aged woman with dark hair and bright red lipstick, was at the reception desk. "Mrs. Atkinson and Beth are both in with Mr. Atkinson." She said to us as we approached the reception desk in the center of the lobby. "We're still trying to get hold of his son at the University in Champaign, but he isn't answering his phone. We left a message, but so far, no call back." Judy bit her lower lip. "I haven't heard how he's doing yet."

The place was empty except for the three of us. I put Gracie's carrier on the floor in front of a row of molded plastic chairs along the wall where Ethel and I were told to wait. It was twenty minutes before the double doors leading into the emergency rooms opened and Tom's wife and daughter Beth came out. The two clung to each other sobbing.

Beth looks like a clone of her mother, medium build, short perm making a dark halo around a flat face, no make up, and no waistline giving them the appearance of wearing a dress over a barrel, with arms and legs sticking out. Ethel rushed over to take Mrs. Atkinson's hand. Beth shook her head to indicate that Tom didn't make it. When Ethel understood, the three women made a circle of grief, wailing loudly, their voices bouncing off the white ceramic tiled walls. The top of Ethel's head reached the other women's armpits, her hands rested on the backs of her keening friends. I sat on a chair along the wall and felt like an outsider.

Judy pushed through the emergency room doors, leaving us alone in the waiting area. I felt helpless. Tears welled up in my eyes and I sat there wishing I could think of something to do.

The three women wept openly together for quite a while. Even though Gracie was asleep, I hugged her on my shoulder while we waited. Finally Judy Calamine came out of the double doors and asked if I could take the women home.

I settled Gracie in her carrier and walked over to the women whose crying abated somewhat when Judy came out. "Come on," I said gently placing my hand on Ethel's back. "I'll take you home." Weeping steadily, Mrs. Atkinson and Ethel held hands and let me guide them toward the sliding glass doors leading outside. Beth fell in step behind us, sobbing quietly into a soggy wad of tissues.

I had them out the doors, a few steps away from the building, when Mrs. Atkinson turned, screamed, "No!" and bolted back into the hospital. "I want to be with Tom," she wailed.

Through the glass double doors, we watched Mrs. Atkinson get as far as Judy Calamine's desk. Judy put an arm around Mrs. Atkinson's shoulders and firmly turned her around, saying something that caused Mrs. Atkinson to sag a little, her expression dazed as she walked obediently with Judy toward the outside doors. "I'm sure you can make arrangements to see your husband at O'Shea's," Judy said after the entrance doors whooshed open and Mrs. Atkinson was outside.

Judy stepped outside on the sidewalk in front of the emergency room with Mrs. Atkinson, her arm around the woman's shoulders. She nodded meaningfully to me and turned back inside. I took one of Mrs. Atkinson's arms, Beth took the other, and we guided her to my van.

It took a while to get everybody settled. Beth climbed into the back of the van with a good deal of effort. She sat behind her mother and Gracie. Ethel rode shotgun. I handed Mrs. Atkinson a box of tissues that I keep in the van.

"Take us to O'Shea's, Julie," Ethel directed. I nodded and pulled out. The women passed the tissues back and forth between themselves as we drove the short distance to O'Shea's Funeral Home which sits on the corner of Main Street and Diversey Avenue. The building is actually a renovated old home surrounded by huge old oak trees and a circular driveway leading to the front entrance with parking in the back.

Entering the front foyer, we were greeted by a very tall, slim gentleman with silver hair. I'm guessing Judy called him from the hospital to tell him to expect us because he greeted us as we opened the door. He directed us into a room off to the right decorated in soft mauve and pale green. "I'm Mr. Edwards," he said as he led Mrs. Atkinson and Ethel by placing his hand beneath their elbows toward cushioned chairs facing a large polished mahogany desk. We all knew someone new in town had been hired to work here, but none of us had met him yet. He seemed competent and was certainly gracious. Beth gravitated next to me on a plush green bench along the back wall. I placed Gracie's carrier on the floor beside me.

Mr. Edwards took three small boxes of tissues from a desk drawer, and gave a box to Ethel, Mrs. Atkinson, and then he came over and handed one to Beth whose shoulders twitched in spasms as she quietly wept.

Waiting patiently until the women's tears subsided somewhat, in a soft, soothing tone of voice, he said, "We at O'Shea want you to know how very sorry we are for your loss and we want you to know that we are ready to serve you in any way that we can at this, the time of your grief." The ladies sniffled a little less as he continued, "May I ask which of you ladies will be making the arrangements?"

This was met with an awkward silence. Mr. Edwards cleared his throat. Mrs. Atkinson put her hand to her throat and stared at Ethel. Ethel worked furiously at getting her nose clear while she wiped at tears. No one spoke for so long that I finally said, "The lady on your right is Mrs. Atkinson and the lady on your left is Ethel Vandergarden." I continued simply because I didn't know what else to do. "Beth here," I nodded at Beth beside me, "she is Mr. Atkinson's daughter, and I'm Julie Armstrong, um, the part-time bookkeeper."

The man's mouth smiled, but the expression in his eyes said, huh?

The awkward silence continued. At last Ethel cleared her throat and sat up a little straighter. "I'm Mr. Atkinson's manager," she said in a husky voice...

"Perhaps Mrs. Atkinson and her daughter would like to make the arrangements privately," he suggested looking at Mrs. Atkinson. The response added to the moment when Mrs. Atkinson shook her head no and Beth gasped audibly.

Mr. Edwards tried again to get control of the situation by saying, "I don't think you need to stay." He nodded in my direction, "Or you, my dear." He came around his desk, bending towards Ethel in an attempt to help her up from her chair.

Ethel swung her arm at the gentlemen's hand, jumped up and said, "First off, I'm the only one here who knows spit about how much we can afford, Sonny." Mrs. Atkinson's head bobbed up and down in agreement. "And second, who are you? Where's Eddie? We're not talking to anybody but Eddie O'Shea himself!"

The man backed away from Ethel and scurried behind his desk. Ethel was clearly in control again. Anger flushed her cheeks. Her eyes glinted behind her oversized glasses. She walked over to me, picked up my hand, and said, "Thank you for bringing us here, Julie. She patted the back of my hand. "If you'd be so kind as to wait for us, we'll still need a ride home, if that's all right, dear." I shook my head to indicate that would be fine. Then she wheeled around and said to the poor guy whose face was now ashen, "And you! If you don't get Eddie over here, I'll call his wife, Gladys and your sorry butt will be out on the pavement before I hang up!" Everybody but Mr. Edwards breathed a sigh of relief. Ethel could take care of Mr. Atkinson in death as she had most of his life.

By the time I got home, it was lunch time but I wasn't hungry. I called Lee's florist and ordered flowers for the wake and funeral. I fed Gracie and put her in the van for a visit to Kline's Department Store.

On the drive over, I wondered what would happen to Tom's store. Would somebody buy it and hire another bookkeeper? I felt a stab of guilt. I'd really miss Tom. He was a big, good natured man. His hands reminded me of bear paws because he had big palms and short fingers. Most of the time Tom was up on a ladder getting something for a customer or he was yelling across the store to ask Ethel where to find something.

Whenever I picked up the receipts from Tom's, Ethel would have them neatly bundled together. Tom always smiled like an overgrown child, letting Ethel do whatever had to be done. It was Ethel who had negotiated my salary, and because Tom's True Value Hardware Store was my first bookkeeping job, it was Ethel who decided on the method of collecting the bills and receipts.

I pulled into the parking lot behind Kline's Department Store. The yellow brick, one story department store stands alone, offering ample parking in front and on both sides of the building. It sits in a prime location on the corner of Central Avenue, and Cottonwood. Behind the store Mr. Kline's silver Beamer sat in the shade of the building at the far end.

A wide passageway runs the length of the building in back. One end is furnished with Mr. Kline's desk and swivel chair, four beige filing cabinets behind the desk, and a folding table with a coffee pot and an electric stapler on it. The employee lunch room is located at the opposite end of the space, and shelves filled with stacks of merchandise line the walls between the employees' area and Mr. Kline's makeshift "office."

The back of the store is strictly "no frills," but in front, the store is filled with quiet music, lots of light, mirrors and plush armchairs scattered all around. Middle-aged sales women dressed well, high-end brand names, and elegant dressing rooms make it a ritzy shopping experience. I know because every Christmas Mr. "K" invites me to choose any item I want, no matter how expensive. So whenever I need a new coat, Mr. Kline supplies it. I charge Mr. Kline less for my services than I charge Al or Mr. Atkinson, but Mr. Kline's the most generous with discounts.

This morning Mr. Kline sat bent over at his desk. He removed his reading glasses when he saw me, and slipped them into an inner pocket in his tan suit jacket as he stood up. His head is rimmed with a narrow fringe of gray hair, but his lively brown eyes and ready laugh make you forget he's not young.

As soon as I reached the desk with Gracie's carrier, he offered me his chair. I put Gracie's carrier on the floor beside the desk while Mr. Kline went to the coffee machine to fill two cups. It was the way he liked to do things. Our routine was that he'd give me coffee and his seat. I'd gather and sort the receipts, bills, time sheets, and register tallies, while he sipped coffee and wandered around the back room until I finished.

"Have you heard about Mr. Atkinson?" I asked before I got started. He nodded that he had and stood looking down like he was going to say something, but instead he took out a handkerchief and turned away abruptly, heading for the employee lunchroom.

When I stood up to leave, Mr. Kline gave me a hard hug. Then he sighed, hung his head and said, "I've known Tom

Atkinson over forty years. He and I started out at about the same time." I put a sympathetic hand on his shoulder and murmured that I was sorry. I didn't know what else to say so I picked up Gracie's carrier, heading for the door when I heard him give a little sob.

I turned around. He was tugging at his suit coat pocket until he'd ripped it. "What are you doing?" I set Gracie's carrier on the floor and rushed back to his side. Tears trickled down his sallow cheeks, dropping onto his tie and shirt front.

"Not to worry, dear," he sniffed, "It's just something I needed to do. I'm fine. Run along and don't worry. I won't rip up any more clothing." He wiped his eyes with his handkerchief, and he hugged me again. Then he walked over and kissed Gracie's head, leaving a wet spot on her downy hair.

"Are you going to be all right?" I was hesitant to leave. He patted my hand, and heaved a noisy sigh. "Tom was my friend," he said simply, and tears rolled down his cheeks again. He turned away and put a hand on the corner of his desk, covering his face with his handkerchief. His jacket hung crooked, the pocket held by the suit's lining. I hated to leave him but didn't know what else to do.

As soon as I got home, I called Mrs. Kline and explained what happened. She told me it was a Jewish sign of respect and not to worry about him. I was relieved to hear he was all right.

I added the bills and receipts from Kline's to the growing mountain of work to be done on my kitchen table. There was too much for my desk, so I stacked everything in piles on the kitchen table, leaving one end clear for meals. It was late afternoon when I started sorting the bills and receipts so I'd know where to begin tomorrow.

When I got up the next morning, I started in on my ledgers and worked steadily on them through most of the day. It was late afternoon when the doorbell startled me. Nobody rang the doorbell at the bottom of the stairs. I opened the upstairs door and stepped onto the landing, peering down the lighted steps. Who is it? I yelled.

"Tom." It sounded exactly like Mr. Atkinson.

"Who?"

"Tom Junior," he called. Relieved, I bounded down the stairs; lost my balance and fell against the door, pushing it out against my visitor. When I pulled the door back, blood oozed from between Tom's fingers as he held his hand over his nose.

I stared at him a split second and then I seized his free hand and pulled it, leading him upstairs. He stumbled along behind me swearing softly. I pulled out a kitchen chair for him. Then I soaked a clean dish towel with cold water and handed it to him. He looked at it bewildered, so I stood behind him, held one end of the towel against his nose and wrapped the rest behind his neck, pulling his head back and nose up, so the back of his head rested against my chest.

"Breathe through your mouth." I said as I pinched his nose closed with the wet towel and waited for the bleeding to stop. We held that pose for a few minutes until he pushed my hand away. His nose gushed fresh blood again.

"Not yet," I yanked his head back into position. "Just relax. It'll stop in a few minutes and you'll be fine." I absently stroked his hair and forehead while I stared out the window and waited. A nice breeze ruffled my yellow curtains. After a few minutes, no fresh blood appeared so I carefully wiped the blood from under his nose and around his mouth and chin. He sat very still with his eyes closed as I cleaned up his face.

"I see you've had experience with this kind of injury," he said when I finished. "Do you wing many visitors with your door?"

I bit my lower lip and shook my head no. I saw that his left eye had begun to puff out underneath. "It's a first," I said. "I'm sorry. I do have two brothers whose noses were bleeding though." I wrapped ice in a dish cloth and handed it to him. "If you don't hold this ice compress on your eye here for ten minutes, it'll puff up some more and be a terrible shiner."

He groaned and held the makeshift ice bag under his eye. "It hurts like a mother," he said. "I just came by to thank you for taking care of my mom and sister yesterday." He shifted the wad of cloth. "I drove back last night when I got home from the lab."

"The lab?"

"I'm in computer engineering at the University of Illinois."

I knew the pain in his nose would be worse later unless he took something for it, so I said, "You need to wait about half an hour for the clotting in your nose to be strong and then take something for pain." I felt awkward with him holding the ice on his face while we tried to hold a conversation around it. Vegetable soup bubbled on the stove, so I said. "Want some homemade vegetable soup and a sandwich?"

He shook his head, winced at the pain and stood up. "I'll take a rain check if you don't mind." He left quickly and I didn't blame him

After supper Margie called to tell me Tom Atkinson's son was home. "I just gave him a bloody nose," I told her. We agreed it was not a great way to meet. Then I caught her up on my day starting with my trip to O'Shea's, then Mr. Kline's behavior, and ending with Tom's bloody nose. After we hung up I made ham and cheese sandwiches for my brothers to go with the homemade vegetable soup.

I couldn't help but wonder if Tom would quit school to run his family's business or if he would sell it. I felt a stab of panic when I thought that Gracie depended on me to support us. Jack's alimony money might not be reliable considering that he wasn't that dependable about getting groceries when he lived with us. If I lost Atkinson's, I would barely make enough to pay the bills. Rent was nonexistent, thankfully, but utilities and food, not to mention insurance now that I had Gracie, and my car was getting old. Suddenly being a single mom felt like the most frightening thing I'd ever had to face.

SIXTEEN

The daily MESSENGER PRESS newspaper announced Mr. Atkinson's wake would be Friday evening and Saturday afternoon. The funeral would be Monday morning at 11 AM. I didn't want to go to the wake alone, so I arranged for Mrs. Costanza to baby-sit Gracie for an hour so that I could pay my respects with my brothers. We arranged to meet at O'Shea's after Shawn and Kevin cleaned up from work Friday evening.

I worked the rest of the week on recopying my ledger sheets. By Gracie's two o'clock bottle that Friday, I'd finished most of Al's books and still had Kline's and True Value Hardware stores to do. My frustration gave way to tears until I told myself to look for something positive or something that might be good about the situation like Gramps always said worked for him. I tossed my pen on the table. Maybe a nice hot bath after I put Gracie down for her nap would help me feel better. At least it would give me time to put a positive spin on recopying all my ledger sheets. After my bath, I hadn't come up with much that could be considered good about my situation. However, it felt good to be rid of Jack and be able to go to college thanks to the break-in, so recopying the ledgers were the price I'd have to pay. It was definitely worth it, in that case. I took a container of chicken and dumplings out of the fridge that I'd made at the same time that I made last evening's meal. Sometimes I find it's easier when I'm cooking anyway, just to do several things at once so I had something on hand later when I didn't want to cook. After I microwaved a package of frozen mixed vegetables, I warmed up the chicken and dumplings and took them over to the house for my brothers after saving a plate of food for myself.

Lorenda Lee Lux

That evening the parking lot at O'Shea's Funeral Home was packed with cars, vans, and pick up trucks crammed into every space available. Vehicles were slowly cruising through the parking lot, as I was, in search of a spot to park. After a few rounds circling the parking lot, I chose a spot two blocks off Central. Gracie's carrier and my diaper bag felt heavy on the walk back to the funeral home. The air felt sultry. The high humidity promised possible rain. When I walked into the funeral home, people stood shoulder to shoulder outside the viewing rooms... I wanted to be alone while I waited for my brothers, so I smiled and hugged friends and neighbors on my way through the throng as I headed for a cushioned bench at the far end of a long vestibule outside the viewing rooms.

Most of the crowd hung around the far end nearest the viewing room where Tom's wake took place. People went in and out of the room, paying their respects and then coming out to commiserate with one another. It was good to have a place to be away from everyone. I placed Gracie's carrier on the floor beside the bench and her diaper bag beside me. The bench was long enough for several people, but nobody else wandered down this far from Tom's viewing room.

I felt really rotten. For one thing, I felt bad about losing Mr. Atkinson, but mostly I felt bad about having to do all the work involved in copying those printer pages onto ledger sheets. It meant that I had to stay alert so that I didn't make an error in any of the columns of numbers and it was tedious and boring. And to top it all off, my parents were not going to get home for the funeral.

It felt stuffy at the end of the vestibule and too warm. Some feeling I couldn't quite identify but didn't like, flooded through me. Everything suddenly piled up in my mind: being a single mom with the possibility of losing one of my jobs, or worse, having to be dependent on Jack for money, plus I couldn't count on my parents and Gram and Gramps were hundreds of miles away. It was all too much.

Tears trickled down my face so I bent my head to hide them while I fished in my purse for a tissue. When comforting arms drew me toward his shoulder, I didn't know if it was Shawn or Kevin, but I let the tears take over. When I felt better, I became aware that whoever held me was quietly crying too. His chin rested on the top of my head as we sat on the bench. Then it hit me that the chest I was slobbering all over wasn't my brother's. I looked up and through bleary eyes saw tears running down Tom Junior's face. His left eye was swollen and purple and he really needed a tissue for his nose.

I peeled off a couple of tissues from a pack out of my diaper bag and handed them to him. He wiped his face and blew his nose. I felt guilty. Here I was crying for myself and Tom probably thought it was for his father. Jeez!

He said in a husky voice, "Thanks. I needed to do that."

I nodded and sniffed a few times to clear a passage in my nose which was, of course, all stuffed up. "I'm sorry I hit you with the door," I said, "and I'm sorry about your father."

"Were you and my dad very close?" His arm was still around my shoulder. I pulled away and shook my head. "Not really. I hate to admit it, but I think I'm crying more for myself than for your father." I hung my head, unable to meet his eyes. "Don't get me wrong. I thought your dad was a wonderful man and I'm sure we'll all miss him."

He nodded, stretched his long legs and gazed at the throngs of people who had come to pay their respects to his father. I thought he'd be heartened by so many well wishers, but he surprised me by saying softly, "I wish I could get a breath of fresh air without being rude."

"Come on," I pulled him up by the hand and we started for the door at the far end of the vestibule that opened out onto the parking lot in back. Outside people passed from the parking lot to the front of the building while we stood in the shadows of the building near the back corner in the fading twilight. Tom inhaled and exhaled several times, blowing out the last breath through his mouth.

"'I'm glad you can breathe okay," I said leaning close to speak softly enough so people wouldn't notice us. "I didn't mean to burst out the door at my place like that but I was so relieved. I mean, your voice, when you said you were Tom," I faltered.

"Oh yeah! I get that a lot. We sound alike, sounded," he corrected himself. He ran his hand down his face and said, "Man, I don't know how I'm going to handle everything."

"Me neither," I said thinking of the mountain of papers on my kitchen table and trying not to think about what the future might hold past that.

"Look," he said taking a shaky breath, "I never got a chance to properly thank you for being so kind to my family. My mom said she doesn't know how they would have managed if you hadn't come along when you did. It was really smart of you to bring Ethel along too. She's been such a godsend. I was going to tell you that I owe you at least a dinner."

"It was Ethel who was smart enough to ask me to take her to the hospital," I said. Besides, after what I did to your eye, I'd say I owe you dinner."

He shook his head no and said, "I need to get back inside but I'd like to call you. I want to hear about what you're upset about but right now..." He didn't need to finish the thought.

"I know," I interrupted and I took a step toward the door. "It's okay." He nodded and we returned to the lobby. He headed back into the room to join his family. I wandered back through the crowd and spotted my brothers talking with a group of their friends.

"Doesn't Kevin look good in a suit," Kathleen Broderick was beaming up at him when I approached them.

Kevin acknowledged Kathleen's compliment with a touch on the end of her nose and a smile that made her giggle like Gracie. Kathleen ducked her chin in, her long blonde hair swung forward to hide her face as Kevin turned to me and asked, "Are you okay?" When I nodded that I was, my brothers and I entered the viewing room to pay our respects.

After the wake, Margie and Brad invited me to join them for pizza. It was good to have a night out at Chuck's with Margie and Brad. We ate pizza and talked about the new deck Brad was adding on to their house. When the pizza was reduced to bits of sausage, peppers, and congealed cheese draping over the wires of the serving pan, Brad leaned back in the booth. His arm rested along the top of the booth behind Margie. I sat across from them with Gracie at the end of the booth. Brad sighed patting his rounded belly and said, "It doesn't get any better than the big three." We clinked our glasses together and drank to our favorite toast, good beer, good pizza, and good company. Ironically, Jack had originally been the one to coin the expression.

"So, Brad," I said, "I hear you think maybe Al stole my books. Do you suspect him of something, or did you base that on his winning personality?"

"I guess I just thought out of the three guys you work for; he'd be the most likely candidate. You have to hand it to Al though, he may be a social zit, but he sure knows his stuff when it comes to fixing cars. He put a new water pump in the Volvo last month. Thing runs like new."

"Except it's twelve years old," Margie said. Margie's battle with the Volvo was epic. "This month it's a water pump. Last month we had to wait a week for Al to order a new radiator. How much was it last month?" She picked at a piece of cheese stuck around the serving rack.

Brad elaborately kissed Margie's cheek with a loud smack and then he picked up a chunk of sausage from the pizza pan. He licked his fingers and scraped a paper napkin over his midnight shadow. "You just don't like the Volvo, face it." Brad smirked and twirled his finger around Margie's earring. "I don't know why you don't like my Volvo. It likes you."

"Maybe I feel sorry for it," Margie said with a smile. She swatted at Brad's finger twirling her earring and laughed. Maybe it's time to give the poor old thing a rest before it conks out in the middle of traffic and somebody gets hurt."

Margie drew her face away from Brad who kept poking at her earring but he only teased her more by tugging on it until she said, "Would you please stop it?"

"Well, since you said please." Brad turned his attention to his almost empty mug of beer.

Thinking out loud, I said, "I've been copying Al's books and I didn't see any Volvo parts. What if he's charging for parts he doesn't actually put in the cars."

"I wouldn't put it past him." Margie said with a satisfied smile.

"He wouldn't try to snooker me," Brad said. "He always shows me the worn out parts," Brad stared into his beer mug with a frown on his face, his previous good mood completely gone. I caught a warning look from Margie.

"How would you know if Al was showing you the parts to your car or the parts to a toaster?" I asked. For some perverse reason, I ignored Margie's pleading look and widened eyes.

Brad shot me a surly look and said, "When my car doesn't work right, Al fixes the problems, so he must use parts. Maybe you just don't remember, Julie." He drained his beer mug and set it down with a little more force than was necessary. "Al might be smuggling drugs in foreign cars, but you're way off base on the repairs being shady."

Margie looked under her brows at me so I said, "You're probably right, Brad. Things have been pretty hectic in my life right now." I tried to lighten up the conversation by talking about Tom asking to take me to dinner but the mood was definitely ruined. Brad went over to pay the bill. We walked in silence to our cars. I thanked Brad for treating me to pizza and we said our goodbyes. It wasn't a happy parting.

When I got home, I went to bed right after Gracie's ten o'clock bottle. My phone rang but when I opened my eyes, it was still dark. The clock read two in the morning. "Hello," I said when I finally got the receiver under my ear on my pillow.

"You've got my record book and I've got yours," a gravely voice wheezed. "If you want your record books back, bring mine to the north end of the park and leave it on the bench by the flagpole tomorrow night at two o'clock. And make sure you come alone or you'll never get your record books back." Then he hung up.

I lay there holding the phone, dazed and half awake. "What?" I said. "What record book? Hey you freaky creep, what are you talking about!" I was yelling into a dead cell phone. My heart had jumped into overdrive. I slammed the phone down on the nightstand between my bed and the crib, and I fumbled with the headboard light. Dazed and upset, I knew there was no way I could just turn over and go back to sleep so I got up and went into the kitchen to make some cocoa.

What am I missing, I asked myself. I sat on the chair in the living room glad the windows were still boarded up, and I sipped hot cocoa. The guy in Florida who I hit might have been trying to break into the camper looking for a record book he thought I had. The holes in the windows here matched the one in Florida. I couldn't connect the dots. Jack must know more about what was going on than he let on, I thought, but I didn't want to ask him. He probably wouldn't tell me anyway.

I shivered at the creaks and groans that I listen to all the time on cool nights. Even with good insulation, the temperature of the air under the floors in a garage apartment is different enough from the temperature in the garage so that the wooden beams creak. My dad had explained all this to me after the first night I moved in. Knowing that was true didn't help much.

Okay Julie, I told myself. You're creeping yourself out. I picked up Gracie, almost hoping she would wake up, but she was limp as a rag doll. I put her into her carrier and slipped into my jeans and shirt. On the way out of my bedroom I grabbed Gracie's diaper bag. I hurried through the kitchen, flipping the lights on as I made my way to the stairs. Before I opened the door at the top of the stairs, I decided to turn on the lights that would illuminate both the stairway and the lights at the corners of the garage which might wake the neighbors. I turned on the garage lights and crept downstairs.

By the time I got outside, the neighborhood dogs barked enough so that the next door neighbor's lights came on. Other neighborhood dogs joined in and lights went on down the street like they were on a relay switch. I felt much better. "No prowlers this time, Mrs. Costanza," I called to the shadow of my neighbor on her back porch.

"So why you waking everybody up?" She called. Her voice was all scratchy. I decided old people don't wake up well. Her back porch light outlined a bubble of plastic she wore to bed to keep her hair in place. She looked like a Martian in the dim light. When the neighbors heard me say no prowlers, doors slammed and lights went out.

Shawn and Kevin came outside in their bare feet and jeans looking pretty surly too. "What's going on?" Shawn asked.

"I had a telephone call from some guy who said he had my record books and I had his. I'm supposed to leave his records on the park bench next to the flagpole at two in the morning tomorrow. Do either of you know anything about what the guy's talking about?"

"Jack," Shawn said through clenched teeth. "We'll find out in the morning. Right now, get in the house and go to bed." When I went into my parents' house, it stunk. "What a mess," I said kicking a pile of old newspapers and pizza cartons stacked on the floor beside the door. "Tell you what I'm going to do for you, since you're going to find out what Jack knows for me. Tomorrow, I'll clean this pig sty for you."

I slept in Kevin's bed. It was the least grungy smelling. It took a while before I could go to sleep. I wondered what the guy would do when I didn't show up tomorrow night. Did he really think I'd go tripping through the park at two in the morning to leave something on a park bench? Oh yeah. That's me all right. I punched the pillow up under my head and within a short time I went to sleep.

SEVENTEEN

It was Saturday morning. The plan was for my brothers to find out from Jack what he knew about the book my caller thought I had. Then tonight, they'd go down to the park with the cops and hopefully catch the guy and get my ledgers back. That would be fantastic. I liked my part. I had to clean the house. I could do my part. I hoped my brothers could do theirs.

I had Aretha Franklin cranked really loud on the Oldies' station as I vacuumed and danced behind the Hoover, really getting into the song "A Little Respect." I pushed the old vacuum forward and turned to make another swath when I spotted Tom leaning against the living room doorway grinning under his purple eye. I jumped, startled, but then I had to grin back. His shoulders bulged nicely under his tee shirt. I had on a ratty tee shirt and jean shorts, and my hair was clipped on top of my head any which way just to keep it off my neck as I worked... The windows and doors were open so a cool breeze came in.

The vacuum handle lay on the floor where I dropped it when Tom startled me. I picked up the vacuum and turned it off. Tom just continued to lean against the doorway, arms crossed on his chest, legs crossed at the ankles. He stood there all casual and sexy. I stood there all sweaty and out of breath.

"I didn't expect company," I laughed wiping my palms against my shorts. "I must look awful."

"Nope. You look good to me." He walked over and took my hand, gently pulling me from the living room to the kitchen. I had a pot of coffee on for my brothers. He took two mugs from the cup rack made of wooden pegs hanging above the counter and he poured out two coffees.

"Time to take a break," he said placing both cups of steaming coffee on the table. He pulled out a chair in front of my cup and waited.

"So what's up?" I said taking the seat. I took a sip of coffee and burned the end of my tongue.

"When I tried to call you this morning, there was no answer," Tom said. He sat at the corner of the table close to me. "I ran into Kevin at Dunkin' Donuts and he told me about your night caller. He also told me I'd find you here."

Tom was two years ahead of me in school, I recalled, but I didn't recall him being so muscular. I smiled up at him, went to take another sip of coffee, remembered it was too hot and wound up blowing at it instead.

"I ought to apologize for last night," Tom said. "I'm sorry I left without finding out what made you so upset. I'm guessing you might have been worried you'd be out of a job." I dropped my eyes and felt my cheeks burn. He took my hand in his and said, "It's okay. I'd wonder too."

"There's been a lot going on lately," I said. I took a deep breath and looked him square in the eyes. I returned a smile he flashed, noting his hazel eyes had golden flecks in the sunlight.

"Your divorce," he asked sympathetically.

"No, actually that's not as bad as I expected. I guess the marriage was over before it began. One of my problems," I said, "is that I have so much work to do to recopy three ledgers from January through July. I wish I could use printouts instead of old fashioned bookkeeping ledgers. I have everything on my computer and a backup copy on a memory stick."

"So why do ledgers?"

"My bosses don't trust computers" I said simply. "They're all used to their old ways I guess."

"Jeez," he snorted. "I have to tell you, I don't know what I'm going to do myself." He got up and started pacing. "My sister, Beth, wants to start college this fall. She's enrolled at Wesleyan and everything's paid up for her first semester, including the dorm room. I don't want to quit my internship either. I'm supposed to get my Master's degree next January." He turned to face me and said, "I'm doing this internship instead of a thesis." I nodded as though I had a clue about what he just said. "I guess I'm supposed to stay home now to run the store." He picked up his cup and stared into the coffee he hadn't touched and his shoulders slumped.

He looked so dejected that I said, "Ethel can run the store. She does anyway." Then I realized what I was saying and felt blood rush to my face again. "1 mean, um, not that your dad didn't actually run things."

Tom burst into such a radiant smile I relaxed and grinned back. "Of course she can!" He put down his cup to hug my shoulders so that I slopped coffee on the table. When he saw what he'd done, he said, "Oops," and went to the sink where he picked up a dishcloth and wiped up the spill while he continued talking." If I was thinking clearly," he said rinsing out the cloth at the sink, "it's the perfect solution. Ethel's practically family. Did you know that she made all the arrangements for the funeral? No," he answered his own question as he neatly hung the wrung out washcloth over the faucet, "Of course you couldn't know that. I'm just so flustered about everything. He yanked a paper towel off the roll hanging under the cabinet over the sink and said, "This morning I almost forgot to put on my shoes. I was all dressed, and went out into the yard in my slippers. If he had turned around to look at me at that point, he'd have seen my mouth hanging open. None of the men I knew clean the table off.

After tossing the paper towel into the trash at the end of the cabinet, he turned and I quickly recovered with a smile. "You just lost your dad," I said. I went over and stood in front of him. "Don't be so hard on yourself."

He cupped my chin in his hand and I thought for one breathless second he was going to kiss me. Instead he smiled and said, "You are so wonderful. I'm so glad you came along in my life." His eyes were smiling and his lips looked soft and inviting and I felt like kissing him. So I did.

"Good grief!" I laughed afterwards, pressing my hands to my flaming cheeks. "I can't believe I just did that."

'I'm glad you did," he said. "It felt good." He kissed me again and it was even better. Even with a purple eye, he was beautiful. To keep from kissing him again, I turned away and sat down so I didn't spontaneously combust.

He took his chair at the corner of the table. "Tell you what," he said taking one hand, "I'll help you copy your books, but now that the old man is gone, I'm making an executive decision. You can use printouts from now on for True Value."

"Oh my gosh!" Thank you so much! I can't tell you how much easier it will be if I can use my printouts from now on," I held my arms out to him and he got up to pull me up into a warm hug. "Plus," I said pulling away, "my brothers might be able to get my ledgers back for me tonight." I told him the plan while he sipped his coffee.

"I have to be at O'Shea's in half an hour," he said looking at his watch, "and I have some stuff I have to do with my mom tomorrow morning." He held both of my hands in his, looked down at me and said, "I have to go back to school Tuesday at the latest." Then he breathed a long sigh and flashed a smile. "But maybe we could get together Sunday after church."

"I'll make dinner," I said.

"Wonderful." He gave me a bear hug and left. My surroundings came back into focus... Faith Hill's song "This Kiss" was blaring on the radio in the living room, which I'd not even been conscious of until he left. I sat at the kitchen table and listened to the words of the song. It expressed everything that I felt at that moment.

After the song, I gulped my coffee and got busy. By early afternoon I finished cleaning the house. I made a mental note to come over and tidy things up and clean more often – not for my brothers, but so Mom wouldn't come home to find their house totally encrusted in layers of crud.

Back in my own kitchen, I decided that supper was going to be something cool since the day had been pretty warm. I put together some tossed salads with chopped chicken tenders on top and I microwaved a recipe for apple cobblers that I'd made up to save time several weeks ago when I'd frozen them. My brothers would eat bread with their salads so I cut a loaf of Italian bread in half and put the chunks in my toaster oven. When my brothers turned up, I'd pop the toaster oven to toast for four minutes and it would be hot and crusty.

Everything was ready so I sat down with my bookkeeping ledgers to see if I could find some tangible proof that Al was maybe cheating when the phone rang. "So you're home," the voice wheezed. I started to hang up to call the police when he said, "While you was cleaning up your brothers' house, I had me a little looksee in your apartment." I felt the hairs on the back of my neck prickle. "I left you a little present," he chuckled and then he hung up.

I hung up bewildered. I'd been in the apartment for a couple of hours and didn't see anything unusual. I looked around the kitchen, and then I crept into the living room to see if there was anything there, but it was fine. I'd used the bathroom off the kitchen, so I knew it was clear, as was my bedroom where Gracie lay on her tummy with her rump in the air. The only room left was Jack's. I glanced around Jack's room and didn't see anything there either. It looked bare, in fact, now that his stuff was gone.

The closet door was closed, so just to satisfy myself that the guy was just trying to scare me, I yanked open the door and was eye to eye with a snake on the shelf overhead. It hissed at me and rattled its tail. Its brown and black head was the size of a lemon, and I swear its tongue was long enough to reach my face from where it lay coiled on the shelf. It raised its head several inches and we both swayed back and forth until I got enough wind to scream and slam the door.

My scream lasted all the way into my bedroom. I knew my brothers weren't home yet so I called the police. Then I stood at the top of the stairs in the kitchen with Gracie in my arms

When Hugh, Louie, and Donald trooped upstairs, I was a tad worked up. I met them at the door barely articulate enough to yell and point, "Snake! Snake!" The three stood clustered around my door on the landing until I grabbed Louie's hand and pulled him toward Jack's room. The others followed. I jumped up on top of Jack's bed and pointed to the closet. Louie opened the closet door and jumped back when he saw it. The thing was backed against the wall, coiled in a giant pile of light brown slime with black splotches on it. It was about the size of a dinosaur poop.

By then I was jumping up and down on the bed pointing to it and screaming, "There it is! There it is!" Gracie, who can sleep through Jack's heavy metal music, woke up and bleated backup.

Louie emitted a verbal sound something like you'd say if a doctor was examining your throat, or maybe your other end, only he yelled it at the same time he slammed the door. The snake hissed on the other side, clearly angry with us all. Hugh and Donald stood behind Louie. "There's a big old bull snake up there," Louie explained to them as I shot past them.

I was in the middle of my bed shushing Gracie to calm her when Louie called out, "It's not dangerous, Julie."

Donald added from Jack's room. "Jack's window's open and there's a hole cut in the glass but whoever left the snake is gone. No need to panic."

"Okay," I called. I stayed in the middle of my bed clutching Gracie. She sighed when I'd stopped screaming and slept on my shoulder. I still had the willies just thinking about those beady eyes and flicking tongue inches from my face. Donald carried the snake past my door, heading downstairs, followed by Hugh and Louie. The snake's body coiled around Donald's arm and was almost as thick as his wrist. Donald held the snake's head away from his body and led the parade downstairs with me and Gracie well back at the end.

The squad car had the neighbors back outside. The snake writhed and fought, tightening around Donald's arm up to his shoulder. It was a regular side show for a few minutes. The men stood around faking hearty guffaws while the women looked crabby and creeped out.

"We haven't had a decent night's sleep since you got back from Florida." Mrs. Arnott snapped.

"I'm sorry about that," I said. "You know I wouldn't call the cops if I wasn't in trouble. But you all could help me by finding the guy who's doing all this to me."

Mr. Spinoza shot his fist in the air and shouted, "We'll help you, Kiddo!"

"The guy who broke into my place the other day and stole my bookkeeping ledgers is a man named Grady. He's also the one responsible for the snake. Jack knows what he looks like. I don't. If you all could put the word out that we need to find this creep, we can all get back to normal."

"Finally," Mr. Spinoza said. "Now we're getting somewhere."

"Mrs. Costanza said, "I get my hair done at nine tomorrow morning. I'll spread the word." We all nodded with relief. Bee's Beauty Shop is gossip central.

"I'll bet we have him before ten-thirty tomorrow morning," Mr. Arnott chuckled.

With that everyone left but the police. Donald said, "I guess your intruder had his fun." He tried to pull the snake loose but it twisted tighter around his arm. I could see he wanted to rid himself of it, even though he was trying to look like it was no big deal. "Kevin should be here in a minute," he said. "Let's get this thing over to the vet's." Louie opened the back door for him to climb into the squad car. Our local vet is also our animal control agent. I wondered what the kindly doctor would think when confronted with this beauty.

The squad car took off. I knew my brothers would turn up any minute. Still, it was suddenly scary after everybody left.

It was early dusk. The house was dark, the trees rustled, the driveway was empty, the neighbors were inside, and I stood in a bright patch under the garage light. Then the Dairy Queen lights went on across the street.

I started up the stairs and stopped midway. What if Grady climbed back in the window and was upstairs? I stood in the stairwell and tried to talk myself out of that idea. Could he have been hiding on the street behind us? Maybe he snuck down the street and when the neighbors left, he snuck back. Maybe I should wait in the house. I started for the back door. About halfway there, I wondered if the cops checked in the house. Did they check the house windows?

I huddled against the door at the bottom of the stairs with Gracie. At least I had the stairway between us if Grady came out of the kitchen. I could run out if he came onto the landing upstairs and the bottom door was bolted. It seemed like a long time, but finally a car pulled into the driveway. I peeked out and saw Kevin's four-by-four peal into the driveway. When he and Shawn got out, I burst into hearty sobs. It was such a relief to feel safe again.

"Why didn't one of those morons stay with you until we got here?" Shawn yelled at me like it was my fault. I started upstairs and he followed me into the bedroom where I placed Gracie in her crib. Then he followed me to the kitchen where I grabbed a wad of tissues. On our way through to the kitchen, Shawn yelled, "If this guy can get into your apartment, you're staying with us in the house, Julie, and that's final."

Part of me wanted to accept Shawn's decree but most of me didn't like the way Shawn was bossing me around. "This guy is supposed to be a harmless weed farmer," I said, "remember? Old Man Grady, the thief in Florida who can cut holes in windows and unlock them. You think he can't get into the house when you're not there? How about finding the jerk and eliminating the problem." Shawn didn't say anything for a second. I could almost see the wheels go round in his head as he put it together. "I told the neighbors to look for

Grady," I said. "And I told everybody that Jack knows what this Grady character looks like."

"Seems to me Kevin and I need to have another little talk with our old buddy Jack," Shawn said.

"Meanwhile, I'm staying here," I said. It was late and he knew I'd argue until dawn if I had to, so he turned around and left without further comment. A few minutes later Kevin and Shawn were nailing boards over all of my windows except the front kitchen window that faced the house. While they worked on making my place Grady-proof, I took the food I'd prepared over to the house. If they caught the guy in the park, I wouldn't need boards on my windows, but I didn't bother to say anything. I just prayed they'd be successful and things really could return to something at least close to normal.

EIGHTEEN

The first thing I wanted to know when Gracie woke me up the next morning was if my brothers and the cops had caught "Old Man Grady, the "harmless weed farmer," last night. But it was too early on a Sunday morning to call my brothers, especially if they had spent the night at the park on my behalf. I expected that if my brothers and the "town clowns" hadn't caught Grady last night, the neighbors would be on it today. Grady would be spotted somewhere and I might even get my ledgers back. By nine o'clock I'd gotten myself and Gracie ready for church when the phone rang. I expected it to be Shawn or Kevin telling me what happened at the park and that Grady had been caught.

"Instead, it was Mrs. Arnash. "Hello, Julie," she said. "I expect you're getting ready for church, but I wanted to catch you before you left to let you know I have your divorce agreement ready to be signed so that I can get it filed with the court. She reminded me again that she could only represent my interests, not Jack's. "However," she said, "if Jack signs the agreement, it will be legal and binding so he can forego a lawyer if he chooses. There isn't a lot of property to divide and since there's nothing being contested, Jack will incur less expense." Mrs. Arnash then offered to bring the papers with her to church to save me a trip out to her place. I thanked her and hung up hopeful that things were finally being resolved and my life would take on a more exciting aspect in a good way. I looked forward to college classes more than I expected. Also, with Jack out of the house, I also discovered that living alone is sometimes easier than living with someone else.

Mrs. Arnash said she would give me both copies of the agreement papers so that I could get Jack's signature, but she said the actual divorce petition would have to be served by a court process server. Everything seemed to be working out well except that I didn't like to think about Gracie's visitation days with Jack. Mrs. Arnash worked it out on the agreement that Jack would get Gracie every other weekend. I'd held out for him having to come to the family gatherings on holidays. I wanted Gracie to see that we both loved her and could be civilized about our divorce.

I was about to call Charlotte's house when the phone rang. "So you thought you was safe after the cops left last night, huh? Well," the now familiar voice wheezed, "I know you don't have my book in yur apartment and neither does Jack." I didn't respond. "Maybe you or Jack has it in one of your cars. I spose I could look there."

"I told you, Mr. Grady, that I know nothing about your book. Jack's the one who must have it." There was a long pause. I had used his name so he now knew we were on to him. I thought maybe he'd be scared enough to drop this nonsense and go back to Florida to tend to his "weeds."

"Ahh," he said finally, "but you, Missy, are the one who's gonna get it fur me. It's a gray composition book like you get fur school. If you don't find it fur me, I up the ante."

"What does that mean?" I asked.

"Next time I take yur kid."

My heart thumped hard all of a sudden and I felt like the wind had been knocked out of me. I did my thinking out loud thing. "I have a plan," I said. "I thought that if Jack came over to sign our agreement papers, I could maybe find out what book this jerk was talking about."

He wheezed, but said nothing.

"Jack's coming here today to get his divorce papers," I said. I'll call him and tell him to bring your book. I'll leave your book by my garage door after you leave mine there."

"You got it backwards, Missy. You leave mine first, or no dice."

"Sorry, but you don't seem like the trustworthy type. If you leave my books, then I'll leave yours." I pressed the off button on the phone.

After a quick flip through the phone book I dialed Charlotte's house. Charlotte answered. "I need to talk with Jack. I want him to come over here around four and sign our divorce agreement."

"Oh okay, Hon, I'll tell him."

"I'd better tell him myself."

"Well okay." She was all chirpy. Then she sang out, "Jaa-ack, telephone."

"Now what?" Jack shouted from another room. Charlotte must have put the phone down because I heard footsteps and muffled voices from another room. I waited. "Hello," Jack said in a petulant voice.

"You know the book you stole?" I said without preamble. "Bring it over here this afternoon at four. If you don't, your 'Old Man Grady' threatened to hurt Gracie." I hung up. Let Charlotte tell him the good news about the divorce papers being ready for him to sign.

I punched the buttons on the phone for the house to tell my brothers that Grady had threatened Gracie but after several rings I knew they weren't home and must be on a side job. My nerves had calmed somewhat and I reasoned that if Jack brought whatever book he must have taken from Grady, I could give it back and that would be that. Besides, I was sure that between the neighbors, the cops, and my brothers, Grady didn't have much chance of being in town without being spotted.

Meanwhile, getting my divorce over with was next on my agenda. I loaded Gracie and her diaper bag into the van to go to church. All I had to do was tell Jack that Gracie's life might be in danger unless he gave me Grady's book. I couldn't imagine that he would risk harm coming to his own baby. Maybe it would all work out as simply as exchanging record books. Who knew? I picked up Gracie and went to church in a much more hopeful frame of mind.

At four, Jack dutifully trudged upstairs to my apartment. He came into the kitchen and slammed his heavy toolbox on the floor against the side of the refrigerator like he always did after work. He looked downright haggard. His clothes were dirty, he was sweaty, and there were dark circles under his eyes. I almost felt sorry for him but I shook my head to rattle the bee-bees in my brain back into place.

"Why did you drag that thing up here," I indicated his toolbox.

"Habit, I guess," he said. He shrugged, took a beer from the fridge, and sat at the table.

"Where's the book you stole??

"Where's the divorce papers?" I must have guessed right since he didn't deny he'd stolen the man's record book.

"Look Jack," I leaned on the table across from him. "This place has been broken into and ransacked. The guy who's doing this said he's going to go after Gracie next time. Do you want to risk something happening to Gracie?"

"She's your kid." He took a long pull of beer as I leaned on the table, frozen. He might as well have broken into fluent French or sung an aria. My mind was on disconnect. He drank his beer while I regained my faculties.

"My kid? Don't even act like she's not yours!"

He leaned back, clasped his hands behind his head and smirked, clearly enjoying my reaction. "Like I said, she's yours." He took another slug of beer and plunked the bottle on the table, punctuating it with a deep, long burp.

When his belching display ended, he crossed his arms on the table and leaned toward me smiling. "Charlotte's cat had kittens last week," he said, "and I think they're cute too." He took another swig of beer and swiped his hand across his mouth. "But they're her kittens, ya know."

Looking into his eyes was same as being face to face with the snake. Only this time my mind snapped into gear.

"In that case, I expect you won't want any visiting rights." He didn't blink. Incredibly, he nodded agreement as he scratched his filthy tee shirt over his belly, smiling before he put his hands back behind his head, relaxed to the max.

I pulled out the agreement papers from a manila envelope on the kitchen counter, crossed out where it said he'd get custody of Gracie every other weekend and I wrote in: No Visitations Whatsoever.

My heart pounded. I wondered if this would be good for Gracie. I wanted time to think. Could I tell her that her father didn't care enough about her to even want to see her? Meanwhile, he sat there with his silly smile pasted on his ugly mug. I pointed to the places on the agreement that were highlighted to show where he should sign. He did. Just like that; he signed without hesitation, or discussion.

A momentary feeling of elation gave way to suspicion. He must be going to pull some trick on me. Would he tear it all up and laugh? I slipped the papers into the envelope. "Could you find it in your heart to at least protect Gracie from the guy whose book you stole? If you give it to me, I think he'll go away."

"Sorry." He headed for the bathroom. "No can do." He closed the door and I heard the toilet lid bang up against the tank. My eyes fell on his toolbox and my skin prickled. Moving quietly, I slid over to the box and carefully undid the latches. I pulled up the top and discovered only tools. But when I peeked under the top tray, a grimy composition book teetered on top of the tools in the bottom of the box. My heart hammered in my throat. I lifted the book out and flipped it under the fridge as the toilet flushed. I hooked the latches and stood beside the kitchen door, praying that I looked casual as I pulled the door open. I was sure he could see something was up.

"Thanks for nothing," I said. He picked up his toolbox and started downstairs. I closed the door, carefully bolted it, and went over and grabbed the phone. Shawn answered.

Thank God my brothers had finished up their side job and were home.

"Shawn, get over here quick!" I hung up and ran over to the kitchen window to check out Jack's truck in the driveway below. Jack threw his toolbox into the cab of his work truck and got in. He gunned the engine and pulled out without looking into his toolbox. Yes! I cheered mentally.

"I've got the book Jack stole from Grady." I grinned down at Shawn as he came up the stairs.

He stopped in the middle of the stairway. "Jack gave you the farmer's book? Just like that?"

I bit at my lower lip and shrugged. Shawn came into the kitchen heading for the refrigerator. He looked as grungy as Jack had. Probably they'd been on the same job. "Jack didn't tell me why he took Grady's record book or anything about it." I said. I wondered now what all Shawn hadn't told me. I waited.

"I can probably tell you that." Shawn got a beer and twisted off the bottle cap.

"Why on God's green earth didn't you tell me everything you know about Grady before now?"

Shawn tossed the bottle cap onto the table and watched it bounce.

After a few seconds of his staring at the bottle cap, I said, "When I told Jack the guy threatened Gracie, he didn't even bat an eye!" My voice had risen to an unpleasant tone, but I didn't care. I waited. I don't know what I expected from Shawn, but standing there in front of my kitchen table with his mouth wrapped around a beer bottle wasn't it. "Are you listening to me?" My neighbors probably heard me by then.

"I heard you." He put a hand on his hip and glared at me like he had a right to be angry. "Why didn't you tell us last night that the jerk threatened Gracie?"

"Didn't I?" I tried to focus on the details of last night, but visions of the snake swirled around in my mind and got stuck there.

"You are definitely going to come back to the house until we can find the bastard." .

"Wait a minute." It took a minute for me to put together the recent events. "First off, the creep didn't tell me last night. I got a breakfast call this morning. Why is this guy so hard to find? Why aren't the cops tapping my phone?" I screamed each thought as it entered my mind. "They could trace the call. What's wrong with everybody that they can't find some dumb old man who has bad asthma?"

"He has emphysema." Shawn said. He straddled a kitchen chair. "This isn't downtown, Julie. We don't have that kind of equipment in this one horse town. You watch too much TV."

I fired up the tea kettle. I definitely needed to calm down...

Shawn set his beer on the table. "Where is the book?" he said.

"It's in a safe place," I said with my back to him. "I told Grady I'd exchange it for my books." I turned around to see what kind of reaction that would produce. I didn't expect him to say anything like what a good idea, Julie. That never happened, but I hoped he'd say he was all set to see that something like that could be worked out.

"Jeez," Shawn swept up his beer from the table and took a swig, wiping his mouth with the back of his hand. He sat there a few minutes looking at his hands, around the room, everywhere but at me..."You can't do that, Julie," He said finally.

"Why not?"

"Because some stuff about me and Kevin in it could cost us work. The guy had a nice little thing going, nothing big, just a little weed for the personal use of a handful of guys. No big deal. But he got greedy. He kept raising the price on us. Then me and the other guys decided to quit using his stuff. It was getting way too expensive."

"So what happened?"

"Jack somehow managed to steal the guy's records. He claimed it's got all Grady's customers in it and some other incriminating stuff. I think there's some big time politician in it or something." Shawn looked around evasively and ran his fingers through his hair. Finally he looked at me. "Jack got the idea he could get some dough back from Grady by holding the book over his head. Me and the other guys thought it was funny -- at first."

"Exactly what other guys are we talking about?" Jack reached for my hands and I held still, "What other guys, Shawn."

"Well, for openers, our cops are in on it." I rolled my eyes. "You know how everybody around here feels. We'd lose a lot of our business, Julie, but they'd lose their jobs. We have to destroy that book."

I yanked my hands free. "How's that going to stop him? You're sucking me and Gracie into a game we don't want to play!" I backed away from him. "I don't want to see anybody lose their jobs but nothing's worth risking Gracie."

"You're right," Shawn rubbed his face with his hands.

"So find the creep. Do whatever you have to do to get him to quit bothering me." Shawn nodded and for the first time in my life, it looked like my brother all but slunk out the door.

NINETEEN

Gracie's warm-up bleats from the other room told me it was six o'clock. I had a baby to feed. On my way in to pick up Gracie, I reminded myself that God gave us a brain and He expects us to use it. I fed Gracie in the living room and went over my options. I could leave the filthy book by my garage door like I told Grady I'd do and hope Grady would leave mine. But would Grady risk coming here to get it? There was also no guarantee he'd return my ledgers anyway. I wasn't sure if Grady was just some dumb farmer trying to scare me, or if he might actually try to harm Gracie. He had gotten inside my apartment but the snake he left ate mice and rats and was actually harmless. That seemed like a scare tactic. Besides, he couldn't cut a hole in my windows anymore unless he did it at the kitchen windows in plain view of everyone since Shawn and Kevin had boarded them all up except for the kitchen windows. That helped me feel somewhat better. Grady's scare tactics might have worked in the short run, but if I knew my brothers, it wouldn't work for him in the long run.

Gracie seemed to be staying awake a while in the early evenings now. She lay on my lap cooing and kicking furiously. Her downy head smelled sweet when I kissed her. I wondered if our cops knew everything about Jack's clever book theft. I decided to call my brothers and see if the cops were up to speed. Between the five of them, and the neighborhood, somebody should be able to find this character. Maybe Jack didn't care what happened to Gracie, but I knew my brothers did

When the phone rang, I pinched my lower lip between my thumb and forefinger and asked myself whether I should ignore it. Did I want to hear anything more from Grady? But it could be Margie or my brothers. I grabbed the phone on the fourth ring.

"I was about to come running," Kevin said. Why didn't you pick up?"

"Actually, I'm glad you called. I have a question. Do the town's dynamic dimwits know everything about Jack's scheme? I mean, between the five of you, one of you guys ought to be able to catch this guy before he hurts someone, like Gracie."

"Yeah well, Shawn and I already figured out a plan. We think you should bring the book over here, give it to us, and when Grady calls, tell him we have it. That'll take the heat off of Gracie and you."

"Right, and then he'll use Gracie or me as bait to get the book from you. Great plan." I hung up. Leave that puppy under the fridge I told myself. Gracie and I spent a few more minutes on the sofa together while I cast about for someone to talk to about my problems.

Usually I talk my problems over with Margie or Gram but I didn't want Gram upset with her heart condition. Margie might help, but she's not usually the one who comes up with solutions to problems. I thought briefly of discussing more than my marital problems with Reverend Hanover, but decided I'd stick to one problem at a time with him. Besides, who knew? He might be part of the twit parade. A minister probably doesn't smoke pot, I thought, but then, I've discovered lately that people aren't always what they seem to be either. I carried Gracie out to the kitchen and put the kettle on for tea.

After I put Gracie in her carrier and got the tea kettle going, I called Margie. I told her the cops hadn't caught Grady and how Grady had threatened to harm Gracie.

"So what happened at the park last night then?" Margie asked.

"I don't know. I forgot to ask." I blew out a long breath. "There's nothing that I can think of to do," I concluded.

"I wish I knew how to help you," Margie said. "You probably won't have to worry for long, though. Your brothers will come through for you. They'll find Grady and straighten him out, you'll see." I hung up feeling better. Margie may not have been able to offer advice, but she was sure comforting.

After I hung up, I went to take Gracie out of her carrier and put her to bed in her crib. "Oh yuk!" I shuddered. Gracie had a major blow-out. Mustard brown stains seeped through her terrycloth sleeper. The phone rang so I grabbed my phone from my nightstand, held Gracie out at arm's length and I carried her to the kitchen counter next to the sink. I have a pad there to use as a changing table. With the receiver tucked under my chin, I said hello while I peeled off Gracie's pajamas.

"Hey, I heard the latest. How you doing?" It was Tom.

"I'm so glad it's you and not Grady," I said. "I'm in the middle of changing Gracie and she pretty much filled her diaper -- and her pajamas."

He laughed. It was a deep, rich laugh. I said to him, "You wouldn't laugh if you could see what I'm looking at. I wish you were here right now, buddy. It's really disgusting."

"I'm not sure I want to get to know Gracie that intimately. But since you asked, I'll be right over." He hung up before I could object.

It took so long to clean Gracie that the doorbell rang before I'd finished. I burped Gracie on the way downstairs to open the door. My hair was wound up in a scrunchie and the tee shirt I had on was old and faded. It didn't matter. First because I liked being free and second, I knew that putting your best foot forward, like Jack and I had done, wasn't a good idea. It's better to see the worst foot too.

"I brought ice cream." Tom held up a paper sack and stepped well back from the door. His smile was great but he still had a big bruise under his eye.

"What flavor ice cream did you bring?" I asked on my way upstairs. Tom followed me into the kitchen, remaining there as I went through to the bedroom with Gracie.

"Chocolate," he called from the kitchen.

"Yum," I called back. When I returned to the kitchen, he'd found bowls and was spooning ice cream into them. I got out some spoons while he tried to cram the half gallon carton into my freezer.

"Boy, you sure have a lot of food for a single lady." He frowned at the packages in my freezer.

I took the ice cream carton from him. "Step aside son. I'll show you how a pro does it." I restacked a few items, fit the container neatly into a niche I'd made, and finished by brushing my hands together.

"You're definitely the freezer meister," he smiled. We sat at the table and ate ice cream in silence for a few minutes. I felt really comfortable with Tom. When we finished, he picked up the empty bowls and spoons and headed for the sink. None of the men in my family helps with the dishes. My jaw was hanging open but he didn't see it. He had his back to me rinsing out the bowls at the sink. "I guess you know everybody's talking about catching this Grady character," he said. I stopped gaping and smiled just as he turned around.

I filled him in on the details, including how my brothers and the cops were involved. He said he'd keep it confidential and I trusted him. By the time I finished, we were drinking peppermint tea in the living room.

"So let's have a look at the book," he said.

He stood behind me while I poked the book out with a wire coat hanger. I became aware that my buns were sticking up as I swept the book from under the fridge and stood up. I gave him a mock glare. "Okay, the show's over." He exaggerated a child sniffling with disappointment. I had to laugh.

We looked at Grady's book on the sofa. There were names followed by dollar amounts on the pages at the front of the book. The entries were exceptionally neat. "My ledgers should look so good," I said.

Tom whistled through his teeth and pointed to the name of a politician we both recognized. The back pages of the book were different. They contained names and addresses followed by two columns. One listed small appliances, such as TV's and DVD players and the other column listed dollar amounts.

"I wish I knew what to do with the book," I said.

"One thing we could do," Tom said, "is to scan the pages into a computer so you have copies of the thing for the newspapers. If enough people know about something, it's a lot harder to cover up."

"I don't have a scanner."

"I do, at my mom's house. Want to go there with me? Mom's not going to wake up. She's been taking sleeping pills since my dad," he couldn't finish the sentence, but I nodded as he looked away.

"That sounds like a great idea. It's something positive that I can do." We got up and I turned off one of the living room lamps while he took the empty cups into the kitchen.

I switched off the second lamp. "What if Grady's watching me turn off the lights from across the street?" I said. I turned off the kitchen light and Tom joined me at the kitchen window. The parking lot of the DQ was empty except for two cars. We didn't see any old men through the DQ windows. "He could be on foot hiding somewhere," I turned on the kitchen light.

"You might be right." He murmured. He stepped back, snapped his fingers and said, "I've got it! Why not put some stuff in a bag for tomorrow and you can sleep in our guest room. No, wait, Mom's sleeping in the guest room now. You can sleep in my parents' room if it wouldn't creep you out."

"It wouldn't bother me, but your mom won't want company at a time like this."

Lorenda Lee Lux

"You don't know my mom. She's as worried about you as everybody else. Besides, by tomorrow night somebody will have spotted Grady and no harm done."

It was an invitation I couldn't refuse

TWENTY

I quickly tucked a pair of clean shorts, a tee shirt, and a pair of sandals into the diaper bag, along with my toothbrush, hair brush, and deodorant. Makeup would be limited to lipstick since it was all I could stuff into the diaper bag. I left my one and only black dress on the hanger to wear to the funeral tomorrow.

Tom made sure Grady wasn't skulking around outside while I went into the house and left a note for my brothers after I clipped Gracie's carrier into the back seat of the van. I tossed the diaper bag on the passenger seat and hung my dress on the hook above the passenger side door. Outside, I said, "You know what? I think I should take my van. I'll follow you. I might want to come home when it's not a good time for you to bring me home. You're going to have your hands full with your mom and sister tomorrow."

"Yeah, I guess you're right." He blew out a long, slow breath. "I really dread tomorrow. I'm glad you're going to be there." Before we headed to his house, I followed Tom's old Ford Taurus as he wound around town to be sure Grady wasn't following us. I pulled into his parents' driveway behind him.

We crept in the back door of his house, tiptoeing quietly up the stairs to his parents' room. I put Gracie, who slept in her carrier, on the floor by the king sized bed. Tom put his arms around me. I rested my forehead against his chest. "All of a sudden I'm beat," I said feeling suddenly very sleepy.

"Tell you what," he said rubbing the back of my neck, "you get to bed and I'll copy the book. You need your rest for the baby and I never sleep more than four or five hours anyway." He stopped at the doorway adding, "At school I'm usually in the computer lab when everybody's gone home to bed."

He went into his room at the other end of the hallway with Grady's book. I hung up my dress and wore my tee shirt and panties to sleep in. I wondered if my being there would be a problem in the morning, but I was so grateful to sleep without worrying about Grady watching me that I stretched out and fell asleep right away.

Gracie woke me up at six. I took a can of formula from my diaper bag and poured it into a bottle. Gracie sweats so much when she eats that it's better for her if her bottles are not warmed up. She emptied her bottle in record time. We both fell asleep again after I changed her diaper and burped her.

The next thing I knew, Tom was tapping on the bedroom door. "Time to get up," he said. I sat up and for a second I didn't remember where I was. Tom looked wonderful in a dark navy suit. I knew my hair was a haystack, and I had on no lipstick. Since I wasn't wearing a bra, and I do have decent "boobage." I yawned and stretched, hoping to distract him from my hair and face.

His smile made me shiver. "There's towels and stuff in the linen closet next to the door there," he pointed. I'm sure I detected a twinkle in his eyes. "Coffee's ready when you come down. I told my mom and sister you're here and they're delighted. Mom said she's been doubly upset knowing that you're having so much trouble with a prowler. Seems you keep the neighbors up at all hours. Some attribute it to your being alone now that Jack's gone." I could imagine the stories being told. I blew out a sigh and nodded that I understood. It couldn't be easy living near us lately. "We have to be at the funeral home at eight," Tom continued. He checked his watch. "It's seven now. Think you can be ready?" I gave him a thumbs up and he closed the door softly.

I accepted the challenge. A quick shower and it took me ten minutes to get downstairs, fully dressed, but with wet hair. My hair takes a long time to dry. Usually I let it hang, fluffing it around my face when it's dry. Today I'd pinned it up into a French twist to keep the wet hair off my dress.

Mrs. Atkinson and Beth were at the table with coffee and sweet rolls. They both smiled but it looked like they were in a stupor. Sleeping pill hangover, I thought. Tom had a bowl of cereal, and held out a bowl to me. We ate in silence except for the crunching that echoed in my head from the Frosted Flakes. Before we left for the funeral, I phoned home and got my brothers' answering machine. I left a message that I'd meet them at the church service. I thought Shawn and Kevin might have gone out for breakfast, so I wasn't worried when there was no answer. Even better, maybe they were taking Grady to jail.

When we got to the church, I looked around for Kevin and Shawn, but they were nowhere to be seen, nor did they come in late for the service. After church, when neither Shawn nor Kevin appeared, Tom said, "Don't worry, Julie. There's probably a good reason they didn't show up. Hey, they could be picking up Grady right now." Now those were some comforting words.

After the church service, Tom rode to the cemetery behind the hearse with his mom and sister. I drove Ethel and her eighty-seven year old sister Chlotilda whose thick hair was pulled into a bun on her head like a gray crown. Heavy and staid, she was nothing like her sister Ethel.

On the way, Ethel told us how she had lined up a lot of senior citizens who were ready to work two or three hour shifts at the store when it reopened. "Everything at the store is going to be hunky-dory," she promised. Tom needn't worry, I thought. When Ethel's in charge, everything's under control. I was grateful to her for that. I didn't want to see Tom have to stop going to school, even though it meant he'd have to leave in a few days.

If only things were under control at my end. My brothers were still missing. I could hardly focus on the minister's words at the cemetery. The weather in July can be delicious every once in a while. This was one of those days, sunny and clear without being too hot. I stood at the gravesite with Gracie's carrier in my hand. Louie sidled up to me, handed me a sealed envelope with nothing written on it.

It was the moment Tom's coffin was being lowered into the grave, so no one spoke. Once the coffin was lowered, everyone lined up to throw flower petals or a handful of soil onto the coffin and to say a silent, farewell prayer for Tom. I moved along in line like a zombie, clutching Gracie in her carrier in one hand and the envelope in the other. I managed to slip the envelope into the diaper bag hanging over my shoulder before it was my turn. I stepped forward, took a handful of silky red rose petals and sprinkled them on the polished oak casket below. A few older people flung a handful of soil from the mound at the base of the flower urn. The soil spread over the coffin with the rose petals.

The drive back to Tom's house was the funeral procession in reverse. I had Ethel and her sister with me again. No one spoke, however, on the drive to the Atkinson's home.

When we drove up to Tom's house, I pulled into the driveway to help Ethel and her sister out of the van. Neighbors and friends had brought homemade casseroles, salads, meats, and desserts to the Atkinson's home. Many of the funeral flowers had been placed in the yard and in the house. The day was so nice that many chose to sit around the patio or yard in lawn chairs supplied by those who lived nearby.

Tom guided Gracie and me upstairs to Tom's parents' room. My first thought, now that the funeral had officially ended, was to go home and see where my brothers were. But Tom had convinced me that it would be safer for Gracie and me to come back to his house so he could go home with me and check out the apartment before I went inside.

"Louie gave me an envelope during the funeral," I told Tom when we were in the bedroom. I put Gracie's carrier on the floor and ripped open the envelope. It read:

I have your brother Kevin. You get him when I get my book. Bring it to the back steps of the police station before

midnight tonight. Do not bring anyone with you or tell
anyone or your brother will be history.

"This has to be bogus," I said. "Nobody could kidnap
Kevin, especially not an old wheezy creep like Grady."

"He might have a gun," Tom said softly. "Or he might have
had help. It says he wants you to leave the book by the police
station?" Tom took the note and read it again He paced back
and forth with it between the foot of the bed and the doorway.
"That must mean the police and Grady are in this together."
Tom Stopped in front of me and took my shoulders. "You
absolutely cannot stay at your house." I couldn't respond.
"I'm going to call the FBI and the state police, Julie." I was
too numb to respond. He went into pace mode again. "Good
thing we have a copy of the book now," he said. Maybe we
should put a couple of copies in envelopes and address them
to the local newspapers, just in case." He came to stand in
front of me again, took my chin and said, "Tonight I can go
to your place after everyone here leaves and pick up whatever
you need for yourself and the baby. You can stay here until
the police catch this guy."

I blinked up at him through tear-filled eyes. "Then Grady
will follow you here," I said. "And your family will be involved."
I collapsed against his chest and took a ragged breath. It was
comforting just to stand there for a minute, resting my forehead
against his soft shirt. Then I looked up and said, "That's not
fair to you or your family, especially at a time like this."

Tom had his arms wrapped around me and since I didn't
know what else to do, I just leaned against him for support
while I fought full blown tears. We heard someone downstairs
ask where Tom had gone so he let go of me, stuffed the note
in his pocket, and said, "You lie down here and rest. We'll
figure out the best plan later, okay?" I nodded and he went
downstairs.

I sat on the edge of the bed feeling weary of everything
and wished I could just lie down and rest. I considered that
maybe the letter was a stupid joke, or maybe Shawn had taken

care of it already. There was still no answer at the house. I left messages on their cell phones feeling twice as anxious. If neither brother answered his cell phone, it meant trouble of some kind.

Gracie shifted in her carrier and I felt tears spill from my eyes as I sat there on the bed and tried to think what to do. I crept to the top of the stairs. Most of the mourners had gone. Hugh stood at the front door. I assumed he was paying his respects to Tom. He shook Tom's hand but Tom yanked Hugh closer and spoke in his face, in a confrontational stance. Hugh turned abruptly and left. I stepped downstairs slowly. Tom, his mother, sister, and Ethel stood at the door to form an informal reception line as people filed out. I stood at the bottom of the stairs, once again the intruder.

"I told my mom and sister you'd be staying here a few days," Tom said when everyone was gone. He draped his arm around my shoulders. "I hope you don't mind." I shook my head no. "I told Hugh that Kevin had been kidnapped according to a note you received from Louie and that the police station was the drop point. I warned him that he was an accessory to a kidnapping. He turned green and said he didn't know anything about it. But he didn't ask questions about it either. It looks like the thick headed numbskulls who man our police station are in on the whole thing. It took quite a while to scan Grady's book but I have it copied onto three disks, and two flash drives for you to keep, in case. He didn't say in case of what. I thought of one possibility. I could leave the book and never see Kevin again. When I looked up at Tom, a lump in my throat formed. I could barely say thank you. Tom went upstairs to call the authorities so that his mother and sister wouldn't be disturbed.

Mrs. Atkinson and Beth sat on the living room couch, hugging one another. "Can I get you something to drink?" I asked Mrs. Atkinson. She nodded, leaning back on the couch with her eyes closed. I brought in a cup of tea for the three of us and sat down opposite them on a matching loveseat.

Gracie chose that moment to cry and I realized it was time to feed her. I went upstairs and brought her back down along with her bottle.

When Gracie finished her bottle, Mrs. Atkinson asked to hold Gracie. "It's so wonderful to hold a baby," she said snuggling Gracie and patting her on the back. I liked that Gracie brought Mrs. Atkinson some comfort. While Beth related her plans to go ahead to college, I told them about my plans to start Owensville Community College at the end of the summer.

"Oh that's wonderful, dear." Mrs. Atkinson said. "But who's going to take care of little Gracie while you're in school?"

"My brothers said they'd pitch in." My throat constricted when I thought of Kevin's easy going smile.

"I wish I could baby-sit Gracie while you're in class," Mrs. Atkinson said. Gracie kicked and cooed on her lap. "My evenings will be so lonesome when Beth leaves for college." She dabbed at her swollen eyes. "I need to do something useful."

I put my teacup on a nearby end table and got up to hug Mrs. Atkinson. "That would be really nice," I said. Tears slid down her cheeks unheeded while she swayed back and forth with Gracie on her shoulder. When Gracie fell asleep in Mrs. Atkinson's arms, I took Gracie so that Mrs. Atkinson could lie down. Beth wanted to talk with Tom about getting some money for books and clothes so I took Gracie upstairs to change her diaper and put her in her carrier.

I sat on the edge of the bed in Tom's parents' room after putting Gracie in her carrier and tried to think what to do. If I delivered Grady's book to the police station and left it as instructed on the note, there was a chance they'd release Kevin. Then again, maybe not. If I contacted a reporter, the media might publicize the involvement of our police which could cost them their jobs. And people in town might not trust Shawn and Kevin again. If the state cops came here after Tom called them, would they take Grady's book or be satisfied with a copy. And then I'd have to explain to Grady that his records were now in the hands of the cops? Oh yeah, that would work! Somehow I had to rescue Kevin and see that nobody got hurt. My brothers had gone to bat for me plenty of times. It was my turn.

I went to the top of the stairs. Tom sat on the couch talking with his sister. Tom's bedroom door was open down the hall so I slipped in and I picked up Grady's book from beside the computer. I scribbled a message on a sheet of printer paper thanking everyone for their concern. I said I was sorry that I'd been so much bother, especially now, and that I didn't want to risk bringing any harm to their family.

I waited near the top of the stairs, with Gracie and my diaper bag, until Tom and Beth headed toward the kitchen. Then I crept downstairs and quietly let myself out the front door.

TWENTY ONE

No lights were on in the house when I drove into my driveway. I knew that Grady might be somewhere watching so I pushed the garage door opener and drove inside the garage. I killed the engine but remained in the van with my doors locked while I pushed the garage door button again to bring them down behind me. Built like a barn, our garage is large enough for four vehicles if you drive two in and then two behind those. I looked around. The camper stood in the back corner to my right, with Kevin's four-by-four parked in front of my van. The space next to the van where the pick-up would be if Shawn were home was empty.

Now that I was home, I couldn't decide what to do next. On the way home I'd left another message on Shawn's cell phone, when he didn't answer, telling him I'd come home. If Kevin really was in danger, Shawn would be out looking for him. I could ignore the note to leave Grady's book at the cop shop, get into my apartment with the door bolted and windows boarded up and wait until morning. Then I could find Shawn and we could both look for Kevin. Unless Grady was just pulling another stunt to scare me and Kevin was actually safe.

On the other hand, Grady could actually be dangerous. And how were the cops involved in this if it was just a scare tactic by Grady? I no longer cared if my ledgers were returned. I had Al's books copied and didn't have to do True Value Hardware Store's, thanks to Tom. That left only Kline's Department Store to do. For one ledger, I didn't want to risk any harm to Kevin. I could take the book over to the cop shop like the note instructed and be rid of the thing. Besides it was all on computer disk now anyway. But there was no way I'd take it anywhere at midnight.

Lorenda Lee Lux

I decided that it now made sense to drop Grady's book off at the police station while it was only twilight and I still had the guts to do it. I'd be rid of the book and, God willing, I'd be rid of my problem with Grady.

I pressed the garage door opener. The garage door rattled up a couple of feet before I noticed Grady's red pickup truck slowly appear directly behind my van. Instantly, I punched the overhead button and the door changed direction and slowly rumbled down.

My heart thumped and I took some deep breaths. My doors were locked. I could spend the night in the van, but that didn't sound good when I thought about feeding Gracie. I was out of formula. If I pushed the button and the door came up, I knew I had enough room to maneuver the van crooked and aim at the empty space next to me. This wasn't the first time I'd been stuck with somebody's car in the driveway behind mine. My hope was that Grady couldn't get out of the truck and break my window or something before I could get past him.

I put the van in reverse, pressed the button, and the door slowly lumbered open. I cut my wheels sharply, aiming at the space where Shawn usually parked. Grady's legs appeared in my rearview mirror as I looked over my shoulder ready to back up fast. As soon as the door cleared my van, I backed alongside the truck before Grady could get back in his truck.

My foot didn't let up on the accelerator as I shot past the truck, backed onto the street and then raced down to Main Street. Dodging between cars, I tore down to Central Avenue and kept speeding. Apparently Grady's truck hadn't been able to keep up because the last time I saw the truck, it receded in my rearview while we were on Main Street. Central Avenue would lead me out to the highway and God only knew where from there. I sped past the north end of town and was about to get onto the expressway ramp when I spotted Shawn's pickup parked in front of Al's garage. At first I was elated but that quickly gave way to caution. What was he doing at Al's? Why wasn't he out looking for Kevin?

Even though there hadn't been any sign of Grady's truck in my rearview for some time, just to be on the safe side, I drove behind the storage buildings next door and then behind Al's. There didn't seem to be any way to tell what was going on in the garage except for me to get out of the van and peek inside the back door. I locked the van doors behind me, and closed the van door quietly so that I wouldn't call attention to myself in case Grady showed up. I crept around the corner of the building to see if Grady was out front. There was no sign of Grady or his truck.

For some reason I felt like it would be prudent to push open the garage's office door and peek in to see if it was clear or if Shawn or Al were inside. It took conscious effort not to gasp out loud when I saw Shawn and Kevin clustered around Al's desk along with Jack! Al lounged against the broken beverage machine. Their heads were close and they were locked into a noisy discussion. I ducked back to the van, unlocked the door with shaking fingers, backed up and peeled out. My brothers were not in trouble and Jack was still their buddy. So it wasn't Grady and the cops who wanted Grady's book, it was my brothers and the cops -- and Jack!

Grady's truck was still nowhere in sight, so I peeled up onto the expressway ramp and jumped to the inner lane away from Frontage Road that runs alongside the garage. So my brothers, who I trusted with my life, were siding with the birdbrain cops and Jack. It made sense. They were all customers of Grady. They probably figured I'd bring them the book and they'd make a show of Kevin being freed. Or even more likely, they'd just take the book, give each other high fives, and tell me not to be a brat.

Instinctively, I headed to Route 65, to Florida. I knew the way by heart, and the thought of Gram and Gramps at the end of the trip gave me something to shoot for. Maybe I could sort it all out from a distance. I stopped at a WalMart on the way and bought some diapers, formula, a toothbrush, and a couple of tee shirts. The first few hours of the trip adrenalin kept me going, and then anger took over. Eventually I was so tired I drove by rote.

Gramps sat at the dining room table, when I walked in and Gram came from the kitchen with a dish that she set on the table. I stumbled over to Gram with Gracie in my arms and all but dumped Gracie into Gram's arms. I kissed her astonished cheek and then I kissed Gramps. They looked confused but pleased. "Oh Gram," I cried out, crumpling onto a chair at the table. I felt too exhausted to even cry. "I drove all night. I'm so tired. Jack and the boys are all creeps and so are the cops. I need to be somewhere safe and Gracie needs to be safe." I wasn't explaining very well, but Gram had always been able to decipher my sobs and tearful pleas.

"Well this is the place to come," Gramps said. He steered me to his bedroom. I threw myself on the bed and fell asleep.

"Have some supper," Gramps said when I heard Gracie's cry for a bottle and I came out of the bedroom. He pointed to a place set for me. Gram rocked Gracie who sucked peacefully on her bottle. Gram and Gramps had finished eating from the looks of their plates. I helped myself to chicken ala-king, homemade biscuits, and candied yams. I put butter on half of a hot biscuit and ate it. Then I spread the other half with the rich creamy sauce, thick with chicken, peas, and mushrooms.

It took a long time to tell them about Grady, as well as getting divorced. They listened without comment which surprised me. I also explained my dream of becoming a CPA and how I'd enrolled in Owensville Community College. They looked pleased at that but not so much so when I told them about my new friend Tom, and Kevin's fake abduction. They were amazed. We talked well into the night. They already knew about Tom Atkinson's death since they kept in touch with their old neighbors. They smiled when I told them about Ethel taking over the business. "She's a pip," Gramps said.

"I can't trust anyone." I said finally. "My brothers, my husband, the police, Al." I felt another cry coming on.

"It's late," Gramps said. "You're getting yourself all worked up. In the morning things will look better. You just stay here and wait until your brothers get things sorted out."

"They're in cahoots with Jack! They're not going to help me. For all I know, they're friends with Grady too. They're probably laughing at the way he's been scaring me!"

"You don't know any of that's true," Gramps said. "Sometimes it's better not to assume you know something until you've gotten all the facts," Gramps came over and wrapped his arms around me, holding me close to his warm, soft cotton shirtfront. "You haven't heard your brothers' side of what's going on."

"I've heard enough to know they've gotten themselves mixed up with idiots!" I pushed back from Gramps and stalked away a few steps. "Oh wait! They're idiots too!"

Gramps put his arm around my shoulders and said, "Sweetie, you need some rest. You know your brothers love you. They may be doing some things you think you understand but unless you wait and see what the truth is, you really don't know what's going on, do you?"

"I guess not," I admitted. I let Gramps guide me to his room and I crawled into his bed feeling totally beaten.

A little before noon the next day Kevin's four-by-four pulled into the driveway. Gram played with Gracie on her lap in her rocking chair. I was reading a magazine on the couch. "I called them, Dear," Gram said when she saw my scowl. She frowned at me. "I know you're angry with your brothers, but they love you and worry about you, you know."

"Is that why they lied to me? Is that why they said Kevin was kidnapped and worried me sick." My voice carried through the open windows. Gram focused her attention on Gracie who kicked and giggled in her lap. She rocked without breaking her rhythm as the hinges on the front screen door squeaked. Kevin strode through the porch and into the living room. "Yeah," he said, "we're so mean to you." Shawn pushed past Kevin without looking at me. They dropped kisses on Gram's upturned face and Gracie's head as they went into the kitchen. I glared at Gram. Oblivious to my mood, she cooed at Gracie in her lap. Bottles clinked in the refrigerator door and then ice crackled as Gram's grapefruit and orange drink was poured into glasses. "Now that's the drink that refreshes," Shawn said from the kitchen. Gram's smile deepened.

I sighed, waiting for them to come back out to the living room. "There's sausage and sauerkraut in the refrigerator if you want me to warm you up a bite," Gram called out. She beamed at Gracie in her lap. Gracie blew happy spit bubbles and waved her chubby fists.

Sure, I thought, feed those angels. Gram was so wrapped up in making Gracie giggle that I had to smile too. Shawn sauntered in, interpreted the smile as me not being mad at him anymore, and plunked down next to me. He set his drink on Gram's cypress coffee table and embraced me in a sideways bear hug.

"You know you can't stay mad at us, Brat." Shawn tried to tickle me in the ribs like we were kids. I dug my elbows into his side and moved to the loveseat. Shawn heaved a martyred sigh, crossed his legs at the knee, and took up his glass. "I have some serious problems, thanks to you two twits," I said.

"We didn't start this," Kevin pointed out, "Jack did." Then Kevin told Gram, "Your good cooking kept us going all night long, Gram." He took Gracie and Gram got up to go heat up something for them to eat. Before she left, Kevin turned his face up for Gram to kiss. She kissed his forehead and then thumped him on the top of his head. Kevin held his head and looked six-years-old.

"That's for scaring your baby sister," Gram said on her way to the kitchen. "You all make some sense before I get back, or nobody eats." We grew up on that threat; it always worked in the past.

Shawn rested his elbows on his knees and leaned toward me. "We didn't want you to be involved in this at all," he said. "And thanks to Jack, it's getting complicated."

"What was it before?" I glared at him with crossed arms, one foot tucked under, the other tapping on the floor,

"Look," Shawn cut in, "The real problem is that Grady made videos of all his transactions. The bastard had a surveillance camera on his porch and made everyone who bought his stuff pay him there."

"Louie and Donald would lose their jobs," Kevin cut in, "and you know how our town is; we'd probably lose our work too. We need to destroy that book."

"What about the videos?"

"Jack has them. He said he went back and got them when he found out that Grady was in Owensville chasing after you."

"Does Grady know Jack took them?"

"Not yet," Shawn answered. "Jack had some fool plan for Grady to pay him to get the videos back. We told Jack he better give us the videos to destroy and that we'd take care of the book."

"That's what you saw us talking about when you came to Al's," Kevin said. "Al's mechanic told us you started to come in but left in a hurry."

"You didn't look like you were threatening Jack to me."

"We'd gotten past that and he agreed. He said he wouldn't think of putting Gracie in harm's way."

"Did he tell you he gave up all rights to Gracie? He doesn't even want to see her after the divorce" They looked at one another with stunned expressions. "There's lots you don't know about your buddy Jack."

"And you didn't tell us that before because?" Shawn accused.

"When? We haven't had much chance to talk lately, have we?" I got to the point. "So your plan is to get the book and videos and destroy them, right?"

"That's about it," Shawn said. "Then we'll find Grady, take care of him so that he doesn't bother anybody again, and nobody loses his job or gets in trouble, get it?"

"So Huey, Lewy, and Donald Duck get protection from you," I snickered. "That's rich."

"Hugh isn't involved." Shawn said. I was about to tell them that Tom accused Hugh of kidnapping and that Hugh had tried to cover up for the other two when Gram brought in steaming bowls of food so we quit talking and moved to the table. Gram had heated up sausage and sauerkraut with new potatoes along with some warmed over candied yams and homemade bread pudding.

Gram held Gracie and we ate in silence for a few minutes. Gramps came in and "got in on the eats," as he put it. Afterwards he and my brothers went out to fish. I put Gracie in bed and helped Gram make stewed tomatoes. The tomatoes weren't the only thing that stewed. I was still angry with everybody, except Tom. Poor Tom; I felt guilty about leaving him without talking things over with him, but at the time it seemed the right thing to do. I still didn't want to get his family involved, or him either.

After we finished the tomatoes, Gram went to her room to lie down for a nap so I took the opportunity to call Tom's house. Mrs. Atkinson said she was relieved to know Gracie and I were safe. She said Tom had gone to my house after reading my note. Apparently my disappearance caused Tom and my brothers to spend the night searching for me. She said Gram called as soon as I arrived in Florida, which was a huge relief to everyone there. I apologized to her and felt twice as guilty about my actions but she seemed to understand. I really liked her a lot.

Later that evening I heard the men tying up at the dock and I went out to meet them. We exchanged pleasantries. Apparently the fish had managed to escape. Gramps and Kevin went in the house but Shawn stayed behind. I stood with my back to the brilliant sunset across the street and stared down at Shawn who fiddled with the bait box. Shawn squinted up from Gramps' aluminum fishing boat. Oil splotches floated on the murky water like iridescent lily pads. Spanish moss drooped from trees lining either side of the canal. "What are you guys going to do now?" I asked.

"Now that we know you're all right, we're going home in the morning. When we find Grady, we'll settle this thing our way. Where's the book?"

"Consider it destroyed," I turned away abruptly. Inside, something perverse in me made me want to keep the book so I slid it under Gram's fridge. The filthy thing seemed to belong under something.

Next morning Kevin and Shawn searched for Grady's book in my van and Gramps' room. I ignored their not overly cautious rifling through my things which included Gracie's diaper bag. I smiled triumphantly as I leaned in the window of the four-by-four to say goodbye.

Shawn scowled up at me. "We can worry about getting the book thing straightened out later." He said quietly so Gram and Gramps wouldn't hear him. Gramps stood on the driver's side saying good-bye to Kevin and Gram had gone back in for a few more things to send home with my brothers.

Pushing back from the car window, I announced over the hood, "Shawn and Kevin told me last night that Jack not only took Grady's book, but he also stole some videos to blackmail Grady with." Shawn flushed looking daggers at me.

"We're going to destroy them so nobody gets hurt," Kevin said shooting death rays at me from behind the wheel. I kept myself from blurting out that Kevin and Shawn didn't want anyone to know they were potheads but I gave the boys a long suffering sigh and cut my eyes at them in disgust.

Kevin kissed Gram when she handed in a plastic grocery bag filled with sandwiches for the trip home and other goodies. They took off and we waved good-bye. I had agreed to stay with Gram and Gramps while the cops and my brothers got the videos from Jack to destroy and found Grady.

TWENTY TWO

By the fourth day at Gram and Gramps my afternoons dragged. Gram and Gracie napped and Gramps was going to drive to Clearwater for a part for his boat motor. He liked to wander around the big True Value Hardware store there, like I browse the mall.

"Can I come?" I had my purse in hand in the driveway where Gramps was preparing to leave.

"I was hoping you would," he grinned, deepening the creases around his blue-gray eyes. "You know I always like to have you come into town with me." He slid behind the wheel of his silver New Yorker and I buckled myself in beside him. We drove in silence for a while. Gramps had to concentrate on the heavy traffic on Route 19.

"How about dropping me off at the Clearwater Hospital while you pick up your stuff?" I was inspired by the hospital sign along the road. I'd already told Gramps about the police call informing me that Grady's son was in the Clearwater Hospital. "I'd like to see how he's doing. Maybe he's out of his coma and I can talk with him."

"You sure you want to do that, Julie?" I nodded so Gramps turned onto Bay-to-Bay Blvd. He dropped me off at the front entrance of the hospital after we agreed to meet in the hospital cafeteria. That way whoever got there first could pick up a magazine or newspaper and get a drink while they waited.

Inside, I went to the information desk where an elderly woman gave me a visitor's pass and directed me to room 319. I walked through a maze of corridors to room 319 and was met outside the closed door by a slight man peering over wire rimmed glasses. He introduced himself as Dr. Burton. "I understand you know this young man?" he asked.

"Not really," I answered in an attempt to be truthful but not get caught in my recent lies about being his sister.

"I was told that you know how he came to receive so many untreated injuries." When I shook my head no again, he said, "Suppose you tell me what you do know about him." Dr. Burton placed his hand firmly under my elbow and escorted me down the hallway to a small office. He closed the door when we entered the room and turned to face me expectantly.

"There's not much to tell," I said. "The guy tried to break into my camper one night a few weeks ago and I hit him on the head with an iron skillet, once behind his ear, and once on top of his head. I assumed he was knocked unconscious. A little while later his father picked him up and drove off with him in a truck. I learned that my intruder was alive just recently and that his father's name is Grady."

The doctor walked over to a narrow window, squinted against the sunlight, and finally turned to me. "That's quite a story." He studied me a long moment before he nodded decisively. "You're right. A Mr. Grady is who brought in my patient. Mr. Grady said the young man's name is Billy. He told us that his son is twenty-four but he's mentally challenged. We were also told that there are no other family members. We haven't seen the father since he brought Billy in. Normally, by now, we'd have released Billy to his family, usually to be sent to a private, long term nursing facility. However, since we haven't been able to locate his father, we're waiting for the paperwork to go through to get him moved to the Pinellas County facility. Billy was comatose when he was brought in. Most of his wounds were healed."

"Were there wounds besides on his head?"

Dr. Burton looked over his glasses and said, "He's been clearly abused -- badly abused, no question about it. Billy's father told us that Billy fell on some rocks, went to sleep, and then didn't wake up." Dr. Burton cleared his throat.

"Now that I've shared what I know," he said, "how about telling me your name and address in case I need to get in touch with you I looked down but he read my thoughts. "Even if you're not family, you might be of some help." It occurred to me that he might not totally believe my story and he probably just wanted to get my name in case I turned out to be his sister or something. I gave him my name and address and we shook hands before he walked with me back to room 319, where he left me to continue down the long corridor.

This time when I got to Billy's room, the door was open. Propped up in bed, Billy waved a spoon around like an infant although he looked middle aged. His thick, dark hair seemed to flow down his face where he badly needed a shave. A plump, young girl mimed Billy's open mouth as she maneuvered the spoon into his mouth. His face turned toward me when I entered the room and he held his mouth open sideways. She successfully landed a spoonful of chocolate ice cream in his mouth. The plastic lapel pin she wore read that she was a nurse's aide named Allison.

"Mind if I feed him," I was so excited to see him awake, I smiled at him and he returned the smile dribbling chocolate ice cream through his teeth.

Allison looked relieved and handed me the spoon. She sang out, "Bye Billy," and left. He opened his mouth wide for each bite of ice cream and as long as I fed him, he didn't bother to use the spoon he held. He ate with such relish that it was a pleasure to feed him. By the time he'd finished the ice cream, his eyes drooped. I set the empty bowl on the tray next to his bed and he scrunched down in bed. He closed his eyes and smiled. "I like it here," he said.

"I'm so glad," I choked around a lump that suddenly developed in my throat.

"I like ice cream." He sighed. All at once his eyes popped open and he glanced around the room furtively. "I don't have to go get no boxes now do I?" He seemed agitated and fearful.

"No, you don't have to go get boxes today, Billy," I said soothingly, patting the back of his hairy hand.

When he saw nobody in the room but the two of us, he took a ragged breath and sank back against his pillows. "I had a shower this morning." His voice was soft and he scooched down on his bed again. "It was like standing in the rain," he crooned," only it was all warm and smelled nice. And I could stay in it as long as I wanted." He smiled remembering the events of his morning in the hospital. "It's nice here; I want to stay here. Can I stay here?" He opened his eyes to get permission from me.

"I'll do everything I can to help you," I promised. And I knew then that I meant it.

He pulled his covers a little higher under his chin and smiled at me. His eyes were soft, dark brown. "Pa makes me get boxes at night when I want to sleep. And he hits me. Don't nobody hit me here and I get ice cream and showers. I don't want to go home." He cringed, craning his head to ascertain that we were still alone in the room. Satisfied, he settled into his pillows.

"It's all right, Billy," I patted his shoulder gently. I realized that he needed to get Grady off his back at least as much as I did. I wanted to find out as much as possible about what Grady and he did so that maybe I could figure out a way to help us both. "Tell me about going out for boxes." I urged.

He yanked at his covers, jutting out a chin so heavily bearded that it would never look clean shaven. "I don't want to go get no boxes," he said fiercely. He scooted further down so that he was flat on the bed, his eyes closed to shut out the world

"What was in the boxes?" I gently prompted.

After a minute, he murmured, "Pa always liked it best when the stuff was still in them. We could use the stuff when we went back for the rest." He rolled into a fetal position with his hands tucked under his chin. A nurse stuck her head in and beckoned to me from the doorway that it was time to leave. By the time I reached the door, Billy snored softly.

Two nurses worked behind a circular counter halfway down the hall. One had her blonde hair done in a neat twist at the nape of her neck. The other nurse had short black hair. Both women smiled when I passed them. On impulse I went back to the counter and asked if they'd heard from Billy's father.

"No, Darlin'," the middle aged blonde nurse said.

"Hasn't anybody been in to see that poor soul, but you all," the older, dark haired nurse said. "Are you the one who knows how he sustained his injuries?"

"His father abused him," I said, "and then I put him in the coma. I'm so grateful that he woke up." I felt tears coming and fought to maintain my composure. It was no use. Embarrassed, I pulled some tissues from my purse and blinked like a windshield wiper that couldn't keep up with a downpour.

"It's all right, Darlin'," the blonde nurse said. She scooted out from around the counter to stand beside me. She put her arm across my shoulders until I could look up. Her hazel eyes swam behind her glasses.

"He's so pathetic," I said. "And I can't believe his own father hasn't been here. Did he even call?"

The dark haired lady stood behind the counter shaking her head no. "I didn't mean to upset you," she said. "It's just that he's so darn grateful for every little thing we do for him, it breaks my heart." She pinched the bridge of her nose with her fingertips.

"His father left us a couple of phone numbers but one never answered and the other is a store up north somewhere. They just say Mr. Grady isn't there," the blonde nurse said. While she spoke I noticed a plastic nametag pinned to her jacket read Vera Jean. The other lady's similar nametag read simply, Carlotta.

"Could I see the phone numbers, please?" I asked. "Maybe I could call at different times and get through to Billy's father."

Vera Jean exchanged a sharp glance with Carlotta and quickly stepped away from me. She marched behind the counter and said in a frosty professional voice, "We aren't allowed to divulge that kind of information,"

"What's going to happen to him?" I asked.

"Billy will be sent to a place for the mentally challenged in Pinellas County," Carlotta answered in a crisp voice. Both women were suddenly busy with papers on their desks.

"Thank God!" I breathed. "The last thing I'd want is for Billy to get back in the clutches of his father."

"Do you know the family?" Vera Jean asked. The frost on her professionalism seemed to have melted.

"No," I answered, "but I talked with his father and let's just say I didn't think he was a very nice man." They nodded.

"Billy's lucky there weren't any beds in the county facility yet," Vera Jean said. "We got his skin and scalp cleared up and everybody tried to help him in what we thought might be his last few days."

"Thank you both," I said. Carlotta left with a clipboard. Vera Jean smiled. I felt like she'd try to be helpful if I trusted her, so I told her how I'd come to bash Billy in the head, and how his father threatened Gracie and me. "So, that ratfink's up in my neck of the woods looking for me. My brothers, the cops, and people in our town are looking for him."

"Sweet Jesus," Vera Jean breathed. "Truth be told, we didn't spend a whole lot of time trying to find the father. Actually, we all hope he never shows up again. That way Billy can go to the Pinellas County home where he'll be well cared for."

"You know, if I could find his father, I think I could get him sent to jail."

Vera Jean and Carlotta, who had returned in time to hear most of my story, looked at one another a moment before Carlotta volunteered, "If we just let things run their course, we can ship Billy to the county facility as temporary lodging until we can locate his father. And we don't intend to do that, just between you, me, and the lamp post."

"I think if I could find his father," I said, "I could get him sent to jail for stealing from snowbirds." Vera Jean gave me a questioning look. "The police think he's the thief who's responsible for the rash of thefts in our area."

I couldn't tell her about the stolen record book. I knew that if Grady got his record book back, though, he might need Billy's help again. I couldn't let that happen. Grady had to be found and put in jail.

"Please give me those phone numbers," I begged. "I have evidence that I think will prove Mr. Grady's a thief. Then he'll be sent to jail and Billy will be safe from him."

"Really." Vera bit the corner of her bottom lip. "Well, if you think the phone numbers might help." I could see she struggled with her wish to help. "You might just want to give a quick peek at the monitor screen there." She pointed to the computer behind the nurses' station. "We need a potty break, right Carlotta?" Carlotta nodded and bent to type in some information before she came around the counter to join Vera Jean on her way down the hallway.

I scrambled around the counter and quickly copied the phone numbers onto a scratch pad near the phone. I left with the piece of paper stuffed in the pocket of my jean shorts. When I passed Vera Jean and Carlotta outside the double doors leading to the ward, I nodded and said "Thanks for everything."

"Good luck, Darlin'" Vera Jean said. "We'll keep our fingers crossed."

"How about a few prayers?" I countered. "We definitely need more powerful help."

TWENTY THREE

Gramps came into the cafeteria while I stood in line to buy an iced tea. He decided to get one for himself and paid for two iced teas "to go." On the drive home I said to Gramps, "Grady absolutely has to be found and sent to jail." I explained what the doctor had said about Grady abusing Billy, and that the nurses had given me a chance to get the phone numbers Grady had given the hospital.

"Man, I sure didn't help Billy any by hitting him over the head," Tears collected in the corner of my eyes. "The doctor said Billy doesn't have a mother." We rode in silence a while and I wondered what Billy's life had been like. Why hadn't any of his neighbors seen that his father was abusing him? "Would you take me to his farm this afternoon?" I asked.

Gramps looked at me and frowned. "What in the world for?"

I shrugged. "I just wanted to see where Billy lived and what Grady's farm looks like. Maybe we'll see his truck there. Maybe that's why nobody can find him in Owensville." It made a lot of sense.

"We don't know where he lives, Julie," Gramps said. "But no doubt the police have been to his place and checked to see if he's there, don't you think?

"Probably," I agreed. "But it's still not settled for me, inside." I looked down and blinked fast, wishing I could put my feelings into words.

Gramps patted the back of my hand and said, "I'd take you, Sweetie, but we don't know where he lives."

"If I can find out, will you take me?" He nodded that he would but he shook his head and sighed.

"Billy talked about his father making him get boxes," I said to change the subject. "He said Grady especially liked boxes with some kind of stuff in them." Gramps flashed me a look of incredulity. "That doesn't make much sense to me either," I said.

For the rest of the ride home, I mulled over what Billy had said about collecting boxes but couldn't make sense out of that idea so I switched to figuring out a way to find out where Grady's farm was located.

As usual, the aroma of Gram's good cooking greeted us as we came in the kitchen through the back door. Gram had prepared tuna salad sandwiches to go with her homemade vegetable soup. We sat down to eat right away.

"Billy said his father made him collect boxes," I told Gram during lunch. She looked at Gramps for an explanation.

"Don't look at me," he said soaking up the remainder of his soup with a corner of his sandwich.

"What kind of stuff would you find in boxes that would make Grady happy?" I asked. Gram looked at me, shrugged and went into the kitchen for dessert. She returned and went to work cutting thick wedges of apple pie and setting slices out on plates. "Billy was afraid I'd make him go out for boxes. What kind of boxes would he have to go out for?" I couldn't let go of the idea. I tried to picture boxes filled with something that would make Grady happy, that his son could find. Usually Gram's apple pie held my full attention, but today I ate without thinking about what I was eating at all. I pictured Grady and Billy in their truck, going out for boxes. But where? And why? "It would have to be boxes you can find outside or would he go into somewhere to steal boxes. Nah, that makes even less sense."

I ate a few more bites of pie and then got up to get a wire coat hanger from the closet. Gram and Gramps followed me into the kitchen and watched me poke under the refrigerator for Grady's record book. "Has that been there all along?" Gramps said as the gray composition book slid out. I nodded and grinned.

Without a word, Gram took Grady's book from me, carried it over to the sink, holding it with her thumb and index finger. She wiped off the cover with a damp cloth before she handed it beck to me. I set it on the dining room table next to Gramps plate of half eaten pie Gramps alternated between taking bites of pie and flipping through pages while Gram and I finished eating.

Gramps continued to look through the book as Gram and I took away the dessert plates and cleaned the table. He whistled at one point and said, "Here's an address up on the point." We started doing dishes in the kitchen while Gramps pored over the pages of Grady's records.

"There's a listing for a television set that was stolen from Ida's place," Gramps said when he'd finished looking at the book and closed it. "Yep, this Grady must be the guy in the papers who's been stealing from homes around here. I can see a couple of other addresses and stolen goods that match." He looked sternly at me. "Julie, you must take this book to the police tomorrow." He waited to see if I'd object.

"If Grady steals television sets and other small appliances, could he be looking for boxes he could put the TVs and appliances into maybe?" Gram offered.

I snapped my fingers and exclaimed, "Packing material! That's what Grady would like to find in empty boxes. I think you're right, Gram. If Grady goes around on trash day and picks up boxes that contained televisions or whatever somebody bought, then maybe wrote down the address..."

"He could go back later and break into the house to steal the new television or whatever was in the box," Gramps finished my train of thought. We smiled at each other and nodded. Yes! Now it made sense.

"And then he could put the appliance back into the original box and do what?" Gram asked.

"Probably sell the stuff," Gramps ventured. "Anyway, tomorrow we'll take the book to the police and let them figure out the rest." I felt a sense of relief. Finally, we could do something to stop Grady – if somebody could find him, that is. My only trepidation was that my brothers' names were in the book as well as our local police. But Gramps hadn't noticed their names, or else he didn't say anything about it. I hadn't looked very carefully but now I wondered if my brothers had actually seen their names in the book or just assumed they were there.

"The front pages of this book might be Grady's marijuana sales," Gramps said flipping through the book again, "and the back pages have the names and addresses with a listing of items he either stole or wanted to steal."

"You know, Gramps," I said as he got up from the table. I wonder if I could just give the cops a computer disk instead of the actual book. That way I could give Grady his book and not tell him the police had a copy of it. What do you think?"

Gramps shrugged. "Why don't you call the police now and ask them?" He went outside while I got busy on the telephone. First I flipped through the front pages of the book looking for Shawn or Kevin's name. They weren't even there. But Jack's name was. Of course, Jack was the customer! I did a mental head slap while I rang up the police.

"Pinellas County Sheriff's Office," a young woman's voice answered.

"I think I need to speak with either Officer Braxton or Daly," I said assuming they'd be the ones who would know what I meant by Grady's record book.

"Officer Braxton here," he said when he answered. I explained my idea about turning in a computer disk and keeping the record book, but he said that the courts would need the original copy of the book in Grady's handwriting, he thought. When I told him I had the book here in Florida, Officer Braxton said he'd be at the bait shop this evening if I could bring it over. "I can't wait to get my hands on that sucker," he said. I agreed to drive it over before I hung up. Gramps said he might as well go to the bait shop with me.

We were about to go out to the car with the book when the phone rang. I held up an index finger for Gramps to wait a minute, and picked up. It was Tom.

I felt a stab of guilt about how I'd left Tom's house, but I reminded myself that Tom didn't need my troubles on top of his own.

"I'm glad to hear from you," I told Tom in what I hoped was a light tone of voice.

"Yeah well, I was ticked off that you ran out on me without even a parting hand shake," he said. "But I know the strain you've been under and I forgive you."

"Tell you what," I said in an effort to soothe him and my own conscience. "I'm driving home tomorrow and I'll be going right by the U. of I. campus. I should be in the area by about six or seven tomorrow night. If you want, I could buy you a meal and thank you in person for not being mad at me."

"Great! I can show you the highlights of campus living. We have a great CPA program here, you know."

"I didn't, I said. We were both straining to keep it casual. "It's good to know. Where should we meet?"

"Take the Market Street exit off Rt. 57, and turn south on Green Street. I'll meet you at the Red Barn Restaurant. It'll be on your left about three blocks south on Green. You can't miss it."

When I hung up, Gram and Gramps had settled at the table and looked at me expectantly so I explained our conversation. They were pleased that I was interested in the CPA program at the University of Illinois, but they were definitely not pleased that I wanted to go home before Grady was caught. "It was a spur of the moment thing," I told them. "If I don't even have Grady's book anymore, and the police do, I can tell him that if he ever calls again. Besides," I added quickly, "I'm really anxious to get my bookkeeping back on track. The bills and receipts must be overflowing by now and I can't afford to lose my jobs." They both looked unhappy, but didn't argue any further.

Gram went to feed Gracie when she woke up and I called the Port Richfield Post Office to talk with Mrs. Krueger, the Post Mistress. She's in her eighties and still runs the post office, calls bingo at church, and is the local information center. "What can you tell me about the Grady family," I asked her.

"Not a heck of a lot," she said. "Mrs. Grady just disappeared one day. Everybody figures she ran off and left her son with his father. He's slow, don't ya know. I never saw the Grady boy much. Sometimes I'd see him waiting outside when his father picked up the mail. The Mister was a surly one; barely said hello."

"I need to know how to get to his place. Do you know?"

"As far as I can recollect, the road next to Syd's Bait Shop runs right out there onto Grady's place. I've never been out there." I was about to thank her and hang up when she added, "Don't really know as how anybody much goes out to the place, come to think of it."

It was late afternoon when Gramps and I took off to see where Grady lived with his son. Gramps agreed to go there first and then take the book to the police later. A long, sandy road ended in front of a shack with a porch hanging off the front of the weathered one story building. The porch had a small yellowed refrigerator at one end and a couple of plastic chairs on either side of an old kitchen table. Three crooked two-by-fours shoved beneath the roof kept the porch from collapsing.

We looked around for any type of vehicle but saw nothing but a rusty old water pump stuck in the middle of the yard. I got out of the car and stepped between patches of sand burrs and weeds to look into a side window of the shack.

The single room inside had a toilet and sink along the back wall, followed by a cabinet and a tiny stove on the other wall. You could literally sit on the "throne", as our family often referred to the commode, and cook your meals. One corner of the room held a card table and two folding chairs, and a dirty, sagging couch that faced a new large-screen television set. An unmade double bed and a small dresser in the opposite corner completed the entire contents of the so-called "house." I sighed heavily.

Gramps walked up beside me and we picked our way through the weeds to the back corner of the building. An old rusty lean-to sagged against the back of the place. It was padlocked. Facing the back of the property, we surveyed a vast area of potted marijuana plants clustered between scrub oaks and palmettos. Undeveloped land surrounded the area in the sweltering heat. Gramps and I shaded our faces with our hands and surveyed Grady's "crop."

Billy must have had an awful life here," I croaked around a now familiar lump forming in my throat. I cleared my throat and added, "How come the police haven't gotten rid of these plants, I wonder?"

"Gramps?" I repeated my question.

"I can't imagine, Julie," he said. "I suspect that nobody has bothered to come out this far besides the owner."

We made our way back to the cool air conditioning of the car as I thought, for all we knew the place was a major shopping center in the world of weed.

Gramps drove me to the bait shop where I handed over Grady's record book to Officer Daly. "Maybe Grady will leave the area and disappear never to be heard from again," he commented as he accepted the book. I hoped that might happen. That would solve everybody's problems.

Gram was on the phone as Gramps and I walked into the kitchen.

"It's Shawn," Gram said holding out the receiver to me. "He just called looking for you."

Before I could tell him anything, Shawn said they still hadn't been able to locate Grady. I don't think I ever heard him sound so dejected. My first instinct was not to say anything about Grady's record book now in the hands of the Florida police. Maybe Shawn would never find out about what really happened to it. On the other hand, if I missed something and a problem did come up for them because of it, I didn't want to have to face either one of them knowing I'd let them down. I took a deep breath and just blurted out, "Grady absolutely has to be found and sent to jail."

"Gee, Ya think?"

I ignored the sarcasm. "So in order to make sure he goes to jail, I had to turn his book over to the Florida cops."

"Are you nuts!" Shawn exploded. "Didn't you hear me when I said Louie and Donald would lose their jobs, not to mention us probably losing work? How could you do such a stupid thing?"

"I have to think of somebody else besides us now."

"Yeah? Like who?"

"Billy, Grady's son." I explained about how pathetic Billy was and how terrible it would be for him to be sent back with his father. "And besides, I'm probably responsible for making the poor guy even more mentally challenged by bopping him over the head with my skillet. I'm going to do everything I can to protect him."

"What about us? Don't we count?"

"I'm sorry, Shawn. The worst that could happen, and probably won't, is Louie and Donald might have to find another job, and maybe a lot of folks won't trade with you anymore, either. But it wouldn't be like what Billy could suffer with his father." I finished with, "You wouldn't want to be responsible for making some innocent guy spend the rest of his life with somebody who abuses him would you?"

"I guess not," Shawn said glumly.

"And for the record, I looked for your names and they weren't even in the book. Only Jack's name was." I felt better when Shawn whooped and said Jack told them they were in the book too. I guess being off the hook was a relief for Shawn, but the problem of what to do to get Grady off my back curtailed his jubilation when I reminded him of it.

Next morning I was getting ready to leave when Gramps said, "I really think you're better off to stay here until Grady is captured. Even a thief can be dangerous if he's cornered." "Don't worry, Gramps," I said. "Shawn and Kevin will watch out for me. You know that." I kissed his cheek and we shared a long hug before he and Gram walked me out to the van. Gram kissed me and hugged me after I'd gotten Gracie in her car carrier strapped into the van. Gram had packed up enough stuff to feed us for a week and Gramps had stowed it in bags in the back seat.

It felt good to be going back, really. I had to get my work at home caught up and I missed Margie and even my brothers as dopey as they sometimes were. By the time I reached the parking lot of the Red Barn Restaurant, I was stiff and more than ready to get out of the car.

Tom waited in his car in the parking lot and ushered us into the noisy restaurant where he ordered a pizza. I told him about Billy, and that I had to give the police Grady's book. "But thanks to you, I can print out another copy." As I said that, it came to me that once Grady knew my brothers and I could make copies of his records anytime, maybe he might just disappear. It seemed like such a good idea that I told Tom so and then I kissed him lightly on the cheek.

Tom smiled at me and hugged me as the waitress placed a large pizza in the center of the table. We sat side-by-side in a booth. Unlike Chuck's bar and grill back home, the Red Barn Restaurant had enormous rooms with high vaulted ceilings. Booths rimmed each room with tables arranged in the center, covered with checkered cloths and quaint little oil lamps. Tom hugged me closer after the waitress left. His smile made me want to climb his frame right there in the restaurant. I hated that I always had improper urges to hide. It was good to see that his face was no longer purple under his left eye.

"I happen to know of an empty bed in one of the dorms where you and Gracie could crash tonight, and then tomorrow I could show you the campus. We really do have a great program here for CPAs, and I'd love to show you my digs. What do you say?"

"That sounds really great." I'd never been on a big university campus before so it was an exciting prospect. "I just have to call my brothers and Gramps so they won't worry."

When I called Shawn, he said, "Why couldn't you just stay put at Gram and Gramps?"

"I need to get home and do some work," I answered, "or I'll lose my jobs. Plus, at the rate you're going, school might start before you catch Grady."

He made me promise I'd leave the University late enough tomorrow so he and Kevin could meet me when they got home from work. I agreed. Then I called Gramps who said he wished he hadn't let me go. I assured him again that my brothers would take care of me. I hung up and it was all set!

Tom took me up to the off campus apartment he shared with three other guys. It was a spacious four bedroom apartment covering the second story of a house that had been converted into apartments. One of Tom's roommates planned to go home for the night so he offered to let me have his room. Next day Tom drove me around the Champaign-Urbana area, taking me to his favorite places. We also visited the University's Financial Aides Office where I picked up information about the business programs offered there. We talked about me transferring to the University of Illinois after I finished at Owensville. It all seemed possible now. I could actually graduate from college and get a job as a CPA with a college degree.

After supper at a little Greek restaurant, I hated to leave. "I'm so looking forward to coming here, if I can," I said as I packed Gracie back into her carrier in the van. Tom said he looked forward to it too and I took off for the last hundred miles of the trip home.

TWENTY FOUR

It was a dark, moonless night when I started up our driveway. Before I was halfway past the house, lights from the corners of the garage flooded the driveway. Both brothers came out of the house to meet me. As soon as I got out of the car, Shawn started bossing me around. "You're sleeping in the house, Julie," he said.

"Here we go again," I said. "I want to sleep in my own bed. Besides, Grady can break into the ground floor windows of the house easier than my boarded up windows."

"We thought you might feel that way," Kevin said, "so we put motion lights on all four corners of your apartment." He pointed to the spotlights under the eaves. "If anybody comes within thirty feet of your place, it'll light up our lives."

My brothers insisted that we walk around the garage to watch each light blaze on as we approached it, and then I let them walk upstairs with me to be sure the place was free of Grady, snakes, or other vermin.

It felt good to be home. I called Tom and Gramps and assured them that all was well. It was late and I was exhausted but I couldn't sleep. Even though there were lights and all kinds of people on the alert, I couldn't relax. I knew I had to do something or I'd never get to sleep.

The only place that I could think of where I could hide in my apartment was the overhead crawl space. I felt around the top of a pile of folded sweaters and sweatshirts on the overhead shelf in my walk in closet until I found the end of a rope pulley. I yanked down a folding wooden ladder. Dust and stale air greeted me as the seven steps swung down on the spring pull. I climbed up enough to poke my head into the rafters above my apartment. A few sheets of thick pressed board covered about a five foot rectangle on top of the ceiling beams. Beyond that the beams were lined with pink paper covered insulation. The area was supposed to be used for storage but I just never used it.

I traipsed downstairs to the garage and hauled my sleeping bag up from the camper along with a flashlight. I spread out my sleeping bag and an afghan my mom made to cover up our "early marriage" hand me down furniture. Then I brought up Gracie in her carrier and my pillow.

About two minutes after I'd snuggled into my hideaway, I had to go to the bathroom. I figured I'd better take up a bucket with some water to go pee in and while I was at it, I grabbed the small plastic hamper I use for Gracie's dirty diapers. Then, just for grins, I arranged a couple of pillows under the covers on my bed to look like me sleeping, like they do in the movies. I was really getting into it. As an afterthought, I got my trusty meat cleaver from the kitchen and put it next to the flashlight by my new upstairs bedroom. I placed the potty bucket on the closed trap door and stretched out on the sleeping bag with my afghan warm and cozy on top. Peaceful at last, I went to sleep.

I didn't hear the new motion lights being shot out with a silencer nor did I hear the door's lock being shot off. I did hear Grady's gruff voice. "I know yur in here," he said from Jack's bedroom below. I was instantly awake. "I seen ya come in." The footsteps moved toward my bedroom. I knew that the rope for the ladder would be easy to spot if Grady looked for it

My heart pounded in my ears along with a ping, ping that ended with a thump. I froze. I'd heard the sound of a silencer in movies enough to be able to put it together. What if he aimed at the ceiling and fired? He might hit Gracie!

I held her carrier up with one hand and felt my way in the dark to the edge of the floor boards with the other. When I reached the end of the flooring, I groped my way out onto the wooden beams. Gracie's carrier balanced between the beams without difficulty so I scooched along on my hands and knees, feeling my way, pushing Gracie carefully along as quietly and quickly as I dared. My ears rang, my heart banged, and suddenly the trapdoor was outlined in light from below where Grady must be shining his flashlight directly on the closed trap door.

"So ya give my book over to the cops, eh Missy? I'm gonna make sure you're real sorry you done that." With one quick yank the ladder was down and my potty pail went over the edge. He yelled as the bucket thumped below. I left Gracie's carrier between two beams and scooted toward the trapdoor.

Grady thrashed about below, clutching the bucket that landed on his head. I pushed the diaper pail over the edge of the trapdoor when he pulled off the bucket. He looked up as the diaper pail fell. One fully loaded diaper exploded smack in his face. He lay on his back gouging Gracie's "big girl" from his eyes.

His gun lay a few inches from his left shoulder. I slid down the ladder on my back, landing with both feet on his fat belly. He let out a loud oomph as I grabbed the gun and whirled around off him, ending up with the barrel of the weapon against the top of his head, while I crouched on hands and knees behind his head.

He reached behind his head, grabbed my wrist with both of his meaty paws and yanked my arm up, causing me to pull the trigger. The shot hit my red suit hanging nearby. He had both hands wrapped around my gun wrist, squeezing painfully. With my free hand, I picked up one of my black high heels and belted him in the face with it as hard as I could. He yelled, let go, and got up. He was quick for a heavy man.

But I was quicker. I sprinted for the kitchen door, screaming as I bolted downstairs, his heavy footsteps right behind me. I had to draw him away from Gracie and hopefully get away myself. I ran for my life.

My brothers managed to get outside in time to see Grady shoot past me, hop in a beat up black Toyota parked on the street and take off.

Shawn had to slap me to stop me from screaming. I doubled over and threw up all over his bare foot. He yelped and hopped around the driveway while I barfed until it became dry heaves. At last I sat on the driveway resting my head on my arms, my wrists dangling across my knees. I didn't know that I still held the gun until Kevin took my hand and tried to pry my fingers loose from it.

"Let go," he ordered. My finger was wrapped firmly around the space under the trigger. Kevin finally pried it loose. I sat on the driveway, eyes closed, with my head between my knees. I picked up my head when Mrs. Costanza handed me a warm, damp cloth. I think there were tears in her eyes, but maybe they were all mine. My neighbors were out in force and the police siren wailed in the distance.

"What's all over this gun?" Shawn asked holding his fingers to his nose. "It smells like...." His widening eyes registered the obvious.

Giggling, I pictured Grady with his face covered in it and the giggling bubbled into hysterical laughter. I couldn't stop. Even when my gut hurt so badly I wanted to stop, I couldn't. Kevin and Shawn pulled me up and tried to lead me toward the house but I struggled to go back to the apartment for Gracie. We struggled a few minutes while they shouted at me to quit being so stubborn as I fought for breath.

"Gracie!" I managed finally, except I got louder and louder until I was screaming Gracie. My brothers each took one of my arms under the armpits and hauled me up to my kitchen. Kevin held my head under the faucet at the sink while Shawn ran into my bedroom to look for Gracie.

Once the cold water soaked through my hair and washed over my head, I got control, stopped screaming, and leaned against the sink. I slurped some water and then held my face under it.

Shawn yelled from the bedroom that Gracie was gone and there was a mess in the closet. Kevin ran into the bedroom while I got a dishtowel and wrapped it around my wet hair. I wobbled into the bedroom, trembling so badly that if my brothers hadn't been there, I would have crawled on my hands and knees to make it.

When I got to my room, my pillows and spread were on the floor. I collapsed on the bed, pointing to the closet. The water bucket and diaper pail lay among Gracie's soiled diapers. The carpet was wet, with blobs of brown splotches that reeked.

"Holy crap!" Kevin gasped.

Hysterical giggles bubbled up again. This time I forced myself to take deep breaths and focus on God.

"What happened here, Julie?" Shawn asked.

"And where's Gracie?" Kevin cut in.

"Attic." I pointed. "Get her." The room smelled like urine, baby poo, and wet carpet. I fell over on my side and sagged into the mattress. I heard one of my brothers on the ladder, closed my eyes, and then became aware that it was daylight and Gracie was crying.

When I started through the living room with Gracie on my shoulder to get her bottle, Kevin sat up on the couch. Shawn stumbled out of Jack's bedroom scratching under his arm. Both of my brothers had stubbly faces, puffy eyes, and snarled hair.

"If only the girls could see you now," I said on my way past them to the kitchen.

"If you didn't keep waking us up at night, maybe we could get some beauty sleep," Kevin said. "The cops have somebody staked out in front and back of here twenty-four seven from now on," Kevin said. I fed Gracie, Kevin made coffee and put the tea kettle on, and Shawn scrambled eggs and made toast. Then he went downstairs for the Saturday papers. I put Gracie in her carrier in the kitchen while I had some tea and toast.

We read the paper and hung out in the kitchen as long as we could. I didn't want to go back into the bedroom closet and even see the mess, much less clean it. Finally I folded my section of the CHICAGO TRIBUNE and admitted that I really didn't want to have to clean up the mess in my closet.

"You should have thought of that when you concocted it," Shawn answered.

"Grady meant to kill you, Julie," Kevin said. "And we can't trust that he won't be back. You've got to go back to Florida and stay with Gram and Gramps until we get this bastard. He can't hide forever."

After last night, I thought it was probably a good idea to go back to Florida too, but I ignored his decree and asked, "So why haven't you been able to get him already?"

"Until last night, we were looking for a truck," Kevin said. "Now we know he's driving a car. Now we know what he looks like too. We can alert the kids who work at the Dairy Queen, and everybody else to be on the lookout for Grady's Toyota and for his truck."

Shawn folded his newspaper and dropped it on the pile on the floor next to his chair. "I want you to go straight back to Florida, Julie," he said. "Grady's not the dopey farmer we thought he was."

Before I could answer, the phone rang. "Think it's Grady?" I asked making no move to pick it up. Shawn shrugged. Kevin gave me an impatient finger bob to pick up.

I was relieved to hear Hugh's voice. "We'd like to station somebody inside your place until Grady's caught," he said. My brothers were elated at the news and decided to take turns with the cops. I was so relieved that there would be somebody else in the apartment at night that I almost cried. Hugh showed up before we finished our coffee and he took the first shift. He nodded to me and then he settled into the chair in the living room with my brothers where they talked while I tackled the closet, which took less time than I thought.

When my brothers left, Hugh watched TV. As I worked on recopying a ledger sheet, I sipped tea at the kitchen table. It hit me then that Grady knew I gave a copy of his book to the cops in Florida when he was clearly still up here in our area. I was going to talk with Hugh about it when I heard tires in the driveway.

The doorbell rang. From the open kitchen window I could see Tom's Ford Taurus in the driveway below. "Hi!" I called down to him. He grinned up at me. "I came to take you away from all this. My mom's making a roast for dinner and we thought you'd like to join us."

"I thought you were at school."

"I came home to help keep an eye on you and to get you away from here, if I can. I heard about what's going on from my mom. She's worried sick about you and the baby."

"She's not the only one." Kevin came down the driveway from the DQ to greet Tom. They shook hands as I headed downstairs. Kevin and Tom stopped talking abruptly when I came up to them as though I'd interrupted something clandestine.

"I think it's a good idea to get you out of here," Kevin said. Tom nodded agreement. Neither of them smiled. If Tom wanted to take me to dinner at his place, it was fine with me.

"You got it." I went up and put clean diapers into the diaper bag and thought that when I came home tonight, I'd have somebody in the apartment with me, even if it was one of the dopey cops. It sounded a lot better than anything so far.

"Do you think we have time to make some pick ups for my work?" I said. "I haven't collected any bills or receipts for over a week."

I think that could be arranged." Tom grinned and put the car in gear. We drove in silence for a while. The hair on the back of his arm was golden in the sunlight as he rested it on the open car window and his sandy hair glowed with blonde highlights. We went to Kline's Department Store and True

Value Hardware Store before we swung out to Al's, which is on the way to Tom's house. Tom waited in the car when I went in.

"You and I have to have an agreement, Al," I said. I stuffed receipts into a WalMart bag. "From now on you don't charge customers for anything you don't install, or I go to the cops and tell everyone in town what you've been up to." I figured he'd either call my bluff or admit the truth.

"Here's the agreement," he snapped, eyes flinty, spit collecting at the corners of his thin lips, "you're fired."

"If I'm fired, I go straight to the cops, and everyone in town will know. You'll not get any customers." I shot back.

"You little bitch." He snarled. "Mind your own business. I pay you. You got nothing to lose from keeping your mouth shut. You want your pay check every month, right?"

"I'm not taking money from a thief." I stood behind his desk and glared at him. He shuffled closer. I was glad we had the desk between us and the open door at my back. He glowered under his bushy brows at me. "Here's the deal, Al. You keep me on as the bookkeeper for as long as I want the job, and I keep my mouth shut, unless you cheat one more person. And I keep all the records on my computer with no ledgers." He propped himself on his fists on the desk and leaned closer toward me. I tossed the bag of his receipts on the desk. Some spilled out. He stared at them and stood up. I knew that he didn't have a clue where he'd get another bookkeeper in town who could take over for me without his books. I put my hands on my hips and waited, wondering if I had to help him put it together.

He held his clenched fists at his sides, looked again at the bills and receipts on his desk, and turned on his heels, throwing a hands down gesture as he walked away. I felt like doing a little dance as I shoved Al's paperwork back into the bag. But I refrained. It was almost as good to tell Tom all about my "agreement" with Al when I got out to his car.

"How did you know he was charging for parts he wasn't installing?"

"I didn't." I said. "Brad and Margie got me to thinking about it and I thought I'd challenge him on it, just in case it was true. It came to me while I was collecting his bills and receipts. If he was innocent of any cheating, he'd at least protest. He doesn't know exactly what I can and can't tell about his inventory on my computer." I shrugged and grinned. Tom laughed, shook his head, and we drove to his house.

TWENTY FIVE

The heady aroma of food cooking made my stomach growl when we came into Tom's house. Mrs. Atkinson greeted us at the door and immediately gathered Gracie into her embrace and held her close. She swayed back and forth with her eyes closed. I love it when people fuss over Gracie. I want everyone to love her.

Tom and I set the table while Mrs. Atkinson took Gracie into the family room to give her a bottle. "Gracie brings out the joy only being a mom can do," I said. Tom shrugged and smiled, obviously glad that his mom found a little respite from her grief. I set the table with country blue napkins while Tom carved a sizzling six-bone standing rib roast. I spooned whipped potatoes into a large serving bowl. Mrs. Atkinson had made steamed baby carrots, a tossed salad and crescent rolls.

"You kids go ahead and start while it's all hot," Mrs. Atkinson said when I went in to tell her the meal was on the table. "I'll hold Gracie until she falls asleep." I knew that wouldn't take long.

The brightly lit kitchen, sparkling blue and white stoneware, and familiar smell of good food gave me a sense of comfort and I relaxed. I took one of Tom's hands in mine and said, "Thanks for bringing me here, Tom. It feels so good to be away from Grady's prying eyes."

Tom put his arms around me and pulled me close. I was enjoying the warmth of his hug when Mrs. Atkinson entered the kitchen, still smiling from leftover Gracie. Tom and I ended our embrace to seat ourselves opposite one another at the table

"I can't seem to get the hang of cooking for only myself now that Beth is at college," Mrs. Atkinson commented as she surveyed the mounds of food on the table. She seated herself saying, "I put Gracie upstairs in my room, but I left her in her carrier. I hope that's all right, dear."

"That's perfect," I said. I smiled and accepted the bowl of potatoes Tom handed me. We filled our plates while Mrs. Atkinson told us about Beth getting into her dorm at college. I felt a twinge of envy. "I'm going to work for good grades at Owensville this year so I can transfer to the University next year." I said. Tom flashed me a smile of approval.

"It's so good to have Tom home," Mrs. Atkinson sighed. "He's promised to come home more often now." Her gray eyes brightened with unshed tears. She blinked rapidly behind her glasses. "I'm really looking forward to watching Gracie when you're in school." Tom and I exchanged a sympathetic glance. "I've never had a job and now that both of my kids are gone off to college," she dabbed her eyes with her napkin, "It's mighty lonesome."

"I hope you know how truly blessed Gracie and I are to have your help," I said. I went over and gave her a hug. When I sat down again, I shared a sudden thought with her. "Maybe you could give Ethel a call. She's gotten together groups of senior citizens who work part time to run the store."

"Why, I never thought of doing that," Mrs. Atkinson said. Her face looked all sunny but then clouded over. "Do you think Ethel will let me work there?" I couldn't look at her or Tom for fear they'd see my reaction to that one. Tom assured his mother that Ethel would surely find something for her to do at the store.

Tom and I helped clear the table but Mrs. Atkinson shooed us out of the kitchen when it came time to stack the dishwasher. Tom took my hand and led me out to the screened-in front porch that ran the length of the brick and frame two story home. Tom sat on an inviting cushioned glider that had three matching floral cushioned wicker chairs. There was room enough for a glass topped coffee table with end tables at either end of the glider. Lots of hanging baskets of red, white and pink geraniums and dark green lamps made the area cheerful and comfortable.

"I'm stuffed," I said. Tom patted a spot beside him on the glider. He put his arm around me and I snuggled against his side.

"Man, I almost forgot what a great cook Mom is," Tom said. "Now that Dad's gone, I'll be able to enjoy it a lot more often. Mom and I always got along fine," I pulled my head away and looked up at him questioningly, so he added, "The truth is, my dad and I never saw eye to eye on anything. I've always been a major disappointment to him." I brushed my hand along the top of his arm. Apparently Tom was in a mood to talk and I wanted to do nothing more than sit out on the porch and listen.

"Dad wanted me to run the store eventually, to be like him. He hated my interest in computers." Now I knew why Mr. Atkinson didn't want to switch to a computerized cash register. All along I'd thought it was Ethel's love of her old cash register. Tom held me close, flexing one leg so that we glided to the cadence of a spring somewhere in the glider straining as we moved back and forth.

"In high school," Tom said, "I spent all of my spare time with my computer teacher who taught me how to put computers together or fix them for people. I tried to get Dad to let me do computer repairs in the store for people, you know, as a service like we fix screens for people and replace glass, that kind of thing. Anyway, he flat out said no. No reason or excuse, just no. What a deal it could have been for everybody."

"You could initiate that in the store now, if you want to." I said.

"Maybe after I get my Master's, I'll come home and add computer services and maybe include computer sales to the store." After a few minutes of quiet, he continued. "Anyway, I won a scholarship to the U.of I. and rarely came home because Dad and I would just end up in a fight. It upset Mom a lot. It hurt her that I never could be close to my dad, but I just couldn't be Mr. Hardware.

After I got my Bachelor's, I won a Fellowship in a Master's program, and I'm working as a T.A. now for one of my professors in order to make ends meet" I looked up again and he explained, ""I'm working as a Teaching Assistant. Anyway, I never asked my dad for a thing after I left." Tom's chin jutted out and he frowned. "Sorry to unload on you like this." He stopped the glider to kiss me before he resumed the glider's motion.

"I was never close to my parents either," I said. I pulled his arm off my shoulders and leaned my head back on the thick cushions cradling his hand on my lap. "All my life my mom and dad talked about traveling when Dad retired. Last June I graduated on the tenth, got married on the eighteenth, and they left town the day after our wedding. It's hard to believe it's only been a year since I married Jack and had Gracie, but the past two months with Gracie makes up for the entire year with Jack." We smiled at each other and I felt more relaxed than I'd felt in a long time.

"My parents call home every Sunday, but they mainly talk with my brothers. I mean, when I'm over at the house, we exchange weather reports, that sort of thing, but what's the use; they're so far away. They don't even know about Grady. Last week they were in British Columbia. A lot of good they could do us from up there. Besides, nobody wants to spoil their dreams." Tom leaned over and was about to kiss me when Mrs. Atkinson came out to join us.

Tom talked about how glad he was that Ethel was running the store. Mrs. Atkinson said how pleased she was that Beth could go ahead with her plans for college. She told us how proud she was of Beth and Tom. Then she yawned and said, "It's almost ten. I'm afraid I'm going to have to say good night."

"I better go get Gracie then," I said. "I'm surprised at how the time slipped away. It's time for Gracie's bottle."

"Relax," Mrs. Atkinson said getting up. "Let me go get her. You two just go ahead and chat. I'll feed Gracie." She was off without looking back.

I smiled up at Tom. Mrs. Atkinson had turned the lamps on low, adding to the warm glow. I settled back against Tom and closed my eyes. "What a perfect evening," I murmured.

Mrs. Atkinson's screams had us both up and running. We bounded upstairs into her bedroom. She stood at the foot of her bed holding her hands to the sides of her face while she screamed hysterically. The bedroom window was shoved up with a circle cut out at the top of one window pane and Gracie was gone.

A quick glance out the window revealed only the dark back yard. "I should have kept her in my arms." I told myself. I turned and raced down the stairs outdistancing Tom and his mother behind me. The bedroom window was a bright rectangle in the back yard with a ladder leaning against the siding below it.

"I'll call the police," Tom called when I sped past him toward the back door. Tom helped support his mother whose body sagged against him, her eyes glazed over. I grabbed my keys from my bag in the kitchen and pounded across the lawn to my van. I shot down residential side streets alternately asking myself why I let Gracie out of my sight and wondering how long Gracie had been gone. The abuse Billy suffered pulled my stomach into a burning knot. Panic mounted with each tree canopied street I shot down. I almost sideswiped a parked car so I pulled over to pray for whatever I needed. I focused on God until my trembling slowed enough for me to drive.

And so I spent the night combing the streets, retracing my steps, and going from one end of town to the other. By five-thirty in the morning my head ached so badly I could barely see. I dragged home and had to use my hands to help me climb my stairs. I called the police.

Marylou Sanders answered. "Oh, my God, Julie, I'm so sorry. Everyone is out looking for your baby, even the FBI." So that's where my brothers must be, I thought fleetingly.

"I'll let everyone know you're home so they can send someone over for you." Then she disconnected.

I took two aspirins and sat at the kitchen table. I rested my head on my arms, too exhausted even to cry. "Please, please help me find Gracie," I begged God. Then I picked up my head and took a deep breath. I knew sitting there wasn't going to get the job done. The phone near my hand on the table jogged my memory of the phone numbers that the nurse at the hospital gave me for Grady.

What was I thinking, I chided myself. I dumped over my chair on my way to the laundry hamper in the bathroom. I tore into the hamper to find the jean shorts that I'd worn the night before. Then it hit me that it had only been last night that I'd gotten home from Florida and Grady tried to kill me.

The slip of paper was still in one of the pockets. I heard myself grunt out each number that I punched on the phone. After a couple of rings, a woman's sing-song voice answered, "New To You." It was Charlotte's voice.

New To You said it all. I yanked a dishtowel off the hook to cover the mouthpiece on the phone and hoped that dumb Charlotte wouldn't recognize my voice. "Could you please tell me how to get to the store?" I asked using a breathy voice. "I want to buy a used DVD player."

It worked. Dumb Charlotte gave me the address and directions on how to get there. It would take half an hour because the place was located in nearby Sherman Oaks. I wasted no time dropping down the stairs two and three at a time. So Charlotte was at Grady's store. I put the van in gear. Grady was probably hiding in Sherman Oaks and Charlotte must have kept him informed about what was going on. Damn Charlotte!

I drove like a maniac, weaving in and out of traffic, foot to the floor, and hoped the cops would show up and use their siren to run interference in the traffic for me. None did.

I didn't know what I'd do if Grady was there to greet me with his gun but I knew I'd have to think of something and play it by ear. It occurred to me as the streets whizzed past in a blur that everyone plays life by ear. Some people seem to be able to stay on key better than others. I hoped I was one of them.

In less than twenty five minutes I found the store and was able to pull into a slot by the front door. I left the van running as I slipped out, eyes darting around for any sign of Grady. New To You was part of a short strip mall in a rundown section of Sherman Oaks. The storefront next door's windows were whitewashed with a "For Lease" sign on the door

Charlotte's eyelids popped up like a cheap doll's, and her jaw dropped when I bolted in, scanning the room as I rushed at her. Before she had time to collect her half a wit, I had her by the throat with both hands. She tried to pull my hands free, but I had such strength that she went limp and clutched my wrists while I throttled her throat.

"Where's Gracie!" I growled through my teeth. She made a noise through her nose like a car engine that wouldn't start when I shook her head. Her teeth clacked together and her head wobbled. Two men in the back of the store skulked along a row of TV sets and out the front door.

When blood dribbled from Charlotte's lips where she'd bitten them, I pressed my nose almost against hers. "If you don't tell me where my baby is, I'll pinch your head off."

Her eyes rolled and I realized that she couldn't breathe so I eased the pressure of my thumbs on her windpipe enough for her to suck in raspy breaths. She tried to pull away again but I held firm. Her whisper was barely audible. "Gracie's with Jack." I gave her pumpkin head a few more shakes and slid my hands down to pin her upper arms. She croaked out, "I was supposed to take care of her but I had to work. Honest."

I don't know why, but I had to shake her a few more times even though I believed she was telling the truth.

When I shoved her away from me, she fell, making a five point landing, elbows, butt, and feet. I turned to beat it back to my van. A movement caught my eye. A door at the back of the store opened, Grady appeared for an instant, and the door closed.

TWENTY SIX

Fearful that Grady went after a gun, I threw myself out the front door and had the van on the highway in a matter of seconds. My mind raced along with the van. I couldn't guess why Jack would take Gracie, but at least I could answer the question of where Grady had been hiding. I drove on auto pilot, numb to my surroundings, until I reached Charlotte's house.

By the time I pulled up behind Jack's car parked behind the wreck on cinder blocks in the driveway, I probably had more adrenalin than blood coursing through my body. Charlotte's small frame house, barely visible behind overgrown shrubs, sits well back from the road on a narrow lot.

I didn't know how long I had before Grady showed up with a gun and I didn't know where Jack was in the house. I left the van running and the car door open close to the street. I pushed aside the thick branch of an evergreen shrub that had been planted too close to the front of the house. The windows behind the shrubs were low, with peeling sills and grimy panes but they were clean enough to see inside.

The shotgun interior allowed me to see through the living room and dining room to where Gracie's carrier sat on the kitchen floor in the doorway, turned sideways to me, but tilted enough so that I could see her tiny fists flail, her face red in muted rage.

The pounding in my head roared in my ears. I was at the front door in a single leap, twisting the doorknob. It was unlocked. If it had been locked, I'd probably have twisted the knob off the door.

Jack's eyes widened above the newspaper he held. Gracie's screams beat against the throbbing in my head. With a flying leap, I landed on top of Jack. I knocked him backwards in his chair. His head bounced on the floor as I landed on top of his chest. Then I clamped my teeth into his throat, pulled back, and ripped out flesh. Blood spurted up and then poured from the wound.

I spit out blood and flesh while I rolled off of him. His hands gripped his throat, his eyes wide as he worked to suck in air. I stood up and vomited on myself even as I reached for Gracie's carrier. Grady could turn up any second. I sprinted through the house, across the lawn and into the van, dropping Gracie's carrier on the floor in front, half expecting Grady to pop out from behind a bush or tree and shoot at us. I had the van in gear and burning rubber between heart beats.

Gracie was probably yelling because she was hungry. Still, I had to be sure so I sped to the hospital. At the emergency entrance, I pulled Gracie, still screaming, from her carrier, hugged her to my chest, and flew into the emergency room. Judy Calamine's face flickered with horror an instant before she became professionally calm. "Call the police," she directed a young girl beside her

Judy helped me onto an examining table in a cubicle and then yanked a green fabric screen around our table. Gracie was smeared with Jack's blood and my vomit.

Dr. Hein rounded the corner. I held out Gracie for him to examine her. Instead he handed Gracie to Judy and tried to examine me. "Check Gracie," I screamed. "It's Jack's blood. I bit him. He kidnapped Gracie. Make sure Gracie's all right."

It took a few seconds for Dr. Hein and Judy to register what I'd said. Dr. Hein took Gracie while I dove for the nearby sink before my insides spilled out. It was a while before my stomach spasms produced nothing more than pain.

"How is my baby?" My head rested on the back of my hands at the edge of a tiny metal sink.

"She's fine as far as I can tell," Dr. Hein said.

"I think I bit Jack to death. I left him bleeding on Charlotte's floor." Dr. Hein handed me a washcloth and turned on the tap. I closed my eyes, thanked God that Gracie was all right, and washed my face and hands. Judy somehow managed to produce a bottle of formula to feed Gracie. I did my best to wipe myself off. Then I took Gracie and started to work on getting her cleaned up too.

I was cleaning between Gracie's fingers when Jack was brought in on a stretcher still alive. Ironically, because I was still his wife legally, they wanted me to sign the forms so they could take him into surgery. My hand hovered over the form barely a second. I already knew what it felt like to think I'd killed someone.

By then my brothers, along with two FBI agents; one male and the other female, and the Owensville police were at the hospital. I explained what happened, ending with my Jack attack. Kevin drove Gracie and me home in his four-by-four and Louie drove my van.

Our driveway was packed with people and cars. Tom and his mother got out of Tom's car and rushed out to the street where we had to park. Margie and Brad came over, as well as our neighbors, and some friends who live across town. People closed in around us. I think they wanted to do a mass hug.

Hugh, Louie, and Donald wound up doing a creditable job of keeping people away from us, without upsetting anybody, so that we could get upstairs to my apartment. Maybe they weren't total clowns after all. It might be that I needed to change the way I looked at them. Too exhausted to contemplate the idea, I put Gracie in her crib and was asleep by the time my body hit the bed -- maybe midair.

I could hear Mrs. Atkinson crooning to Gracie in the kitchen when I woke up. Along with bedhead, I had on my blood and vomit crusted clothes which at this point really stunk I peeled off my clothes and put my robe on over my stinky body, barely able to breathe in the stench without wanting to hurl. Mrs. Atkinson was feeding Gracie and Tom sat at the table talking with Louie. "Would you like some breakfast, dear?" Mrs. Atkinson said when she saw me.

"The only thing that sounds good to me is a shower," I answered. I hurried past everyone to get to the bathroom before Tom saw too much of me and before the stench of my clothing got to them. I dumped my tee shirt and shorts in the plastic bag lining my waste basket and tied it closed. There was no way I'd ever wear those again. I stepped into the shower, letting the hot water stream over me. It reminded me of Billy's joy when he took a shower at the hospital.

"It's my turn to watch the place in case Grady turns up," Louie told everyone at the table when I came out of the bathroom in my bathrobe. Louie put his plate in the sink, Tom walked over to put his arms around me, and the phone rang, all at the same time.

"How are you?" It was Shawn.

"I'll live."

"Jack made it through surgery. The FBI is going to hold him on kidnapping charges. I'm on my way home."

Louie filled me in on what happened, while I sipped peppermint tea at the kitchen table. "Charlotte's house and Grady's store are both under surveillance," Louie said. "Charlotte was picked up, but not Grady. Charlotte was questioned and told the FBI everything she knew."

"That must have taken all of a minute," I said.

Louis continued after a few appreciative chuckles. "She told the police that she and Jack were only babysitting for Grady. She said Grady did the actual kidnapping."

"So basically she just covered her own butt."

"Not really. Listen to this. The deal was Grady had a lawyer all set up to have Gracie adopted by some couple who paid the lawyer. Charlotte and Jack were to get ten thousand dollars to watch Gracie for the day. She was screaming about not being paid what she was due, and being inconvenienced by the FBI. Can you believe it?"

I could only nod my head and roll my eyes along with everyone else.

"If you hadn't found Gracie yesterday afternoon, she'd have been gone by evening," Mrs. Atkinson said.

"And if I hadn't gotten the phone numbers from the nurse in Clearwater, I wouldn't have been able to find her." I said.

"I guess things work out the way they're meant to," Mrs. Atkinson said. She looked away and I knew she was thinking of Tom Sr.

"And," I said with conviction, "if God hadn't given me the strength I needed, I don't think I could have done what I did." There were nods of agreement all around.

"The fact that Charlotte was working for Grady at his store," Tom said, "made it possible for Grady to stay informed while he hid out in the back rooms he used as a second home when he came up here from Florida."

Shawn came in with more news. "Charlotte gave the FBI the name of the lawyer who was going to sell Gracie. They think they'll be able to find out who the couple was that wanted to buy Gracie and maybe find others. Catching that crooked lawyer is a major plus, Julie,"

I had to agree. "I wish they'd catch Grady, though."

"For a fat dude, Grady sure can make himself invisible somehow. I wonder if he wears a disguise or something." We looked at one another, shrugged and almost sighed in unison. Nobody had the answer to that one.

"We have flyers circulating with a photo of Grady now," Louie said. "It shouldn't be much longer before he's captured."

"How'd you get a photo of him?"

"Shawn worked with the FBI people. They did a computer generated picture of him," Kevin said.

"You need to go back to Florida," Shawn said, "and stay there until Grady is captured."

"I'll drive and see that you get there safely," Tom said. "Then I can go back to school."

"And we'll let you both know when we pick up Grady," Louie said.

There wasn't much I could say except, "When do we leave."

"Get whatever you need together and let's go now," Tom said.

I dressed and wound my hair into a French twist in record time. Everyone helped me pile my things into Tom's car. We agreed that it might be a good idea to leave my van in the driveway so that Grady might think I was still somewhere in the area. I gathered my bookkeeping records, and Shawn helped me take my desktop computer. I wasn't sure where I'd set up all my bookkeeping stuff, but I badly needed to get some work done, and I felt sure Gramps would come up with a spot for me to work.

We pulled in to Gram and Gramps' way past their bedtime but they were both up waiting for us. Gram hugged me and then Tom. She told him how sorry she and Gramps were to hear about his dad. Tom and Gramps shook hands. Since Tom and I were beat, I went in to sleep in Gramps' room, Tom slept on the couch, and Gramps slept on the daybed on the front porch.

When I woke up, it was past breakfast time. Gramps was cleaning Buddy, his M1 Army rifle. Gramps calls his rifle Buddy because it saved his life during the war. It had been a while since I'd seen it. Mostly Gramps shot it off on New Year's Eve, the Fourth of July, or for target practice.

Gramps nodded at me when I came into the dining room. Gram came in with Tom. She carried a steaming cup of tea for me and Tom held Gracie over his shoulder. We chatted a while and then Tom left for the University. Gramps put up a long folding table on the front porch for me to set up my computer. A breeze swept through the open windows and there was plenty of room to stack my books and papers. I breathed a sigh of relief.

I worked nonstop on my bookwork and by the end of the following week I had my bookkeeping all caught up. I went to bed with the satisfaction that I could be ready for school next month, assuming Grady was caught by then. Thinking about my options made it hard to sleep. There didn't seem to be much I could do but wait.

"Grady could go to another state and start a new business dealing in stolen goods or start a new farm somewhere." Gramps said at breakfast next morning. "We may never find him."

"So there's barely a month before I either have to go back and risk having Gracie stolen or stay here and mss school," I said glumly. My head rested in my upturned hands as my elbows rested on the dining room table.

Gram said, "It's in God's capable hands, Julie. You've done everything you can. Now you just have to wait."

"I want to know and I want to know now," I said with a smile. I tried to make it sound like a joke but they knew better.

After breakfast, I called the nursing station at the Clearwater hospital. Vera Jean answered. I caught her up on what all happened, ending with the fact that Billy's father was still out there.

"Billy's been transferred to the Pinellas County facility," Vera Jean said. "I sure hope his father doesn't come back and mess things up."

"I don't think you have to worry about it. Grady can hardly waltz in and pick up Billy now. He's wanted for kidnapping and attempted murder." I had to explain to Vera Jean how Grady had broken into my apartment and tried to shoot me. After we hung up, it occurred to me that Grady might try to kidnap Billy. It seemed like the nightmare would never end.

Gramps came in from the back porch and said he needed to do some errands. He took Gram, Gracie, and me into town, telling us he wasn't leaving anybody home alone. It was fine with me. We were in the S&W Department Store. Gram said, "Your grandfather must be pretty worried for all his talk about Grady being out of the area." I didn't have to ask why. Gramps was following us around the store like a hound dog.

We shopped for Gram some new shoes and me something to wear to school. It felt great, like the first day of school when I would get a new outfit to wear along with a new pencil case in grade school.

It took all morning to find Gram shoes and a pair of jeans and a top that I liked. We ate lunch at the Four Square Diner and I fed Gracie her two o'clock bottle in the car on the way home. Afterwards, she and I played with her little cuddly kitty for a while. She stayed awake a little longer each day it seemed.

Kevin called after I'd put Gracie down for her nap. "Nobody can believe that we haven't found Grady yet," he said. "Hugh and Donald found his truck in a garage near his store. At least we only have one vehicle to look for now, although it's possible he ditched the Toyota and got something else."

I felt sorry for my brothers. For the first time, they couldn't bully their way through their problems, or mine. It was a first step into reality for both of us.

"The doctors worked miracles on Jack's throat," Kevin said. "After he gets out of the hospital, he'll have to go to court, of course." Kevin's voice dropped, "And you'll have to testify against him."

"That won't be a problem." I said without hesitation. We hung up and I brought Gram up to speed about Jack. Gram said she was disappointed in him. She said shopping wore her out and she went into her room to take a nap. Gramps said he was going down to the point to fish. I was glad he decided to finally leave the house and take some time to fish. He'd been hanging around the place as though he felt Grady might show up at any moment. But Gramps was probably right. Grady wasn't going to take a chance on being caught. He was probably long gone.

There was nothing on TV. I went into Gramps' room to lie on the bed next to Gracie. Just to be sure, I checked the window and left the curtains open and the shade up. It was pleasant lying in the quiet house with the sunshine streaming in. I thought about Jack. Who knows what he might have done if I hadn't gotten there at that precise moment. I shuddered.

Since Grady still hadn't been found, it made sense that he would relocate and start up another shady operation. The only thing that made me uneasy now was how to convince my brothers to let me come home to go to school on time.

I dozed off but woke up when my arms were yanked behind my back. Rough hands slipped a rope around one wrist and then the other bringing them together so tight that both my wrists and shoulders hurt. Then Grady yanked me up by an elbow and flipped me onto my back, wrenching my shoulder.

Grady stood over me, rubbery lips sliced wide across dark stubble. His squinty black eyes glittered. I took a breath to scream but he said, "Scream all you want, Missy. I saw yur granny's hearing aide on the nightstand. An' I saw yur old Granddad walking down the road with his fishing pole."

"Why are you still after me?" I shouted. Pain wracked my arms and shoulders as I lay on them and the rope bit into my wrists. I squirmed sideways in an effort to sit up but Grady pushed down painfully on one shoulder, pinning me to the bed as he bent his head close to my face.

"I can't sell nothing anymore, thanks to you. But I might make enough on yur kid to make up fur it." I froze at that, feeling my scalp prickle. His breath was hot and smelly as he leaned within an inch of my face. "And afore I take care of you, I'm gonna have me some good woman for a change. I ain't had me no women in a long time." He stood to unbutton his pants, and pull down the zipper. I lifted my legs to kick him, but he caught my ankles and laughed. "No old codger kin help you now."

"One old codger can," Gramps said. He pointed Buddy at the back of Grady's neck. Grady's jaw dropped. He zipped his pants in one swipe and buckled his belt.

"Get on the floor, face down, legs spread, hands behind your head." Gramps said. "Do it nice and slow." I rolled into a sitting position. Grady did as Gramps asked.

For a second I wondered how Gramps could untie me and still hold the gun on Grady. Then it dawned on me; he couldn't. I had to do something. So I inched over to the nightstand, backed up against it and felt for the phone. One thing I know by feel is the keypad. I pressed 911 until I faintly heard a voice.

"Send the Port Richfield police to the second house on Old Gulf Road," I yelled bending down as close as I could get to the phone. "Tell the police the gun pointing at Mr. Grady is old and might go off any second." Gramps winked at me over his grin.

I sat on the bed to wait for the police. Gramps didn't take his eyes from Grady, his rifle steady in his hands. "I knew you'd figure out something, Julie," he said. "You always did know how to take care of yourself."

"I have a lot of help, Gramps," I said pointing upward with my chin and eyes. He got my message and nodded.

The police put Grady in jail to be held without bond for kidnapping and attempted murder. Billy will stay at the Pinellas County facility and I made it on time for my first day of college which turned out to be another story and a new beginning.

www.ingramcontent.com/pod-product-compliance
Lightning Source LLC
Chambersburg PA
CBHW070112260626
47160CB00004B/1434